The 12 Games of Christmas

KB Badger

Copyright © 2021 KB Badger

All rights reserved.

ISBN: 9798757702964

DEDICATION

With deepest love and gratitude to my wife, Kathleen, who supports and believes in all of my wildest artistic endeavors. And to my children, Mae, and Cary, who may one day read this book: I love you more than Christmastime – thanks for being my two best pals.

ACKNOWLEDGMENTS

Thanks to my family, Bill, Cindy, Tammy, and Mike, for your endless support. Special thanks to Will and Maria for your editing, publishing, and marketing help.

PROLOGUE

It was an emergency. Not a fire or an earthquake, but a big enough issue to call a Saturday morning meeting, and that was rare. Mr. DuPonte lumbered toward the elevator, and mulled the bad news. In the past, when he'd been forced to deliver bad news, he had always tried to delegate it. Not out of laziness, but because he hated to see the looks of disappointment on his employees' faces. Today was different though, this was not delegable. The news had to come from him.

Ponty – as he was known in the bullpen – pushed the call button and resisted scrolling through his phone while he waited. When the doors slid open, he caught sight of the peeling carpet and the brown-smudged buttons, faded after years of being mashed by journalists rushing to meet copy deadlines. He was embarrassed by the unsightliness, but the budget always had more-pressing needs. The smell came second, but that part was okay. A mixture of drying ink, and sweat, the aroma was nostalgic. As a kid, Ponty had played on the elevator for hours, pretending to be an astronaut or superhero, while his grandfather barked orders at junior editors.

The boardroom was already full when Ponty arrived. He appraised the group as he approached. His employees were wearing hoodies, jeans, and t-shirts and sat chattering with one another or thumbing through social media. There was no dress code on Saturdays, and that was a relief. Ponty felt better that they looked casual, crammed into the mish-mash of worn and well-loved chairs. Normally, the office wore business attire, and the employees' neatly pressed suits were in stark juxtaposition with the careworn boardroom. His employees greeted him with a friendly mix of nods, smiles, and "good morning"s as he moved to the head of the table.

"The paper's hurting," Ponty said, without preamble or affectation. The chatter stopped, and people lowered their phones. "I know I don't have to explain the Gazette's pedigree to any of you, but suffice it to say I don't want to be responsible for overseeing the failure of my family's legacy." He paused. "And that's the least of my worries. It's your jobs, your healthcare, and, of course, keeping this town informed. Without us, it's only national outlets." He paused and swallowed the lump forming in his throat. His paper, The Daily Gazette, had been in his family for three generations, and Ponty had steered the ship for over 50 years. Now, thanks to online rags, social media, and a news-weary public, paying readership was on a precipitous downward trend and the paper was bleeding subscribers.

"How long do we have?" a voice called out.

Ponty shook his head. "Don't worry. This meeting's not about layoffs. Everyone is keeping their job."

Several employees sighed simultaneously.

"I called you in here to brainstorm." He scanned the room. "Where's Alex?"

"Here," said a squeaky voice from the back corner. Alex, rotund and balding, emerged from behind the group. Unlike his colleagues, he was dressed up in a gray three-piece suit, but it had seen better days – wrinkled, greasy, the threads stretching at the seams.

"Alex," Ponty said, "tell them our current projections, please."

Alex scuffled his way to the front. He cleared his throat. "Sure, Ponty," he started, his voice quivering slightly. "At our current staffing rate, if subscriptions do not change…that is, if subscriptions do not increase – substantially – our paper can operate for," he paused, less for dramatic effect and more for fear of the reaction his news would cause, "no more than a year, year and a half."

The boardroom exploded with chatter. "You just said this wasn't about layoffs!" yelled one employee. "Sounds like we do need to look for new jobs!" shouted another.

Ponty held his hands up, and the chatter simmered. "Please," he said, "I understand you're upset, but we're not laying anyone off. Nobody is going anywhere. As I said, I didn't call this meeting to scare you, I called it so we could discuss things." He gestured toward the group. "I want to open the floor to any suggestions."

Barb Weissman, a longtime colleague of Ponty's, reached her arm to the sky. He nodded at her. "Go ahead. And you don't need to raise your hand, Barb."

"I agree we need to fight. This town loves the Gazette. We just need to remind them why."

"I'm listening."

"Maybe more advertising? Perhaps we can squeeze some money from the budget somewhere and run more ads to attract more subscribers."

Ponty looked at Alex who was frantically shuffling through the sheaf of paper in his hands. "Our advertising has been a bit ineffective of late." Alex said. "We haven't seen a correlated rise in subscriptions with increased advertising expenditures."

"But that could be chalked up to the way the way we're advertising," Barb countered, "right?"

"That's right," Ponty responded. "But that still brings us back to how to advertise more effectively."

Across the room, a junior editor raised her hand slightly, then quickly pulled it back down. The movement caught Ponty's eye. "Go ahead, Rachael," he urged, "and please, you don't need to raise your hands, people."

The gaze of the room fell on her. Rachael slumped and shifted in her seat. "Never mind, It's stupid."

Ponty flashed an easy smile. "It's only stupid if what you don't say could have helped."

Rachael sat up. "Okay. I was thinking we could have a competition. Like, ya' know, a contest. For money. For our readers."

Ponty paused. He'd had a similar thought on the drive to work that morning, but Alex's gloomy forecasts had squashed the idea. "A good suggestion," he said, "but considering we're maxed on our advertising budget. I think a competition would be hard to swing right now."

Rachael nodded.

"Any other ideas?"

Rachael's friend, Marc, kicked her under the table. "Ow!" she exclaimed, staring at him.

Marc raised his eyebrows and cocked his head sideways, motioning toward Ponty. "Keep going," he whispered.

"Shhh," she countered, but it came out louder than expected and drew the attention of the room.

Ponty turned toward her. "Were you not finished?"

Rachael's face flushed. "Uh…sorry…" Under the table, Marc kicked her again. This time in the other leg.

Rachael continued. "I mean, what I was getting at was a sales promotion. A contest. People love contests. If we go big, we could put The Daily Gazette back on the map." As Rachael spoke, she seemed to find her confidence a bit. "The truth is, before you even called this meeting, Marc and I had been spit-balling ideas to grow readership. We came up with a long-shot idea we were planning on pitching to you in the new year. It sounds crazy, but it might actually work. It's a contest where we give away…" she paused and shot Marc a wry smile. "I'll let Marc fill you in on the details."

Marc grinned. "We want to have a grand prize of $100,000." Laughter erupted across the room. "We're serious," Marc continued. "A contest with that kind of a prize would attract huge attention. We might even go viral on a national level. We can run the whole contest through our app and website. Think about it. 100K will drive crazy site traffic – advertisers will be salivating. That alone could be more than enough to recoup the investment."

Rachael stood up. "And it won't just be some random lottery. It'll be an actual competition. Whoever wins will win based on merit." She paused to let the drama percolate. "Here's the hook: for the customer, it's no pay, no play. We run a large discount for new annual subscriptions and only subscribers will be eligible to compete and win. We'll be double dipping just like all the streaming services on your TV. You pay the subscription fee, but they still make you watch ads."

The boardroom buzzed with chatter. Marc beamed and looked at Ponty whose expression gave away nothing. "Wait, we didn't tell you the best part." he said. "Rachael and I devised a fail-safe. In the coming weeks, we divert all of our advertising to the competition – really hype it up. We can get the local news involved, blast social media, and everything else in between. But in the fine print we have a caveat saying we're only running the competition if we reach a certain threshold of new subscribers. If we don't reach it, people and advertisers can cancel for full refunds. That way we'll know before we even start whether the competition will be viable. It's that simple." Marc spread his arms palms up and looked like he was about to shout "ta-daa," but he said nothing more.

All eyes turned to Ponty, who was still stone-faced. Seconds ticked by and a nervous energy filled the room. Finally, Ponty turned to Alex. "Is this realistic?"

Alex furiously shuffled the papers in front of him once again. "There's always risk, but I…I think if we can hit around 15,000 new subscribers, I really don't see why not."

Ponty nodded slowly and turned back to the group. "All in favor?" Hands shot to the sky with most of the Gazette employees confirming their assent. "The ayes have it." Ponty turned to Rachael and Marc. "What will the competition be about?"

"We came up with an idea for that too," Rachael said. "We don't need to reinvent the wheel. We want to show our prospective readers and our ink-and-paper subscribers that our digital editions have more than the news. You know the Christmas contest we run every year, with the puzzles?"

Ponty nodded.

"We make that the competition, we run it through that."

A grin spread slowly across Ponty's face. "The Twelve Games of Christmas it is."

CHAPTER 1

The mortgage penalty was looming. Nothing could change that now. The ink on the loan documents had been dry for almost ten years. Mia had agreed to the terms, hardly skimming them as she excitedly scribbled her name on the dotted lines. Back then, the loan seemed solid: a fixed rate with manageable payments and low interest. To a fearless college graduate, all Mia needed to know was where to sign. The paperwork was littered with caveats and contingencies about what the bank could do in the event of late or nonpayment – trivialities which Mia hadn't concerned herself with at the time. In her mind, the store was a sure thing. But that was before the pandemic. Who had need of an airplane neck pillow, or travel mugs, or car games, during a lockdown? Over the last year, the Snow Valley Treasures' mortgage had been paid late on more occasions than it had been paid on time. The bank sent letters warning her, but Mia couldn't bear to read them. There was nothing she could do about them anyway. Mercifully, the vaccines had come, but the vast majority of shopping was still being done online, and the threatening envelopes kept stacking up.

Mia popped open her weather app as she trudged toward work. All suns. There was zero snow in the forecast – and no snow meant slow business. Her store, Snow Valley Treasures, stood on the corner of Main and 3rd Street, right across from the park. It was a perfect location, and while the building itself wasn't much to get excited about – a single-story, brown brick building with a wooden door – there were two large windows in front which Mia decorated every Christmas, doing her best Macy's imitation. Snow helped the complete the theme.

Across the street, Mia noticed Christmas decorations adorning some of the local businesses. A half-inflated snowman looked out-of-place slumped on the dry lawn of the beauty salon. The pet shop next door featured a beautiful Santa's sleigh on its porch. She couldn't help thinking if Santa took off from there, his sleigh would probably kick up sparks. But it wasn't just an aesthetic concern. The snow was an issue. Without it, foot traffic to and from the park's sledding hill would be next-to-nothing. With no precipitation in the forecast, the chances of selling gloves, hats, sleds, and last-minute gifts was diminishing.

"Ugh." She closed the weather app and stuffed her phone back in her coat. At the shop's entrance, she caught a glimpse of herself in one of the windows. Mia still had the same small frame and mousy brown hair she'd had when the store first opened, but a few new wrinkles had found their way into the reflection. "Smile lines," she tried to convince herself, but couldn't suppress the thought they might just as well be from stress.

Inside, her employee, Richard, sat sipping coffee and hardly looked up. "You'll have to do better than that," he said.

Mia laughed. Richard's husky frame was stuffed into a red and white striped shirt, and solid red pants. "What time did you get up this morning?" she asked, motioning at his outfit. "I like the candy cane theme, by the way."

"Thanks, my boyfriend picked it out. And if you want to beat me here, you better put a cot in the back."

Mia laughed again. "You know I'm not afraid to do that."

"Until then, score another point for me."

Richard and Mia had been friends for more than a decade, and he was Snow Valley Treasures' sole employee. In December, it had become an annual game to see who could get to the store first. The game had started out of necessity, back when people would cram themselves into stores on Black Friday, and the Christmas rush kept them busy all season. Now, post-pandemic, their need to come into the store at dawn had evaporated. But Richard kept the game going, and his optimism helped Mia to not lose hope on the business. Mia had met Richard in college, and when he was laid off from a corporate gig a few years after graduation, she offered him a job. It was only meant to be temporary, but they had worked together ever since as de facto partners, and Mia was grateful for it. She liked the company. Plus, Richard was a hard worker. The only time the two butted heads was when Richard suggested they expand more into the online space. Mia was an old soul in that regard. She wanted the community, and tourists, to have a traditional, old-timey experience in her shop. In truth, she worried about her store becoming a dinosaur, but it had always been her baby and she bristled at the thought of needing to ask anyone for help.

Richard was still thumbing through his phone.

"What're you reading?" Mia asked. "Is that a crossword?"

"Yes, and you're not helping me. This one's mine." He locked his phone and tucked it in his pocket. "I know what time of year it is."

"Not yet. The Twelve Games of Christmas doesn't start for a few days. I just want to warm up."

"Have you heard about the changes they're making to the Games?"

Mia cocked her head. "No. I hope they're not changing anything. What have you heard?"

"I don't even know if it's true, but people were saying on social media that the Gazette is gonna run some kind of competition in the Games this year."

She arched her eyebrows. "That's weird. I hope that's not true. The Games are perfect the way they are."

"Just telling you what I heard." Richard popped his app back open.

"Ok. Here's a warm up for you. What's a nine-letter word for showing you care?" He smirked. "Not that you'd ever know the answer to that one."

"Haw-haw," Mia said sarcastically. She wrinkled her brow and considered the question. "Hmm. I don't know. I've gotta think about it."

"Great, another two weeks with your nose stuck in a puzzle."

"Excuse me," she said, smiling. "They're a Christmas tradition." She darted behind Richard and tried to snatch the phone from his hands. He countered by locking and stuffing it back into his pocket. "And you're saying you're not obsessed?"

It was true Mia could become fanatical about the Twelve Games of Christmas. They were her guilty pleasure. The Games were a progressive set of puzzles of increasing difficulty which built on each other from one day to the next. The way they were structured, it was not possible to solve day two's puzzle without first solving day one; just as it was not possible to solve day three without day two, and so on. Mia loved the puzzles because of the challenge, and when she was honest with herself, enjoyed the romantic holiday theming as well. She was surprised and embarrassed Richard had noticed.

"Don't worry," Richard said, seeming to sense her embarrassment. "At this time of year, everyone sounds like that. You just take it to a whole new level." His phone had resurfaced.

"Affection!" Mia yelled.

"What?"

She reached for the phone again and this time managed to slip it out of Richard's grasp. She tapped in the answer to the puzzle.

Richard laughed. "Just don't get too sucked in, 'cause you still have a store to run." He paused. "Or, you know what, do get sucked in. Let me take over for a bit. Go on vacation."

Mia squinted. Unfortunately, this was a tune she'd danced to before – her parents and friends had both made similar comments in the past. As a nine-year-old, Mia changed a flat tire by herself when she and her mom had gotten stuck in the middle of nowhere. Rather than waiting for someone to come along, she'd read the operator's manual, and popped on the spare. The story got told over and over at family gatherings, and had slowly warped from a story of heroics to "Mia never needs to ask for help." That mantra was solidified when, as a teenager, Mia worked nearly full-time while also balancing high school and varsity volleyball. In college, Mia paid her tuition and her own room and board by working at a restaurant in the evenings, in addition to her coursework. But rather than being rewarded for her efforts, she had too often been dismissed as overly career driven. "So," she thought, "I don't need to be told I need a vacation. I can handle it." But knowing Richard's intentions were good, she only said, "I'll think about it."

At that moment, the bell on the front door of the shop jingled and a little girl and her mother spilled inside. The girl was pulling on her mother's reluctant arm, saying "this way, this way!"

"Welcome to Snow Valley Treasures." Mia said, warmly.

The girl's mother nodded at Mia, as her daughter tugged her further into the shop. As they passed, Mia noticed the rubber sole on one of the girl's shoes was coming unglued. Her coat was smudged and looked like it had probably fit better last Christmas, or the one before.

The girl scanned the room and then dashed in the direction of a science display. The table was in the "Discover" section of the store, and featured eggs with dinosaur bones for excavating; volcanoes meant for vinegar and baking soda eruptions; and small construction kits, which, once assembled, taught children basic computer coding and machine engineering. The girl picked up a kit and examined it. Mia looked on, smiling.

"Mom, look! They have it!" the girl cried out, as she triumphantly held the kit in the air like a trophy. "This is the one where you can build a robot. I saw it on YouTube."

The girl's mother moved quickly in her direction. "Don't hold it up like that," she said. "I told you we're not getting anything today."

Her smile faded and she placed the kit back on the table. "Sorry, Mom."

"It's okay. Let's go."

"Wait." She stuck her hand in her pocket, fished around, and pulled out a twenty-dollar bill. "Is this enough?"

"Where'd you get that money?"

"It's my birthday money, from Grandma."

The mother looked at Mia. "How much are these robot things?"

"$27.99," Mia responded.

The girl's eyes fell. She glanced at her mother. "Do you think maybe I could get it for Christmas?"

"Tess, it's expensive." the mother said under her breath. "We'll have to see." She pulled her daughter toward the door.

Mia shot a sympathetic glance at Richard. "Wait!" she yelled, rushing after them. "Don't leave yet!" She stretched her arms in front of the door and barred the exit, smiling at the seemingly-startled pair. "You were looking at a CityBot kit, right?"

Tess looked at her mother timidly, as if unsure what to do next. She nodded.

Mia feigned a relieved look. "I'm glad I caught you. The CityBots are on sale this week. 50% off."

Tess looked confused. "So, do I have enough, then?"

"Yes, you do…as long as it's okay with your mom."

Tess's eyes widened and a smile spread across her face. "You mean it?" she shouted. "Can I, Mom?"

The mother nodded slowly, and Tess let out a whoop as she bounded back toward the Discover section. When she was out of earshot her mother turned toward Mia, mouth taut. "We don't need charity. I want to make this right." She unzipped her purse and rooted around inside.

Mia held up her hand in protest. "It's not charity. That toy's on sale."

The mother pointed to the display. "Why isn't it marked?"

"It's still early. We just opened."

The mother's expression softened, and she removed her hand from her purse. Seconds later, Tess bounced up to the cash register clutching a CityBot in both arms. "I want this one!"

Richard grabbed the kit and beeped it. "Excellent choice! Concrete Pete is the best of the CityBots!" Tess handed him the crumpled $20. "Thank you." He bagged the robot and gave it back to her along with $14 change. "Have a Merry Christmas!"

Tess's mother wore a relieved smile. "What do you say?" she asked.

"Thank you! Merry Christmas to you, too!" Tess shouted.

Mia laughed and waved as the pair left the store. Richard sidled up next to her. "On sale huh? Where'd you come up with that?"

"Don't start. This is no different than our Toys for Tots drive. It just happened in real-time, that's all. Anyway, I didn't see you come up with any better ideas."

Richard nodded. "It was sweet. It's just…" he trailed off.

"Just what?"

"Just that now is not the best time to be giving toys away. We really need every penny."

"Don't worry, Grinch, this one's coming out of my pocket."

Richard pursed his lips. "I mean it, Mia. I got the bill from my inventory source in China yesterday. It's not pretty. And we're lucky to even have him. The way he connects us to exclusive inventory – he could charge us a lot more."

Mia absorbed the news. For the last year, to compete with Jungle.com, they had pivoted from selling common items – the kind one might find at Target, or Wal-Mart, or Jungle – to selling unique, hard-to-come-by gifts. This was a taller task than they'd anticipated, and Mia and Richard spent a good deal of money, and a great deal of time, sourcing exclusive inventory, both locally and as far away as China. Mia's theory was that even if online sales were dominant, brick-and-mortars would never fully go away. People liked to shop in-store. They liked to feel the packages in their hands; to try-on different sizes of hats and gloves; to play with toys before buying them. But Jungle was always there. Swallowing up more and more mom-and-pop stores. Always increasing its own inventory. Often, when Mia and Richard found something perfect for the store, there it was on Jungle. Everyone used Jungle, and who could blame them? The convenience was unparalleled. Fast, free, same-day delivery. Mia herself frequented the site when she was low on time. But still, she held fast to her business plan. There were plenty of retail businesses that had survived the retail apocalypse: COVID-19 and the online boom. Best Buy was one shining example, and there were plenty of small businesses too. The key was adaptation. But adaptation was expensive.

Mia pulled a twenty-dollar bill from her pocket and walked to the register. The CityBot was still "rung up" on the screen, which showed $13.99 owing. She put the money in the drawer and collected her change. "Happy?"

"Yes, but that's not all." Richard reached under the counter and pulled out a stack of mail. He held it out to Mia. "We can't ignore these, forever."

"We'll be fine. When the snow comes, tourists will too. But this was never only about the bottom line for me. I wanted to provide a service and to make people happy. If we forget that, then what's the point of running this business in the first place?"

"I hope you're right."

Mia chuckled dryly and narrowed her eyes. "Are you on my side, or not?"

Richard smiled. "Of course, I am. I'm ready to do whatever it takes. I just think we need some help."

"We're fine," Mia insisted. "We'll be fine."

CHAPTER 2

Sunlight poured in through the sheer curtains next to Noah's hotel bed. Another beautiful day. He stretched his muscular 6' 2" frame out across the white, high-thread-count sheets. Luxurious, soft, expensive, just the way he liked them. Bleary eyed, he reached for his phone and scrolled through the day's headlines. Nothing interesting. Next, he scrolled through the stock outlook. That was better. The predictions based on pre-opening trading were strong. Things had been looking up for the economy month-over-month, after the COVID vaccines became widely available. To be sure, there was still work to be done – many businesses were still trying to pick up the pieces – but things were headed in the right direction. Noah wasn't a day-trader himself, but he had a few investments and liked to keep abreast of any larger trends. Lastly, he tapped the weather app. Ten straight days of sun. "Perfect," he thought. "Just like living in Phoenix." Not that he hated snow; he just didn't see its utility. Snow had been fun when he was a kid, but now it seemed like an inconvenience. Snow caused traffic jams, power outages, and shut down businesses. No thanks.

He closed the app and rested his phone on the side table. "So far, so good," he thought. "This place may work out."

His workout was brisk – some intense calisthenics and cardio – and it was easy to complete from a hotel room. That was one of the few beneficial byproducts of the pandemic – learning to get by in small spaces. His only hiccup was finding which suitcase housed his workout gear. Noah had only been in the hotel for a couple of nights but he was already tired of living out of a suitcase. His new condo was opening across town the following day. He knew he'd miss the luxury of being waited on in a five-star suite, but was looking forward to getting back into his own space.

Before his plane landed – three days prior – it had been more than a decade since Noah had last set foot in Snow Valley. He had some family in the city, but as his career grew more demanding, the visits had become less-and-less regular. However, when the position of Regional Asset Interim Director opened, he'd jumped at the chance. It was offered to him as a temporary position – a placeholder until a permanent director could be found. But Noah had different plans. He was intent on doing such a bang-up-job, those responsible for finding a permanent director, wouldn't have to look very far. The new position meant a move across the country, and working in an office he was unfamiliar with, but it was a big promotion, and the salary bump was significant, too. Considering he didn't have a wife or kids, and his mom already lived out-of-state anyway, the move made sense. It was a big step in the right direction. Today he'd take a tour of the new office, meet his new boss, and get the lay of the land. He anxiously fidgeted with the buttons on his suit, as he walked out of the hotel.

Noah ordered a Rydeshare to the new offices, and took in his surroundings on the way. Snow Valley's skyline was majestic, giant buildings of chrome and glass twisting skyward, set against a backdrop of snow-capped mountains. The city's architecture was a mix of old and new. A century-old train station had been restored and recommissioned as an outdoor mall. There were several skyscrapers which rivaled those in Manhattan and Chicago. He pulled out his business card holder and popped it open. He read and re-read one of the new cards, hot off the presses: "Noah Caffrey, Regional Acquisition Interim Director." He chuckled out loud. R-A-I-D. "How apt," he thought. A Regional Acquisition Director was responsible for surveying and acquiring prospective businesses. With the additional "I" for interim, Noah's title actually spelled out RAID, an irony which was not lost on him. He knew asset directors had been called "corporate raiders," – and much worse – on blogs and social media. That was just the name of the game though. What he did was perfectly legal. It wasn't his fault if disgruntled employees from companies who'd been absorbed or disbanded, were upset with the change.

The Rydeshare pulled up in front of a towering, ultra-modern building. The driver turned back to Noah. "This it?"

"Yep."

"Wow, you work here?"

"Yep."

"You're lucky, man."

"Thanks."

Noah did feel lucky. He smiled politely, tipped the driver in the app, and clambered out of the car. Before walking inside, he took a minute to gather himself, and looked up at his new building. It was at least sixty stories tall, made entirely of reflective glass. About half way up, in giant letters was the company's logo: Jungle.com.

CHAPTER 3

Outside of work, Mia's condo was her sanctuary. It had marble countertops, vaulted ceilings, and a balcony with a nice view of the lake. In the summer, she'd watch the small sailboats, and dinghies putter across the water. In winter, ice skaters would brave the frozen lake, and Mia would have a front-row seat to all the twirls, spins, and spills. One time, she even saw a proposal right in the middle of the ice. It was romantic, and Mia couldn't help but feel a tinge of jealousy. The condo wasn't perfect though. The elevator occasionally broke down, and always, it seemed, when she had her arms full of groceries, or whenever she'd had a particularly hard day at work. Also, the paint needed some freshening up, and she knew she could do with some interior decoration help. But it was home, and it meant a lot to her. Thanks to the vaulted ceilings, every Christmas, Mia would put up a giant tree in the corner of the living room. Last year she'd bought a ten-footer and had to buy a full-size ladder just to decorate it.

On this day though, Mia wasn't thinking about her condo, or Christmas, or anything other than how to help her shop. The elevator was working, a small miracle considering her stressful day, and she rode to the top floor lost in abject thought. When the doors opened, Mia stepped off and tripped over a box lying in the middle of the floor. She stumbled forward arms flailing, and tried to grab onto the bare wall in front of her, before crumbling all the way to the ground. Other than a small bump on the knee, she was fine. "Who in the world left this here?" she called out, but no one was around. Mia looked down the hallway toward her door. It was littered with several more taped, brown, moving boxes. They were strewn haphazardly, as if they'd been dumped there in a hurry. The most substantial pile was stacked near the condo marked 2B, and one box propped the door open.

Mia picked herself up and brushed herself off, shaking her head. The box she'd tripped over was mangled, the cardboard torn, and pot and pan handles were poking out of the newly-ripped hole. She bent over and shoved the box out of the way of the elevator door. It tumbled onto its side and two pans fell out. "Serves them right," she said, and turned to head down the hallway.

As she passed 2B, Mia looked inside the open door. From her point of view, the condo was empty, and only one light was on. While she was gawking, a familiar voice rang out and startled her.

"Hi!"

Mia recognized the voice. It was her octogenarian neighbor, Dorothy, who'd always reminded her of Ethel from "I Love Lucy" reruns. Dorothy had lived in 2C for as long as Mia had lived in the building. Mia had heard, from another tenant, that Dorothy was the original occupant of 2C, from when the condos were built, but Mia had never inquired, worrying such a question would be impolite. She smiled. "Hi, Dorothy. What's going on?"

"Looks like someone's moving in."

"I saw. They almost killed me by the elevator. I tripped over one of the boxes. Have you seen who it is, and maybe asked her why she put her boxes all over the floor?"

"It's a he." Dorothy stated proudly. "I saw him carrying boxes from my window…and my door." Mia smiled and cocked her head sideways. Dorothy continued. "He's handsome too, ya' know. I might have to go and introduce myself later."

Mia laughed. "How old is he?"

"Age is a state of mind, my dear."

"Okay, well what's his…" Mia raised her hands and air quoted, "state of mind."

Dorothy laughed. "I'd say it's mid-thirties."

"Isn't that a bit young for you?"

"I'm like a fine wine. I just get better with age."

Mia laughed again. "Well, cheers to that. And good luck. But if you successfully woo this guy, tell him to clean up his boxes."

"Will do."

They said goodbye, and Mia pushed open her condo door. Her large tree sat in the corner, and after it was plugged in, it lit up the room in a dazzling LED glow. No matter how stressful her days were, she always felt more relaxed under the twinkle of Christmas lights. She made her way to the kitchen and groaned at a sticky note she'd left on her fridge that morning: "Remember!!" it said, "Get groceries on your way home!" Mia kicked herself for forgetting, but she popped open the fridge anyway, just in case. Old Mother Hubbard would have been proud. "I'm gonna have to stick these notes to my forehead," she thought. She grabbed her coat and headed back out the door.

After navigating the labyrinth of boxes strewn about the hallway, Mia stepped onto the elevator. The box she'd shoved was still sitting on its side, its contents spilling out. As the elevator doors closed, a hand reached in and sent them flying back open. Mia rolled her eyes surreptitiously. The hand was followed by a body belonging to a tall, well-built, man. He had brown hair, a bit of face stubble, and was sporting slacks and a blue button-down shirt. The shirt was covered in sweat stains on the neck, armpits, and chest, and the man was out-of-breath. He stepped onto the elevator and flashed a quick smile.

"Sorry about that," he said.

"It's ok."

"I've been chasing this elevator all night. The doors close way too quickly." The man shook his head in frustration. "I don't know who would set it up that way."

"That'd be the HOA." Mia offered.

"Well those guys make questionable decisions."

Mia pressed her lips together and extended her hand. "I'm Mia. President of the HOA committee."

The man grimaced and his face flushed. He shook Mia's hand. "You didn't let me finish...I meant they make questionable decisions, in difficult situations, that are probably very...sound and well thought out."

"Nice try," Mia interrupted.

"Thanks. I was drowning there. I'm Noah. I'm moving into 2B." He was still shaking Mia's hand and she pulled it away.

"I noticed. I nearly killed myself on the boxes you left all over the hallway."

"Sorry about that. The movers never showed, and I've been running back and forth all night."

"It's fine," she said, curtly.

Noah stared at the ground and looked like he was struggling to think of something to say. "So," he said, finally, "what do you do besides arrange for elevators to close like guillotines?"

"Wow! Doubling down?" she said, but couldn't stop herself from chuckling at the joke.

"I'm joking, I'm joking. I really am sorry about leaving my boxes everywhere."

She nodded. "I'm in retail."

"Me too. Online retail. I work for Jungle.com."

Mia's eyes closed slowly. "Of course, you do."

"What is that supposed to mean? Usually people are interested in my job."

"I guess I'm not a usual person."

"Trust me, I can see that."

"What is that supposed to mean?" she asked.

"Nothing. So, where do you work?"

At that moment, the elevator doors opened and Mia practically jumped off the elevator.

"I work at Snow Valley Treasures," she said, without turning, "and clean up those boxes." With that, she pushed her way out into the cold.

CHAPTER 4

The Jungle.com office building was "techy" in every respect. There were pool and ping-pong tables in the common areas, brightly painted walls, open ceilings with purposefully exposed wiring and HVAC systems, and glass offices. Noah didn't particularly care for the design, but then again, he didn't particularly care about it either. He had bigger fish to fry. Noah had worked hard to get where he was: near the top of his class at State University with a degree in English Literature, then an MBA from a prestigious school in the northeast. After graduation, he'd hit the ground running on the job hunt. The timing was bad, even for someone with his impressive credentials. He finished school in 2009, well before the bounce-back from the 2008 crash. At first, he tried to leverage his contacts, but they were meager. His dad had been killed in a car crash before he was born. His mom had received a bachelor's degree and had dabbled in the corporate world, but eventually opened a small business and focused on motherhood. She didn't know anybody who knew anybody either. So, Noah blanketed the city with job applications. He received a few responses from sales teams offering him immediate work and promising commissions of up to "100K per month" but he let those opportunities pass.

Finally, he got an offer from Jungle.com to work as an assistant. The salary was small, but the experience would be unparalleled, at least according to the job breakdown. He accepted, and began work the following week. Over the years that followed, Noah proved himself time and again to his superiors. In the ensuing ten years – while his college roommates were getting married and starting families – Noah was promoted, then promoted again. Occasionally he'd see pictures of friends on vacations with their kids, or celebrating their kids' first birthdays, and he'd wonder what a life like that would feel like. But as soon as those thoughts crept in, he'd push them back out. He was focused. During his last few years at work, things had stagnated a bit and Noah worried about his career prospects going forward. But then the RAID position opened up, and Noah was on a plane the next week.

The elevator arrived at the 46th floor, and Noah marched to his office. He popped open his laptop and navigated to a search bar where he typed the words "Snow Valley Treasures." The top hit showed a thumbnail of Mia standing in front of her store smiling. Noah clicked the link. The website was modest, no flashy videos or music, and it was clear it had been made by someone with little web design experience. Still, it got the job done.

The store boasted unique and one-of-a-kind games, toys, and trinkets, for sale. Noah navigated to the "About Us" section and began reading. "Hi, and thanks for stopping by," welcomed the site. He continued scrolling, "My name is Mia Gallagher, I'm the owner and operator of Snow Valley Treasures. We are a local treasure shop dedicated to giving back to our community. I started Snow Valley Treasures because I love to try products out before buying them. When I was little, there were only big-box retailers who never let kids play with toys before buying them." Noah paused and smiled. He remembered being scolded by a store employee once, when he'd taken a toy out of the box. He hadn't intended to steal or to damage it, he just wanted to try it out. Noah continued reading, "At Snow Valley Treasures, you can try ANY toy, game, or clothing in the store before you buy it. We will gladly unwrap it if there is not a demo model on the floor. Please stop on by, and come play with us!"

"Clever business model," Noah thought to himself. He grabbed a notebook, a pen, and paper and jotted down information from the site. "This is perfect." Next, Noah navigated to Snow Valley's dot-gov website which listed small business information. When he found what he was looking for, he smiled and picked up the phone.

An hour later, Noah emerged from his office and made a beeline to one of the glass-exposed boardrooms on the 50th floor. A group of casually-dressed 20-somethings, his coworkers, were seated around the boardroom table. The meeting was about to begin, and Noah dived into a chair. At the front of the room, Noah's boss, Nadine, stood and addressed the group.

"This will be short and sweet, I promise. I know we all have things that need attention. If you'll please direct your gazes to the slide show on the projector…" Nadine started into what turned out to be an hour-long slog. The meeting, as most meetings tend to be, was a grind and probably could have been accomplished with an email or two. Noah tried to pay attention but couldn't keep his mind from drifting. He tuned back in as Nadine was finishing up.

"Now," she said, "because we are getting close to the end of the year, I want to ask each department to briefly rundown where they are currently, and their Q1 goals. These last three weeks of the year need to be strong, and all of us need to come up with ideas for how to grow in Q1 of next year." Noah sat up. That meant he'd have the opportunity to pitch his new idea. Nadine continued. "The focus needs to be on expansion. If we're not expanding we're contracting, so let's get contract-ing," she said, putting the emphasis in the word "contract." Several people around the table subtly rolled their eyes, and an audible, but faint groan could be heard. Nadine proceeded to go around the table asking the respective executives and department heads about their plans and goals.

The Q&A session was pushing the meeting toward the end

of hour two, and Noah felt his mind start to drift again. Next to him, one of Noah's colleagues from IT was doing his best to parry questions from Nadine. Noah shook off the drowsiness and listened in again. "I understand what you're saying about efficiency," she said, "but I'm still failing to see how your suggestion that the entire IT department be issued new laptops, will be an asset and not a liability. How could we hope to make up that initial outlay of cash?"

The man hesitated. "We could look to outsource some of the… non-essential jobs."

Another groan from the group. Across the table, someone else piped up, "You're non-essential." The room erupted. Even Nadine choked back laughter as she said, "Let's play nice people." She composed herself and addressed the group again. "I'm talking about Q1 goals, I'm talking about expansion. I don't want to hear about more coffee machines, or pool tables," she looked directly at the IT employee, "or better laptops for the IT department." Nadine motioned to Noah. "Everyone, this is Noah Caffrey. He's our new Asset Director…on an interim basis only," she added, annoyingly. "He's here by way of the Sun Valley office. Previously an Associate Director." She looked at Noah. "Not to put you on the spot – I know you just landed here the other day – but if you have anything to add, go ahead."

Noah gave a half wave to the group and cleared his throat. "Thank you," he said to Nadine. "Actually, I have one suggestion."

"I'm all ears." she said, halfheartedly.

"Well I know in the Sun Valley office we discussed increasing our footprint in brick-and-mortar stores. And I know company policy is to 'behave and think as one,'" he said, using air quotes, "so I presume the same thought processes apply here?"

Nadine nodded. "Yes, that's generally correct, but there are several caveats. First, real estate is considerably cheaper in Sun Valley, so brick-and-mortars make more sense there. Second, we don't expand just for the sake of expansion. It has to be viable. It has to make sense."

Noah nodded along. "Of course," he said. "Well, I may have

stumbled into a viable, make sense expansion opportunity.

"I'm listening."

Noah continued. "Last night I found a cute little boutique store fairly close to here. I did some digging, made a few calls to the bank this morning, and found out they're not doing so hot. The COVID lockdown basically wiped them out."

"This sounds bad, so far." Nadine interrupted. The group chuckled.

"I know, but I think we could easily, and affordably, acquire them and make them our trial store in this market."

"Why would we want a failing business?"

"Because it has good bones. The pandemic squeezed thousands of good businesses, but it seems like things were fine beforehand. The owner seems solid, too. Maybe she'd stay on as a Jungle employee and still run the day-to-day."

"I still don't see what's special about this place." Nadine interrupted again, sounding increasingly impatient.

Noah sat forward. "Our data indicates the biggest missing puzzle piece from online sales is customers frustrated by not getting what they think they're getting, right? Pictures just don't always suffice. We take a bath every month in shipping costs for returns. Imagine a place where kids could come in and play with toys, people could try on clothes, chefs could hold pots in their hands, and they could either buy them there, or be sent links to buy them online."

"That sounds like a retail store," Nadine said. More laughter.

"Yeah, but here's the twist," Noah countered, "when they have something shipped to the store, they pay nothing. Not just nothing for shipping, nothing at all. It's a free trial. Normally the purchase is made first, and the return is the hassle. The customer has to risk their money and hope they like what they bought. No longer. We can add a "Try It Free" button next to items on the website. And here's the best part, once people come in to try out their items, it's impulse purchase time. We can have interactive kiosks set up for browsing, as well as a large in-store inventory of attractive SKUs. No more complaints from angry parents. No more mountains of returns. No more fear of purchasing something because you don't know if it will fit, or if it's cheaply made. Everything would be fully integrated."

Nadine nodded along as Noah spoke. "Try it before you buy it, huh? I like it," she said. "Have you spoken to the owner about selling?"

"Not yet. But I don't anticipate that being a problem."

"What's the store called?" she asked.

"Snow Valley Treasures."

Nadine smirked. "Not for long." The group laughed again. "Good job, Noah. Way to come out swinging. You can make this your priority. Go find out everything you can about that little boutique. Get to know the staff, take a peek at their financials if you can. I'll need to run this up the flag pole, so I expect a full proposal a week from today. Is that doable?"

Noah sat back in his chair and a grin spread across his face. "Absolutely."

CHAPTER 5

The sign outside read: "Valley Mutual Bank, A pillar of trust and security since 1952." The logo featured two hands clasped in a handshake, all encircled by a padlock. Mia remembered the padlock, all right, albeit for different reasons. She found a parking spot near the front, and dragged her feet towards the entrance. The sign logo was also stenciled on the door. She took a deep breath.

Mia hated banks – the way they smelled, the way they looked, the way the way they made you think they had your best interests in mind – and her distaste for banks was not new. When she was young, she hated banks because they were boring. All that interminable waiting. Going on errands with her mom, Mia was expected to be on her best behavior. Banks were stuffy, and more than once she'd been scolded her for being too rambunctious. When she was older she hated the bank for a more legitimate reason: her parents' foreclosure. Mia's dad lost his teaching job when his school district decided to prioritize theater over music. The budget was thin, and it could only afford one art elective. Music was out. Her parents scrambled to find work, picking up odd jobs, but it wasn't enough to keep them afloat. Though they tried to hide it, Mia was old enough to read the threatening letters, and more importantly, to read the tension in the household. Her parents pled and fought with the bank, but, apparently, only so many grace periods can be granted.

After they were evicted, Mia made a habit of pedaling past her old house on the way to school. A large white paper labeled "Eviction" was stuck to the door, but it was the lock she remembered most. A simple padlock hung from two plates connecting the door and doorframe. She'd been locked out of her own house. She watched as the grass grew out of control, and weeds choked out the garden her mom had spent so much time tending. It was a hopeless feeling, one she swore she'd never encounter again. But now that same lock was staring her in the face, in the form of a corporate logo. Mia clenched her teeth and yanked on the doors.

Inside, a straight-faced bank manager approached and extended his hand. He flashed a closed-lip smile. "Ms. Gallagher," he said, "please follow me." The manager led Mia past the row of cubicles which provided only the smallest modicum of privacy, behind which people divulged their deepest financial secrets. He entered his office and pointed to a chair.

"At least I get the office treatment," Mia thought.

"Have a seat." The manager sat across from Mia and opened with the standard pleasantries. "Cold out there, huh?"

"Sure is."

"They're saying it's going to hit single digits tomorrow night."

"I hadn't heard," Mia responded.

The manager gathered some papers in front of him. "Ms. Gallagher, I'll cut to the chase. I called you in today, because I have something important to discuss. A matter which cannot, or at least should not be discussed over the phone."

"So much for cutting to the chase," Mia thought.

The manager continued. "It's about your balloon payment, for your mortgage on…" his voice trailed off as he rifled through the papers in front of him.

"Snow Valley Treasures." Mia offered.

"Yes, that's it, Snow Valley Treasures. Thank you. Now, Ms.

Gallagher, you've been receiving our delinquency letters for some time. Is that fair?"

"Fair?"

"Is that correct, I mean?"

"Yes, I have them."

"Good. Then as you're aware, all of the COVID forbearance and relief has been extinguished. We've done all we can do."

"I understand."

"And you also know that under the terms of your loan, in the event the bank receives payment for less than the full balance six or more times in a calendar year, the bank can exercise the option to call a larger amount due, as a protection, up to and including the full loan balance."

"I read that too," Mia responded dryly, her pulse quickening.

"Good. I hate to give you this news in light of the holiday season, but you must understand the bank must do what it must do."

"And what must it do?"

"The bank is demanding 25% of the remainder of the mortgage. As a security. And that amount must be received by the first of the year, or we will have no choice but begin the foreclosure process."

Mia's thoughts raced back to the day when her parents received their eviction notice. She closed her eyes and absorbed the information. "What are you talking about?"

"I'm sorry," the bank manager said. "I wish I could delay things, but I have no say in this."

"25%!" Mia asked, nearly shouting. "How much is 25%? Why not just demand the full balance?"

"We could. As I said, that was within our rights to do. You should be happy the bank is only calling for 25%."

"I should be happy?"

"I'm sorry…" the manager stammered. "That's not what I meant. I mean it's good the bank has not exercised that option."

"How much is 25%?" Mia pressed again.

The manager picked up the file and looked through more papers. "It's…ninety-six thousand and change."

Mia was stunned. "Ninety-six thousand." She repeated to herself. The bank manager might as well have said ninety-six million. Mia had a bit of money in savings, but nowhere near a hundred grand. Her condo had some equity, but not much, and she couldn't even sell it in time if she'd wanted to. "Ninety-six thousand," she said again.

"I'm afraid so." The manager got up from his chair. "Let me get you a bottle of water." He scurried out of the room.

Mia was numb. She knew she owed money, and she knew about the potential of a delinquency penalty. But now sitting here and hearing it first-hand, was just like being 9-years-old again, and hearing the foreclosure news from her parents. All of the angry, hopeless feelings she remembered from her childhood washed over her. She hung her head in defeat.

But as she looked down, something caught her eye. There, tucked under her mortgage papers on the bank manager's desk, the top of the Daily Gazette was peeking out. The headline, though she could only make out a bit of it, said, "$100,000 Grand Prize!" She grabbed the paper and yanked it out from below the stack.

At that moment, the bank manager returned bearing two bottles of water.

"Is this today's paper?" Mia asked.

"Yes."

"Do you mind?" she said, motioning at it with her head.

"Not at all. I'm finished with it." Mia was pouring over the words in the article. After a moment, the bank manager cleared his throat. "Any more questions for me, Ms. Gallagher?"

Mia looked up, startled. "No, I'm on my way now. Don't start the foreclosure process. You'll get your money."

"I hope so. As I said, you have until the first of the year." Mia stood up to leave. "Best of luck," the manager called after her.

She made her way to the lobby and chose a seat meant for would-be credit card applicants. She flipped the paper open and began reading. There it was, the front-page headline in dark bold typeface: "Annual 'Twelve Games of Christmas' Puzzle Contest

to Offer First Prize of $100,000!"
 Mia's hands were shaking. "This is it!"

CHAPTER 6

Noah had never been across town. In fact, he was so new to Snow Valley, he'd never really been anywhere. So, despite the traffic, he enjoyed his slow drive across the city in his newly-leased SUV. He chose "alternate route" on the GPS in the hope of avoiding freeways, and getting to know some of the city's backroads. The SUV was a splurge in celebration of his new position. It was also a necessity of sorts – he needed a car, just maybe not one with built-in seat massagers. The (upgraded) Bose speakers softly piped out Charles Dickins' "A Christmas Carol," on audiobook while Noah drove. As an English Lit major, he always made time to fit in the classics.

The first stop he made was the donut shop. One dozen assorted. The dot-gov listing only showed Snow Valley Treasures as having two employees, but Noah wasn't sure how accurate that was. Better to be safe than sorry, especially when trying to butter people up. Back in the car, he plugged Snow Valley Treasures into the GPS. The "alternate route" led him through busy thoroughfares, and back alleys. Twenty minutes later, he pulled up to the corner of Main and 3rd, and was underwhelmed. The building wasn't ugly, but it certainly wasn't eye-catching. The location was perfect, though. One didn't need to be an expert on Snow Valley real estate to see that. A retail shop on a busy corner, right across from the entrance to a park. Location, location, location. He pulled the car over and parallel parked – or rather, the car's autonomous parking feature parallel parked itself (another upgrade) – in an available spot across the street from the shop. On the SUV speakers, he heard Scrooge tell the ghost of Marley "there's more of gravy than of grave about you," before shutting the engine off. Noah grabbed the donuts and headed toward the entrance.

Inside, Richard was busy stocking shelves. A tedious task, but one Mia cared deeply about. She'd told Richard the shelves could never appear empty. The store always needed to look like it was bursting at the seams with inventory. Richard had pointed out if the shelves were emptier, it would look more like a high-end boutique, and might drum up more business. Or perhaps even a supply and demand type scenario. It was Mia's call though, and she wouldn't hear of it. She wanted her shelves to seem as deep and endless as an online catalogue, so, Richard restocked.

As he was putting one last luxury teddy bear on a high shelf, the bell above the door jingled. Noah stepped inside, carrying a box of donuts. Richard smiled. "Oooh, I hope those are for me," he said, joking.

"They are, actually."

"Then it's my lucky day. To what do I owe this pleasure?" he said as he climbed down from the ladder.

"I'm here to talk to Mia. Is she around?"

"I'm afraid she's out." Richard looked at his watch. "But she should be back soon. Are you a friend of hers?"

"Yes, well, not exactly. I'm her neighbor."

"Wow. Nice to meet you." Richard had made his way across the room and shook hands with Noah. Noah handed him the box of donuts. "Thank you so much. So, you said these are for Mia?"

"No, no. I brought them for all the employees."

"Then it really is my lucky day, 'cuz it's just me." Richard slid the top off the box of donuts and selected a chocolate-raised with Christmas sprinkles. He took a bite. "Fank ooo," he said through a stuffed mouth.

"Don't mention it."

"Do you want me to give Mia a call? Is she expecting you?"

"That's ok. You said she'll be back soon, right?" Richard nodded. "I don't mind hanging out until she gets here."

"No problem. Follow me." Richard waved his hand and beckoned Noah to the back office. "Sorry," he said, "this is really the only place that has any chairs. Take a seat." Noah thanked Richard and plopped down in a 70s-style rolling computer chair.

The back office was less an office and more of a clutter space. True, there was a desk, a computer, and a phone, but that was about as close to an office qua office as the space would allow. Richard and Mia mainly utilized it for dumping old boxes on their way to be recycled. Occasionally, the two would take lunch in the room, but only when the weather was so bad there was no choice but to stay in. There were only two chairs in the room, the one currently occupied by Noah, and another ripped, leather chair behind the desk.

Richard walked around the table and sat in the chair facing the desktop computer. "Let me just check Mia's schedule," he said. He tapped the spacebar and the monitor sprang to life. He punched in a password, and navigated the mouse to a calendar app. "Okay, it looks like she's free for the rest of the afternoon. No dentist appointments or anything." Noah chuckled politely.

Seconds later, they heard the jingle of the bell over the front door. "Excuse me," Richard said, "that might be her now." He smiled cordially, and made his way back out into the store, without locking the computer.

"No problem."

From the other room, Noah heard Richard's voice. "Welcome to Snow Valley Treasures, can I help you find anything?"

"Thanks," came the response. "Do you guys have the gloves with…"

Noah had trouble making out the rest of the conversation. It sounded like a customer was asking about snow gloves that could be used with a smartphone. As Richard and the customer engaged in a back and forth, Noah checked over his shoulder to ensure he was alone. His gaze fell to the opposite side of the desk. The computer sat glowing. Another glance over his shoulder while he listened. The customer was still talking. It sounded like she wanted a bigger size of glove. Noah jumped to his feet and sidled around the desk. On the screen was the calendar Richard had been looking at. There wasn't much listed. Most days were completely blank. Every other Friday at 4:00, there was a listing for "Inventory Arrival." Noah looked at the schedule for that day: a meeting with Eric Reynolds, of Valley Mutual Bank. Noah stole a quick glance over his shoulder again, then pulled out his phone, and opened the camera app. He snapped a picture of the information on the monitor.

"Thanks, and come see us again," he heard Richard call out from the other room. The bell of the front door jingled.

Noah turned to sit back down, when one more calendar entry caught his eye. He enlarged it to get a better look: "Call with Zhang Wei – New Inventory Discussion." The entry also had a phone number listed. Hands shaking, Noah slid his phone out of his pocket, and almost dropped it. Corporate espionage was new for him. Again, he tapped open his camera and snapped a picture of the screen.

"Sorry to keep you waiting," he heard Richard say, from just outside the door. Noah jammed his phone back in his pocket and clicked the "X" on the calendar entry, but it was too late to make it back to his seat. Richard rounded the corner into the back office.

"No problem at all," Noah said. He was still standing behind the desk but was staring intently at the leather chair. "Is this an antique? It looks beautiful."

A small crease appeared on Richard's brow. "Er…no, I don't think so. It's just a chair." Richard clocked the computer screen as he drew near Noah. Nothing seemed to be out of place.

"I'm fascinated by antiques," Noah said, trying to sound casual. He moved back around the table and sat in the rolling chair again. "Do you ever watch the Antiques Roadshow?" He said, trying to sound casual.

Richard grabbed the mouse and locked the computer screen, but he smiled. "I've seen it. I don't know much about antiques, but I love it when the people bring in something they think is junk, and then they find out it's worth a million bucks."

"Me too."

At that moment, the front door chimed again. "Richard," Mia's voice called out. "You're not gonna believe it."

CHAPTER 7

Mia was out of breath and had a smile painted on her face. Richard looked relieved to see her. "I'm glad you're here," he said. "There's someone…"

Mia either didn't hear, or didn't care to hear what Richard had to say. "This is it! Look." She waved the newspaper above her head like a Wall Street trader after the bell.

"What is it?" Richard asked. "Another puzzle?"

"No…well, yes actually. But that's not the point. This is special. You were right."

Richard looked unimpressed. He stood closer to her and lowered his voice. "Mia, listen. There's someone…"

Mia put up her hand to silence him. "Hang on. Hang on. You'll like this. Look." She unfolded the newspaper and pointed to the front page. "You were right. They're changing the Twelve Games contest."

"So? Changing it how?"

"The prize. Guess what they're giving away."

Richard shrugged. "Dunno. A Starbucks giftcard?"

Mia laughed. She pointed to the headline. "Annual 'Twelve Games of Christmas' Puzzle Contest to Offer First Prize of $100,000!"

"Whoa. That can't be real."

THE 12 GAMES OF CHRISTMAS

"I think it is. It's put on by the Gazette and they printed this themselves. Their social media page is buzzing about it, too. Listen." She read out loud from the newspaper. "The Twelve Games of Christmas. Perplexing puzzles and a citywide scavenger hunt. A $100,000 prize is up for grabs! Rules: Download the Gazette-on-the-Go app to play. Every day for twelve days, a new game or puzzle will appear in the app. The puzzle's solution will contain clues revealing a secret location. Be one of the first three people to find the location and take a selfie there, to score a point for the day. At the end of the twelve days, the contestant with the most points will win." Mia finished reading and nearly panted from lack of breath.

"So?" Richard said.

"So? What do you mean, so? Don't you see? This is a sign."

Richard looked over his shoulder toward the back room. He walked over to the cashier's counter and again grabbed an envelope with a red stamp which read, "Important! Open Immediately." He held the letter up facing Mia. "No. This is a sign. The bank isn't going away."

The smile melted off her face. "I know. I met with them earlier."

"What'd they say?"

"It's not good. We need to come up with 25% of the mortgage, by the first of the year, or we're outta here. This contest may be our last hope, as silly as that sounds."

Richard held his finger up to his lip in a shushing motion, and he looked over his shoulder toward the back room. "Well it doesn't sound very realistic."

"What do you keep looking at," Mia asked.

"I've been trying to tell you! Your neighbor's here to see you."

"What? My neighbor, Dorothy? Is everything ok?"

Richard slapped the palm of his hand against his forehead. "No, it's not Dorothy. It's…I actually didn't catch his name. All I know is he's waiting in the back office."

Mia whispered. "Who is it, Rich. What if he's a burglar or something?"

"He didn't look like a burglar. Plus, we have nothing left to steal, remember? He'd only be taking on our debt if he got the deed to this place."

Mia chuckled. "True. Did he at least tell you what he wanted?"

"Just said he came to talk to you. I assumed you were friends." Richard pointed to the counter. "He brought donuts."

Mia was nonplussed. She shrugged and walked to the back room. Noah was still seated in the small rolling chair, tapping away at his phone. Seeing his tall frame squatting in that tiny chair conjured up an image of a circus bear riding a tricycle. It would have made Mia laugh, but she was too stunned to find anything funny. "What are you doing here?" she asked.

Noah turned and flashed a large, toothy smile. "That excited to see me, huh?"

Mia stepped over several boxes, and made her way around the desk to the leather chair to take a seat. "I'm sorry. I just didn't expect you. What can I help you with?"

"As a matter of fact, I think I can help you."

Mia cocked her head sideways. "I don't think I need help."

Noah continued. "I want to tell you, I…we love this shop. It's perfect."

At his mention of the word "we" Mia had a moment of panic. She glanced past Noah and gave the room a quick once-over to make sure she hadn't missed someone. "Thanks, I guess. Who is we?"

"My employer. Jungle.com."

"Perfect for what?"

He leaned forward. "Right now, we're expanding into brick-and-mortar stores. We're looking for ideal locations to test our pilot program. To be frank, we think this place could be it." Noah finished speaking and the wide grin remained plastered on his face.

Mia was stone-faced. "I'm sorry. I feel like I'm just catching up. You mean, you're asking me to sell my store?"

"Think of it as a growth opportunity. For both of us. It's a chance for you to partner with one of the biggest online retailers in the world…"

Mia waited for him to continue, but he said nothing else. "Is that it?"

"Is what it?"

"The end of your pitch. I thought…never mind. It doesn't matter. No thank you."

Noah's mouth fell open a bit. Mia's "no" had clearly not been the response he'd been anticipating. "Wait. No, that's not it. I didn't know what you meant. I haven't told you the proposal yet. You wouldn't have to quit doing what you're doing. You could still work here."

Mia was shaking her head before Noah finished speaking. "Look, Mr…"

"Noah. We met the other night. I'm your new neighbor."

"Mr. Noah."

"No, that's my first…"

Mia cut him off. "Mr. Noah, I'm not interested in your proposal to buy out the store I built, that I love, so I can become another soulless employee of Jungle.com." She paused. "No offense."

"I'm happy to hear you think so highly of us."

"I said, no offense."

Noah smiled again. It looked genuine. He seemed to like the back and forth. "No offense taken. But I think you're missing the big picture here. This buyout could save your store. It could save your employees' jobs."

Mia screwed up her face. "What makes you think we're in need of saving? We're doing just fine."

"It's customary for Jungle to look into any potential investment transaction."

"This is the problem. You guys have no sense of propriety, or decency. My store is about serving the community. Not just about serving the bottom line. I know you. I know what you're like. You go sneaking around in my personal business so you can surprise me with some bogus offer, and when I refuse, you try to prey on my vulnerability with scare tactics."

Noah raised his hands in protest. "No, no, no. I promise I

didn't mean to…"

"I think that's exactly what you meant to do."

"You're getting the wrong idea. We love this place. We want to keep the romance and charm exactly the way it is."

Mia stood and weaved between the clutter toward the door. "You wouldn't know romance if it slapped you in the face." She grabbed the door and stood by it, holding it open. "No offense."

Noah smiled and stood. "None taken. Thanks for your time." He handed his business card to Mia. "Let me know if you change your mind." With that, he turned and walked out. Mia followed him and watched him exit the main entrance. As soon as the door closed behind him, Richard rushed over.

"What are you thinking? You just let the answer to all our problems walk out that door."

"First of all, you're not supposed to be listening to my conversations."

Richard clutched his heart as if her comment was so shocking, he'd gone into cardiac arrest. "It's not my fault. These walls are super thin. Plus, that was business-related. I should have been in there."

Mia considered that. "True, but do you really think that's the answer? They'd buy us, change everything, and fire us within months."

"You're probably right. But don't worry. While you were talking, I came up with an idea."

A few hours later, Mia and Richard huddled around the desk in the back office. Mia had offered the large leather chair to Richard because he was bigger, and he'd obliged. That left the broken rolly chair for Mia, which meant she had to stand rather than risking life and limb sitting on it.

"What's this plan of yours," Mia asked.

"I've been thinking of a way to help the store. What you said about the bank is pretty dire. And I was thinking we need to do a flash sale."

"How is a sale gonna help us?"

"Not just any sale. We need fast cash, right?"

"That's right."

"Well let's mark everything in the store down, 50% off at least. Maybe even below wholesale."

Mia laughed. "Sorry to laugh, Rich, but if we mark everything down that much, we'll be out of business before January first."

"But you just said it." Richard countered. "We're going out of business anyway. At least this way we have a chance. Just hear me out."

"Ok, I'm listening."

"We mark everything down at least 50%, and we can dip below wholesale on the stuff we have a lot of. Then we plaster social media with our sale price. That'll boost huge sales volumes from our regulars, who will probably tell their friends. Even though we'll be going into the red on inventory, hopefully we'll raise enough quick cash to satisfy the balloon loan. That keeps us in business. Then we can negotiate with our suppliers who aren't as exacting as the bank, and work our way out of debt to them over the coming year."

Mia was quiet, looking off in the distance, considering Richard's proposal.

"What do you think," he asked.

"It's not the worst idea you've ever come up with. I mean, it's worth a shot, right? What else do we have to lose? Worst case, we don't make the money. We'd have to liquidate and we'd sell all our assets at a discount anyway. So, we either get the cash, or we have a head start on a going-out-of-business sale."

"Don't sound so chipper when you say that."

Mia chuckled. "Okay. Let's do it."

An hour or so later Richard called Mia into the back office. She found him crouched in front of a computer which was resting on the ground. The computer was old. It had a curved glass screen, and a fat backside.

"Why'd you plug that dinosaur in?" Mia asked.

"It's the only computer in here that has illustration software." Richard motioned to the screen. "Look at this." On the monitor was a bright green banner ad which read,

"Everything 50% Off or More! Pre-Christmas Sale! Everything in the store marked down! No exceptions! Today 'til Tuesday!"

"What do you think?" he asked.

"Are you sure it doesn't sound too much like a going-out-of-business sale?"

"Like you said, it will be if we can't get some fast cash."

"Post it."

"You got it, boss." Richard moved the mouse over and clicked open an internet window.

"I'm surprised you could even get WiFi on that thing."

"I didn't." He pointed to an Ethernet cord poking out of the back of the computer tower.

"Wow."

Richard prepared the post for submission. "It's ready. Once it's out there, there is no going back. We doing this?"

"Do it."

He clicked the submit button on the screen.

"What happens now," Mia asked.

"Now we wait, but we're in business. Everyone who's ever liked us or followed us on social media will see that ad. I hope you can get some sleep tonight, because tomorrow's gonna be crazy."

CHAPTER 8

Scrooge's gravelly voice poured through the car speakers. "Old Fezziwig. He has the power to render us happy or unhappy; to make our service light or burdensome…" Noah reached up and switched the audiobook off. His SUV rumbled down the road, headed back to the Jungle offices. He tapped the "Call" button on his steering wheel.

"Who would you like to call?" prompted an electronic voice.

"Call Nadine."

The phone connected. "How did it go?" Nadine demanded.

"I wouldn't call the relocation team just yet. But, on balance, it wasn't a total loss."

Noah relayed the conversation he'd had with Mia to Nadine. "What's your next move? she asked.

"As I said, it wasn't a total loss. I lucked into some interesting information." He told Nadine what he'd overheard between Mia and Richard, and he told her about the pictures he'd taken of the calendar.

"You really are ruthless," Nadine said, sounding impressed. "They won't know what hit 'em." It was meant as a compliment, but the comment made Noah's stomach drop a bit.

"Yeah, I guess so."

"Good stuff. You handle Zhang Wei, and I'll take care of

anything bank related."

"You got it." Noah discontinued the call made his way back to Jungle. He parked on the lower deck and took the elevator back to the 46th, where his office was. He shut the glass door and picked up his landline phone. Looking at Zhang Wei's number from the cell phone picture, Noah carefully dialed out – a complicated process considering he'd never dialed China before. After several rings, a groggy voice picked up.

"Nǐ hǎo?"

Noah froze. He'd just assumed the person on the other end would speak English. "Hi…is this Mr. Wei?"

"Yeah, this is Zhang. Who are you and why are you calling me at 2:30 in the morning?" Zhang said in a perfect American accent.

Noah glanced and the clock and slapped his hand over his face. "I'm so sorry, I didn't realize what time it was for you."

"What do you want?"

"My name is Noah Caffrey. I work with Jungle.com in Snow Valley. I have a proposal for you."

"I'm listening," said Zhang.

Nadine sat in her office in front of a glowing computer. She was alone on her floor, and most of the other lights were out. She glanced at the clock. 12:03 a.m. She pointed her mouse to the search bar and typed in "Snow Valley Treasures, Facebook." She tapped her login info into the box and looked at the store's page. The top post was a banner ad from that day. The ad promised a 50% or more discount on all inventory. Nadine scrolled down the page. The banner ad was getting noticed. It had already been shared over 2,500 times, and had only been posted a few hours earlier. Nadine clicked the X to close the window. She looked at the clock again. 12:08. "Is that too late to call?" she wondered to herself, then grabbed the phone and punched in a number.

"Hi, Ryan? We need to talk about setting up a local promotion, pronto."

CHAPTER 9

The line at On the Grind Coffee stretched all the way out the door. It was a favorite pre-work stop for both Mia and Richard, and was always worth the wait. The coffee was fresh and piping hot, and during December, they offered a delicious peppermint creamer. Today, the line moved like molasses. Mia assumed it was due to the line's length, but as she got closer, she realized there weren't as many people in line as she'd thought. The line was stretched because people were spaced about six feet apart – old habits. What was really causing the drag, she determined, was that everybody was glued to their phones, their heads and necks craned downwards. To be fair, Mia liked to use her phone as much as the next person, but tried to limit that use when others were waiting on her. The rise in smart phone addiction had created a generation of bad drivers, bad pedestrians, bad conversationalists, and even bad friends. Not to mention bad posture. "Some spine and neck doctor is going to make a mint in twenty years," Mia thought as she waited.

After an agonizing wait, she reached the front of the queue. The barista had elected to take an in-between-customer break, and was leaning against the back counter, flicking through her phone.

"Excuse me," Mia said.

The barista looked up, scowling. "I'll be with you shortly, Ma'am." she said, before diving back into her phone. Mia waited awkwardly for a few seconds, and then noticed a bell. It was affixed to the counter and had a sign in front of it which read: "If we've given you great service, please ring." Mia slammed the ringer, and bell chimed loudly. The barista jumped and pocketed her phone.

"Sorry, I was just picking up some of these Jungle deals."

"What Jungle deals?"

"You didn't hear? They surprise-dropped their pre-Christmas deals early."

"I didn't hear."

"Most stuff is 25% off, but they're also beating any other store's price by, like, 10%. All you have to do is upload the UPC. It's crazy."

Mia felt like everything was in slow motion as the words spilled off the barista's tongue. "No," she finally managed.

"No, what?"

"No, I don't want anything. Never mind." She turned to exit, her face white as cotton. The barista looked confused, shrugged, and pulled her phone back out of her pocket.

Mia jogged down the street toward her shop. It was still early, but the street seemed to be unusually quiet. Very few pedestrians were out, and cars which usually zoomed by, seemed to be in short supply. The only sound to be heard was the plodding of Mia's feet on the pavement, and a street sweeper down the block. "I'd hoped there'd be a bit more foot traffic than this," Mia said to herself. As she rounded the corner, she noticed the front of Snow Valley Treasures was also empty: no line, no stampede of customers, no cars circling looking for parking. She quickened her pace and pushed through the front door. Mia scanned the room quickly, looking for customers. Richard was the only one there. "That bad, huh?" she said.

"Did you see? Those snakes at Jungle.com must've stolen our idea. Your neighbor came in. Maybe he was a spy or something."

Mia shared Richard's frustration, but didn't feel right pinning the sale idea on Noah. "I don't think so. I don't like the guy, but you didn't tell me your sale idea until after he left."

"That's true. Unless…you don't think he planted a bug and is listening to us, do you?"

Mia laughed. "This isn't a spy novel. People don't plant bugs in real life. Besides, to Jungle.com we are a bug. They can squash us whenever they want."

Richard nodded. "Well it's still early. Maybe more people will come." As he was speaking, the bell on the front door jingled. The both looked at the door expectantly, but it was a mailperson who entered.

"G'mornin'," she said.

Mia was deflated. "Good morning."

The mailperson crossed the room and handed a stack of letters to Mia. "Have a good day." She turned to exit. When she reached out for the door handle, she was knocked backward a bit as a dad and son entered the shop. The mailperson scooted around the two and exited, closing the door after her.

Mia approached them with a wide smile. "Hi, can I help you?"

The father was staring at his phone and didn't respond. The boy looked up at Mia and blurted, "Where are the Action Andys? Do you have any?"

"We sure do. They're right this way. Follow me."

Mia walked to the other side of the room. The boy followed but his father didn't. "Daaad. Are you coming?" The boy called out.

The father momentarily looked up from his phone. "Do they have him?"

"We have every kind of Action Andy on the market." Mia said.

"Perfect."

Mia turned back toward the boy. "Do you watch Action Andy on TV?"

"I dunno. Sometimes. I watch it on my tablet mostly." He looked past Mia and noticed the display, then dashed toward it.

"Yes! Action Andy with battle gear!" He snatched the toy off the shelf and raised it triumphantly in the air, but the movement was so abrupt, it knocked several other dolls to the ground. The boy either didn't notice or didn't care. Mia smiled graciously, and bent down to pick up the mess. The boy ran the Action Andy doll over to his father, and stepped on the packaging of one of the dolls he'd dislodged on the way. Mia flinched, but resisted the urge to tell the boy to be careful. He shoved the doll in his father's face. "See? It's the Action Andy with battle gear and the Night Strider costume."

"Are you sure this is the one you want?" his dad asked.

"Yes," he responded, practically shouting. "I'm sure! I told you I want the one with battle gear. This one has battle gear, doesn't it?"

Richard crossed the room toward the group. "Cute kid," he said.

The father said nothing, but his eyes narrowed as if he wasn't sure the compliment was genuine. He turned toward Mia. "Glad to come to a place where he can mess with the toys before we buy 'em. Just to make sure we're getting the right one."

"Thank you," Mia responded.

"Serious." He gestured toward the open room. "These places are a dying breed. I hope you guys stick around."

"We do too." Mia paused trying to think of something to say. "You know, those Action Andys are 50% off today."

"I know it. That's why we're here."

Mia glanced over at Richard who was giving her an I-told-you-so smirk.

"Oh, good. You heard about the sale," she said.

"Of course. Everybody heard about it."

The father beckoned his son over and reached out his hands. "Lemme' take a look at that doll," he said. The boy reluctantly handed it to him. He spun the box in his hands, as if he was looking for something.

Mia pointed at the box. "The accessory list is right there on the side."

"That's not what I'm looking for. Oh, here." The man

pointed to the barcode on the bottom of the Action Andy box. Then, he pulled his cell phone from his pocket and aimed it at the barcode. A loud chime emanated from the phone. "There." He bent down and gave the Action Andy back to his son.

Mia glanced over at Richard who shared a confused look.

The father continued tapping on his screen. Finally, he looked up. "Ok, bud. Action Andy's on the way."

"Yes!" the boy shouted.

The father looked at Mia. "Thank goodness Jungle's is doing their big sale. Those Andys usually cost a fortune."

Mia's mouth fell open. She was too stunned to respond.

"Let's go, bud," The father said to his son. The boy dropped the Action Andy in the middle of the floor, right where he'd been standing and walked out the door. Mia watched in utter disbelief.

"What just happened?" Richard asked.

"I've never seen anything like that," Mia said. "I knew people did that. I knew it happened, but it's never been so brazen, never right in front of my face."

Richard walked over to Mia and put his arm around her. "The day is young. We'll see how things go."

Eight hours later, Mia made her way to the door to flip the "Open" sign to "Closed." After officially closing the store, she turned to Richard. "Our promotion led to one of the slowest days we've had all year."

"I'm sorry. There's no way I could have known what Jungle was planning."

"It's not your fault."

"Maybe it's time to seriously think about other options."

"What else did you have in mind? I thought this was our last option."

Richard reached under a shelf near the cash register. He rifled around, until he resurfaced clutching Noah's business card.

"No. No way," she said.

"Why not just hear what they have to say?"

"I heard it already. And I told you, they'll decimate us."

Richard laid the card down on the counter and looked at Mia. "Please, Mia. Just go talk to them and find out what they want. I've been a loyal employee for years and I've never asked you for anything."

"Ok. I'll go."

CHAPTER 10

Noah poked his head out of the elevator and looked down the hallway. The coast was clear. Quietly he tiptoed down to his condo and slipped inside. He didn't know Nadine had planned to undercut Mia's sale. In fact, he didn't even know Mia was having a sale to undercut. But he certainly wasn't ready to accidentally bump into her in the hallway and have to explain what was going on. Earlier that day, Noah had accessed Jungle.com's sales data and narrowed by region. Purchases in Snow Valley had swelled by more than 60% during the sale. He felt momentary pity. "Surely some of that uptick would've gone to Mia had we not run a competing sale," he thought. But he shrugged it off just as quickly. That's business. Only the strong survive. All's fair in love and war. And any other cliché he could throw at it.

Inside, Noah twisted the deadbolt into place, as if an enraged Mia was going to come smash down his door demanding answers. He kicked off his shoes, grabbed his laptop, and headed to his bed. Normally he'd have sat on the couch, but his was still with the movers, in transit across the country. Cardboard boxes were stacked in every room, very few having been touched. Noah opened his laptop and navigated to YouTube. With no TV, it was the next-best option. He started with clips from late-night hosts – Conan; Fallon; Kimmel – but they were political, and while normally that was ok, at the moment he just wanted to unplug. Next, he watched America's Funniest Home Videos, the ultimate unplug, and had a good laugh at a segment on ski and snowboard crashes. At last, he clicked on a video titled "CuTeSt ChRiStMaS PrOpOsAl EvEr – man proposes to girlfriend with new puppy." Sure enough, a little spotted beagle was wrapped up in a box under the Christmas tree. When the girlfriend opened it up she squealed with delight as the puppy climbed up and licked her all over her cheeks. Then she noticed the engagement ring attached to his collar and began to weep. Noah fought back a lump forming in his throat. He was surprised the simple video was making him so emotional. He felt heart-warmed, and jealous, and lonely, all at the same time.

When he moved to click on the next video, his phone buzzed. He tapped the speaker phone button. "Hi Mom," he said.

"Hi sweetie." She was calling to remind him about his aunt's surprise birthday party in January, but, as often happened, it turned into an interrogation. "Yes, I'm still planning on coming, Mom – No, I'm not bringing a guest – yes, I remember she doesn't like seafood – Okay, I'll bring a suit – No, I don't mind sleeping on the pullout." Years earlier, during his undergrad, Noah had made the mistake of telling his mom he was going to become a writer. She had fallen in love with the idea, and when Noah had decided to do the "sure thing" instead, and go to business school, she was crestfallen. Despite Noah's having worked for Jungle for nearly ten years, she still asked what he was writing almost every time they spoke.

"Working on anything new?" she said.

He'd given up trying to convince her he was a businessman. "Nope," he said, dryly. "Nothing new."

"I wish you would. You're so talented."

As she spoke, Noah's email box pinged. He clicked it open. It was from Mia. "I gotta go, Mom. I love you."

"Love you too."

Noah disconnected and slid his laptop closer. He could feel his pulse pumping. "How'd she get my email?" he thought, and then remembered the business card. "At least she's not kicking down the door." He prepared himself for the verbal abuse he was sure was waiting in his inbox and clicked it open. Instead, the subject line read: Chat about SVT. He relaxed a little and double-clicked the email.

"Dear Mr. Caffrey," it began. "Thank you for your recent visit to Snow Valley Treasures (SVT). When we spoke, you mentioned Jungle.com's potential interest in partnering with SVT. Having discussed the matter with my business partner, I would welcome the opportunity to sit down with you, at your convenience, and discuss the matter further. I can make myself available tomorrow should you still have any interest. Please just let me know what time works best."

Noah was stunned. It worked. Here he was, thinking she was writing to chew him out, and really, she just wanted to talk business. He'd be a hero at work. A brilliant new marketing plan, acquiring a brick-and-mortar, and saving a local business, all in the first week. He tapped out a quick reply to Mia.

"Hi Mia, thanks for your response. I'd be delighted to discuss things with you. Please meet me at the Jungle.com offices at 11:00 am, tomorrow. The address is 3427 Peacock Blvd. I'm looking forward to it."

He pushed "Send" and then sent an email to Nadine.

"Nadine, it worked. The owner of Snow Valley Treasures wants to discuss things. I told her to come in at 11. Does that work for you? If not, I can handle."

Nadine responded almost immediately. "Lol. Perfect. I'll be there."

CHAPTER 11

Mia was up early enough that if she'd wanted to beat Richard into the shop, she could have. But the shop was not on the agenda today. At least not initially. Today was Jungle, and heaven only knew what that meant. The first issue was how to dress. On the one hand, Mia needed to be taken seriously, so casual was out. On the other, she didn't want to seem eager, so professional was out too. She ransacked her closet looking for the perfect outfit, but nothing seemed to work. "This isn't a job interview," she reminded herself. But she was surprised by caring so much about what she looked like. Ultimately, business-casual won the day. She chose a grey blazer over a white top and khaki slacks. She also picked red pumps (festive and powerful) and her mom's elegant pearl necklace. Then, she was out the door.

The Jungle.com offices were different than Mia had pictured in her head. She had imagined white marble floors, gilded door handles, and red oak paneling, instead of the modern urban-chic vibe which she encountered. She was more at ease in the relaxed environment though, and wondered if she'd overdressed. She really felt out-of-place when several people scurried by in hoodies and jeans. As she approached the desk she noted that at least the secretary was dressed up. That gave her some relief.

The secretary handled an endless barrage of calls, putting nearly every caller on hold. She could hardly get a word in edgewise before handling another call. It was – "Jungle.com, how may I direct? – hold please – Jungle.com, how may I direct? – hold please," on an endless loop. It reminded Mia of operator switchboards from movies set in the 40s. The frenetic pace was almost anxiety inducing. Mercifully a friendly-looking receptionist approached.

"Mia?"

"Yes?"

"Ms. Campbell and Mr. Caffrey will see you now."

Mia followed the receptionist past a maze of contemporary open-air cubicles and glass offices. They came to a stop in front of a giant glass boardroom, outside of which was a breathtaking view of Snow Valley. Inside, Noah sat accompanied by a tall, female colleague. Both Noah and the woman were dressed in business suits. The receptionist knocked lightly, then led Mia into the room and introduced her. The tall woman strode effortlessly across the room and extended her hand. Mia shook it, politely.

"Mia," she said, "can I call you that?"

"I…"

"Mia," the woman continued, "My name is Nadine, this is my colleague Noah, whom you know. I'm very glad you agreed to meet with us today. We have a lot of great things in mind for…what was it?" Nadine looked at Noah to fill in the gap.

"Snow Valley Treasures."

"Snow Valley Treasures, right." She flashed Mia a patronizing grin. "Such a cute name."

Mia retracted her hand from Nadine's grip. She didn't appreciate the condescending "cute" nor did she like the woman cutting her off. "I'm glad you're glad," she said, defensively, "but as I told Noah when he stopped by, I have no intention of selling anything. I'm just here to gather information."

Nadine smirked. "Of course, of course. We would never dream of pressuring you. It seems like you're getting plenty of that from the bank."

The meeting was off to a bad start. Mia shot a look at Noah who shrugged innocently. "Let's hear it, then."

Nadine turned her back on Mia and moved to the front of the room. "It's no great secret your business is in trouble. You know it. We know it. The bank knows it. You wouldn't be in this room talking to me, if that weren't the case. Am I right?"

Mia despised being put in this position. Having some corporate "suit" talk down to her because her business was flagging. Still, what Nadine said was true. Mia nodded, reluctantly.

Nadine continued, "Look at this." She pointed to a white screen hanging down from the wall, and clicked a button on a remote control. An overhead slide presentation jumped to life on the screen. The first slide was a picture depicting the exterior of Snow Valley Treasures, but instead of the SVT logo, a new sign above the door read, "Jungle.com Try'n'Buy." Nadine spun to face Mia.

"What do you think?"

"Um…"

"Welcome to the new era of internet shopping. This will be the first seamless nexus of online and retail-based shopping. A Jungle.com Try'n'Buy. Customers can try anything in the store, no questions asked. It will be revolutionary." She looked Mia in the eyes. "And you have the chance to be part of it all." Nadine pressed the button on her clicker and the screen jumped to the next slide. Now, the picture showed the interior of Snow Valley Treasures, but like the previous slide, this picture had also been digitally altered. Instead of the quaint charm of the store, the room was changed to look ultra-modern, and was accented by the distinct green and yellow of Jungle.com's logo. In front of every shelf, and clothes rack was a digital scanner of some kind, and every item had a small, black, electronic box attached to it. Nadine continued talking. "You're looking at the future here, Mia. Of course, you'll need to make way for our inventory. But it will be the most technically advanced retail store in the world. Kids will be able to play with the toys, adults can try on clothes, and with the touch of one button, automatically add anything to their online shopping cart. No sales actually need take place at the store."

Mia was confused. "No sales? And I'm supposed to do what?"

"Encourage the people to buy more, obviously. The more they try stuff – the more stuff they add to the cart – the more they add to the cart – the more they will buy. It's simple, really. Just business."

"It sounds greasy to me."

"I'm surprised you feel that way. But maybe it makes sense. Maybe that kind of thinking is why you're in the financial position you're in. You need to open your mind here a bit. Think of the possibilities."

Mia recoiled at the words and glowered at Noah. "This your idea?" she said to him. "Thanks for the invite." To her surprise she thought Noah actually looked embarrassed.

Noah jumped to his feet. "Nadine, I thought we discussed integration and keeping their business model similar to how it is now."

"We're way past that. This is the future." Out of the corner of her eyes, Mia thought she saw Noah subtly shake his head. "What do you say, Mia?" Nadine pressed.

Mia considered her next words carefully. She wanted to explode, but it was unlike her to lose her cool. "I don't know what to say," she said, finally. "Except no. I would never do that to my store, no matter how much trouble I'm in. That's not a boutique shop it's… it's…entrapment."

Noah laughed out loud at Mia's comment, but she couldn't tell if he was laughing at her or with her – though, to be fair, she wasn't laughing at all, so "with" seemed the less likely of the two. Mia rose and headed for the door. Nadine called after her. "You're drowning, Mia. We'll get that gift shop one way or another, but at least with us you might get a little money."

Mia was halfway out the door, but spun back around. "Are you gonna get my little dog, Toto, too?" As the door slammed behind her, Mia could have been sure she heard more laughter coming from Noah. She didn't look back, and stormed from the building.

Richard was busy ringing up a customer – a cute, well-dressed grandma who was purchasing a tea set for her granddaughter. Mia pushed the door open like a whirlwind and a rush of cold air came twirling in behind her. "That's it! I've had enough!" she yelled, slamming the door closed. Richard made eye contact with her, raised his eyebrows, and motioned with his head toward the customer. It was too late. The grandma was staring at Mia, surprised.

"I'm so sorry. I didn't see you there." Mia said.

The grandmother laughed gamely. "That's quite alright. I yell too sometimes, when I've had a hard day."

Richard rushed to finish the transaction. He handed the woman her receipt. "Thank you very much for your business. We hope to see you again."

"You will," the grandma responded. "I love this store. So quaint." Then she shot Mia a wry smile. "When there's not as much shouting, that is."

All three laughed at the joke, and Mia and Richard thanked the woman again as she exited. Once she was gone, Richard turned toward Mia. "Let's hear what was so important you had to chase away one of our last customers."

"I'm doing it. I'm gonna save the shop."

"Whoa, whoa, whoa. Doing what? What are you talking about? What happened at the meeting?"

"I can't believe I have to live next to that snake."

Richard's brow furrowed. He looked bewildered by Mia's whirlwind stream-of-consciousness. "Who? What?"

"Noah. The guy from Jungle? My new neighbor?"

"Oh yeah. What happened?"

"And he…they ambushed me. They never wanted to help save the store. They wanted to strip it and turn it into an online sales trap. It was disgusting."

Richard nodded. "Sorry. But I'm confused. What do you mean you're doing it?"

Mia grabbed Richard by the shoulders and looked him in the eye. "I'm doing this, Rich. I'm gonna win the Twelve Games of Christmas."

CHAPTER 12

In the postmortem with Nadine, Noah peppered her with questions about how she'd handled the meeting. He was careful not to overstep – she was his boss, after all – but still, he felt the meeting could have been handled with considerably more tact. Plus, something else was bothering him. Mia had given Noah a look before she walked out of the room. She hadn't looked angry, or sad, or any other way Noah might have expected. Instead, she looked at him like she'd been betrayed, and the look had Noah reeling. Nadine insisted her method was the best way to handle things. "Fear is a stronger motivator than greed," she said.

"If you say so," he responded.

Nadine picked up on Noah's apparent insincerity. "Noah, you're the interim director. Emphasis on interim. I can help you get rid of that "interim" part, but I need to know you're on board." Noah opened his mouth to respond but Nadine continued. "I've liked what you've done here so far. And when you applied for this position, I'm the one who greenlit everything."

"I know. I wasn't trying to—"

"So, don't question my intuition, or methodologies." she interrupted. "Please. And the next time you're tempted to do so, just remember it was my same intuition that gave you this job."

Noah nodded, sufficiently chastised. "You're right. Thank you," he said, as Nadine turned and left the room.

Noah trudged back to his office, his thoughts swirling. He couldn't stop thinking about the look Mia had given him. Add to that the aggressive dressing-down from Nadine, and work was a non-starter. He dragged his mouse around his computer screen, opened a few files, responded to some emails, but nothing substantive was happening. Eventually, he grabbed his coat and headed for the elevator.

The soft leather of Noah's new car cheered him a bit, as did the smell. In the past few years, he'd grown accustomed to luxury, even though that's not at all how he'd grown up. As a child of a struggling single parent, Noah had learned to go without, through most of his childhood. Now that he was well-paid, and could afford the finer things, he liked to treat himself – and his mother, to a taste of the good life. His first purchases after commanding a large salary were a new truck for his mom, and a watch for himself. It was expensive, and ostentatious, and he wore it proudly. Occasionally, though, when the newness and excitement of his most-recent gadget had worn off, Noah could feel the hollowness of filling the holes in his life with "stuff." Those moments were the loneliest. But for now, the leather smelled good, and the seat heater warmed him to his core. And that was good enough.

Noah pointed his car toward a cheesesteak quick-service restaurant his co-workers had told him about. Maybe food would take the edge off. Mia's look popped back in his head, and he tried to shake it off. "It's not my fault her business is flagging," he thought, but her look lingered. Noah hadn't started out with the goal of destroying businesses. When he began work with Jungle, he'd never even heard of an Acquisition Director. He'd taken an entry-level position, and worked his way up the ladder, but it wasn't always a vertical climb. His first role was in data entry. A role for which he was entirely over-qualified and was consequently promoted out of only a few weeks later. Next, he moved into management. Noah was a natural leader, and thrived in the role, quickly moving up to senior manager. It wasn't until a vacancy opened in the Acquisition department that he even considered it. The move had been lateral, but it had the possibility of leading to bigger things. And Noah was living those bigger things now. The chance to become the permanent Regional Acquisition Director, was too big to pass up, notwithstanding the queasiness he felt when he thought of Mia's look. He'd do what he had to.

CHAPTER 13

The cold hit her like a brick wall. "There's a thin line between freezing and burning." Mia thought as she stepped into the wind, her skin on fire. She fastened the top button of her coat and buried her face in her scarf. It helped. Normally, she would have ordered a Rydeshare, but tonight she wanted to think, and walking helped clear her thoughts. She rooted around in her purse and found a pair of flats she kept for emergencies, then swapped the red pumps out for them. They were warmer, and more comfortable – much more suitable for walking. Mia shuffled down Main Street and considered her predicament. The contest, if she won, would solve every financial issue – at least in the immediate, but it was a long shot. Jungle, on the other hand, was willing to give her a real, concrete offer, one that might let Richard keep his job. She owed him that much, at least. Mia glanced at the Christmas lights lining the buildings as she passed. The beauty of the bright colors did nothing to cheer her, as they usually would have. "Maybe I made a mistake storming out," she thought. "Maybe I should call them back and hear the full offer."

Near the end of the street, the Christmas lights gave way to bright, flickering, red and green neon. The bulbs spelled out "Nick's Diner" in cursive. The Christmassy red and green appeared to be coincidental, though, as several other colored bulbs were burnt out. Mia had passed the diner a thousand times before, but had never stopped in. Her stomach growled and she decided a burger might be just the thing she needed for some clarity.

If the neon outside evoked a feeling of Christmas, the inside did the opposite. Maroon booths and a checkerboard floor, the diner was devoid of Christmas decorations, and it seemed, of life. One line cook sat staring up at a mounted TV and didn't turn at the sound of the door. There was no hostess, and no servers. Mia appraised the situation and decided she'd eat elsewhere. As she turned to leave, an elderly woman emerged from the back. She was dressed in a teal uniform, with an apron and hat, and looked straight out of a 50s movie. The woman smiled as she approached. "Snow Valley Treasures, am I right?"

Mia did a double-take. It was the grandmother who had bought the tea set from her shop earlier today. She returned a warm smile. "That's right. You were in the store today. How did your granddaughter like her tea set?"

The grandmother patted a plastic bag sitting behind the host stand. "I've still got it here. It's going to be her Christmas gift."

"It's a lovely choice. I'm sure she'll be very happy."

"I hope so," she said, staring at the ground, "although, I won't be there to see it." She paused and looked off in the distance. "Just you tonight?"

Mia felt her cheeks flush slightly. "Just me, thanks."

"No shame in that. Follow me." The woman led her to a booth near the back of the restaurant. "This booth is right under the heater. It's my favorite."

"It's perfect," she said. Mia looked over the menu and went with a bacon cheeseburger, cheese fries, and a cup of hot chocolate. She considered a bowl of clam chowder, but the way the waitress scrunched up her face when asked about it, gave her restraint.

When the waitress brought Mia's food, she introduced herself. "I'm Edith."

Mia shook her hand. "Mia. Nice to meet you." She waited a

second, then delicately laid out her next question. "You mentioned you won't see your granddaughter open her gift. Does she live far away?"

"She lives quite close, actually. It's just…" Edith trailed off. "I'm sure I'm boring you with all this."

"No, I'm interested." she said, and then turned red. "I'm sorry. I didn't mean to pry."

"Not at all. Not at all."

The front door chimed and another waitress strolled in, clutching her apron in her hands. Her eyes met Edith's. "You can clock out, hon. Thanks for covering."

"Thanks Melinda," she responded. Then she turned back to Mia. "Looks like I'm off. Mind if I join you?"

"On the contrary, I'd love some company. Have you already eaten?"

Edith broke into a wide smile. "I guess eating a greasy burger one more time won't kill me." She looked back at Melinda. "Linda, do you mind asking Tony to throw another burger on for me?"

"No problem, hon." Melinda responded.

Edith untied her apron and sat down opposite Mia. "It's a cold one out there tonight." Mia said.

"It is. But I like cold for Christmas. My late-husband always wanted to go to Florida for the holidays, a snowbird you know, and I never got used to palm trees and 80-degree weather for Christmas. Just didn't feel the same."

"I agree completely, and I'm sorry to hear about your husband."

Edith looked surprised and then laughed. "It's nothing recent. Winston's been gone almost 14 years. I still miss him every day, but I've learned how to get along." Edith switched gears. "So, tell me, how long have you worked at Snow Valley Treasures?"

"As long as it's been there. I'm the owner."

Edith's eyes widened a bit. "The owner, that's wonderful! It's a lovely store. I shop there as often as I can."

"I thought you looked familiar! It's so nice for us to have

repeat customers. Thank you. I just hope you're able to come back sometime."

"What do you mean?"

Mia told her about the business's financial dire straits. Edith listened intently, and offered sympathy and encouragement as appropriate. "That's why you came in shouting earlier."

Mia flushed and nodded. She decided to switch gears. Having been so open herself, pried again. "I don't mean to impose, but I was curious why you won't see your granddaughter open her gift, if she lives close."

Edith's gaze left the diner and she looked out the window for a few seconds. "It's no imposition at all," she said, slowly. "The truth is, my daughter and I haven't spoken in almost two years. We had an argument, and I haven't seen her or my granddaughter since."

"That's terrible. I'm so sorry."

Edith bit her lower lip, and looked as though she was fighting back tears. "So am I. I always send presents to Renee – that's my granddaughter – for every birthday, and Christmas, and Valentines, but I never hear from her or my daughter. I'm not even sure she's getting them."

Mia felt awful but wasn't sure what to say, or how to help. "I'm sure she's getting them, and playing with them, and loving them."

"I hope so."

"Have you tried reaching out to your daughter, you know, to reconcile."

"I doubt she'd want to hear from me."

"What makes you so sure?"

"When I last talked to her, we argued about…" she paused, "that's the thing, I hardly even remember what started the argument. Something silly like what type of diaper cream she should use on Renee's diaper rash. I was stuck in my ways and insisted I knew best. She told me she was a mother now and would be doing things her way. I don't even remember what happened, I got too pushy and said some things I regret. Next thing I know, two years have gone by and I lost the two most important relationships in my life."

Mia reached across the table and rested her hand on Edith's. "I'm so sorry."

At that moment, Melinda approached carrying Edith's burger. "Tony wants to know if you want the bill or if you this to come out of your check."

"Put it on my tab." Mia interjected.

"I couldn't possibly." Edith objected.

"Please. It's my treat. I was feeling pretty low, and it's been nice to have a friend."

"Okay, then. Thank you, sweetie."

Melinda walked back to the kitchen and Edith dug into her burger. "Pretty good, huh?"

"Really good," Mia said with her mouth full. The two continued to eat for a bit without saying much. Then Mia broke the silence. "I'm sure you've already considered this, but I feel like it needs to be said. Why don't you just reach out to your daughter? You can apologize, and then who knows what will happen."

"I've thought about it. It's almost all I think about. But I'm scared. Right now, I can hope she'll take me back, and that's what gets me from day-to-day, but if she says no, I'll have nothing left to hope for."

Mia considered Edith's words solemnly. "You'll never know until you try."

"I know, but I don't think I can. At least not yet."

Mia felt like she'd invaded Edith's private life enough. She tried to change the subject. "So, what are your plans for Christmas Eve?"

"I – I don't have any."

"My friend Richard and I – you met Richard today at the store – eat Christmas dinner together every year, and there is always room for more. You interested?"

Edith beamed at the invitation. "I'd love to. Thank you."

"Good. It's settled."

Mia and Edith continued eating and chatting. At the end of the meal they bid each other a warm goodbye. Exhausted, Mia ordered a Rydeshare and headed home.

CHAPTER 14

Noah liked his new condo, but he missed his old apartment. It had been eclectic – at least he liked to think so. There were books everywhere, and knick-knacks from his travels; a faux tiger skin rug on the floor; and a rolling ladder which led to a loft. He also had art, though he'd never studied it. Noah never understood what made one painting objectively great and others inferior – but he hung paintings he liked and that suited him just fine. His favorite painting depicted a giant whale poking vertically out of the water, balancing an old pirate ship on its nose. When a colleague from work visited Noah's apartment she'd commented that the whale painting was "pedestrian" and "amateurish." The words had stung at the time, but Noah kept the painting, reminding himself that art is subjective, and as long as he liked it, that was the point.

His new condo was not nearly as visually appealing as his old place. There was no loft, no original hardwood floors, no rolling ladder. But it was quaint, and when the sun shone through the windows and brightened the room, Noah could see the appeal.

Amidst a pile of still-packed boxes Noah's bed and box spring mattress lay on the ground. He stretched and sat up, yawning. The sun was up and his alarm clock – which was plugged in across the room and rested on the carpet – showed 7:42 A.M. He reached for his cell phone and saw a voicemail from Nadine. She'd called in the middle of the night at 2:32. "Wow, she's relentless," Noah thought. He clicked the voicemail open and held the phone to his ear to listen. Nadine's voice came through.

"Noah, are you there? Are you awake? If not, wake up and call me back. This is urgent."

"I'm sure it is," he thought. Noah pressed the redial button and his phone connected. After one ring Nadine answered.

"Where are you?"

"I'm at home."

"When are you coming in," Nadine demanded.

"It's Saturday."

"I don't care what day it is. We don't pay you to take vacation whenever you want. We need to get on this Treasure Trove, or whatever the name is, pronto. I've got some ideas you need to incorporate."

"Ok. I'm—" The line went dead. Noah looked at his phone and rolled his eyes, annoyed. Sure, he'd head in to the office, but he'd take his time getting there. He stood and began unpacking one of the many boxes in the room.

When he finally stepped into the hallway, several hours had passed. He knew it was a dangerous idea to cross swords with Nadine, but he was still upset about the previous day's meeting. He glanced down towards Mia's door. All was quiet. Last night he'd made the decision to apologize to her. Initially, he'd typed out a short email message, but it felt too impersonal. He figured an apology was a good idea for several reasons: one, it made good business sense. If Nadine really wanted to work with Mia, it would be better to not have the two hate each other; two, they were neighbors, and Noah didn't like the idea of having to hide in his own condo for the rest of his life; three – and most importantly – he hadn't been able to shake the feeling he'd gotten when Mia had been so upset. He wanted to set things right.

Noah walked to Mia's door and gave a light knock. He could

feel his heart pounding in his chest. There was no answer. He tried again, this time louder. No sounds of movement came from inside.

"You got the wrong door. I'm right here." Dorothy's voice called out from behind him.

"Aaah!" Noah yelled, startled.

Dorothy broke into a belly laugh. "Somebody's had too many cups of coffee this morning."

Noah spun around and smiled at her. "Good morning, Dorothy."

"She ain't here."

"She's not? I was just...I just wanted to tell her...I mean...Do you know when she'll be back?"

Dorothy looked unimpressed as Noah stumbled over his words. "She's doing the Twelve Games. Could be all day."

"What are the Twelve Games?"

Dorothy chuckled. "You've got a lot to learn."

CHAPTER 15

The clock radio clicked on. "It's another cold day out there, folks, so make sure you bundle up…" Mia's eyes shot open. The radio continued, "Experts say temperatures could reach as low as 15-degrees today. Stay indoors if you can, but if you absolutely must go out, make sure to layer."

Another voice chimed in, "That's right, Chip, but I suspect a lot of people are going out anyway because today's the first day of the Twelve Games of Christmas. And this year they have the special award of $100,000…"

Mia sat up with a start and slammed the "Off" button the radio. She grabbed her cell phone and scrolled to Richard's contact. She pushed the green button to connect, and a groggy voice answered.

"Hey, Rich. Sorry to call so early, but I need you to know I might be a bit MIA today." Mia said.

"Really, why?"

"Because I'm doing the Games, remember?"

"That's right. Do you need any help?"

"I think I'll be fine. Just hold down the fort for me. I'll take care of any logistical stuff from here."

"You got it, boss."

Mia jumped out of bed and rushed a shower – no need to shave, she'd be bundled up anyway. Once ready, she tapped the Gazette-on-the-Go app. A nifty animation sprang to life: "On the 1st Game of Christmas, my Daily sent to me: a crossword for puzzle points, three," it read, and then morphed into a blank crossword puzzle board. "That's cute," Mia thought. Before she could begin the game, a notification popped up with all of the standard legalese and warnings. Mia clicked the "I agree" button and was then prompted to put in all of her personal info, and verify her email. At last, she was ready to begin.

The puzzle was huge. It would be classified as a "jumbo" by those familiar with crosswords. With over 100 rows and columns, and 206 clues altogether, it was a behemoth. Mia was undaunted, though. A puzzle that size would be a turn-off to casual players. Apparently, the Daily Gazette wanted to separate the wheat from the chaff, early.

"Let's do this." Mia laid her phone on the counter and tapped the first clue. One across: "City of lights." Mia looked out her window, and considered the possibilities. "Five letters," she thought, "that's gotta be Paris." Mia had visited Paris years before, and vaguely remembered the nickname. Plus, she remembered reading about a controversy over the sparkly, flashing lights that had been added to the Eiffel Tower. She typed the answer into the corresponding boxes. The app automatically jumped to two across. "The most famous reindeer." This one didn't require much thought. "Rudolph," she typed in. Mia's pulse quickened a bit. If all the clues were this easy, maybe there'd be more contenders than she thought. Three across: "Singer, Crosby." She typed in the letters. "B-I-N-G." Her worry was increasing now. "That one's a little harder," she thought, "but still. Bing's a Christmas institution." The clue for four across popped up: "Classic holiday movie featuring Big Bang Theory's Johnny Galecki." The clue was a long one, 16 letters. "Finally, a hard one." Mia thought. She had seen some episodes of the Big Bang Theory, and knew who Johnny Galecki was, but didn't know he'd been in any holiday classics. She felt the sudden urge to Google the answer, but resisted. She'd promised herself if she were going to win the prize money, it'd be fair and square. She clicked the next clue. Twelve letters for "Nutcracker villain." As a little girl, Mia's mom had taken her to the Nutcracker ballet every Christmas. She typed in the answer immediately: "Rat king," but that didn't fit. She tried "the rat king," but it was still too short. "Weird," she thought. "I know this is the right answer. Maybe they mean a henchman or something." But she couldn't think of anything that worked.

As she was considering the answer, her phone vibrated. It was Ron, a shipping manager. Mia reluctantly pushed the "Accept" button.

"Hi, Ron."

"Mia. Got a minute?"

She pushed the speaker button, and looked at her crossword. Only a handful of clues solved, and literally hundreds to go. She wanted to bump the call to later, but the logistics with Ron was something she handled, and it wouldn't be fair to pass it off to Richard. Mia looked at the clock. "Go ahead," she said.

"I'm calling to go over next week's shipment. I want to discuss your inventory and make sure we are on the same page."

"That's fine. I am kinda tied up though, how long do you think it'll take to go through your list."

"Shouldn't be longer than an hour."

Mia sighed. "I can take care of it. Let's get started."

After exactly one hour and three excruciating minutes, the call ended and Mia was back to the puzzle. During the call, she'd jotted down a list of classic holiday movies to see if any would fit: It's a Wonderful Life – too many letters, and Johnny Galecki wasn't alive when it was filmed; The Christmas Story – close, but still too many letters and probably filmed too long ago; Love Actually – not enough letters; the Holiday – not enough letters; Christmas Vacation – letters worked, but it was Chevy Chase, and probably filmed too long ago. Nevertheless, she tapped "Christmas Vacation" in as a placeholder, and decided to work on some Down clues to see if it was correct. To her surprise, she solved several clues that crossed correctly with Christmas Vacation and confirmed it was the right answer. "I'll have to look up what role Johnny Galecki played, when this is all over." she told herself.

When she clicked 10 across, her phone buzzed again. She picked it up without checking the caller ID.

"This is Mia."

"Mia, this is Janie from Pendleton Manufacturing. How are you?"

Mia's heart sank. Janie was a valued contact, but was very slow-moving. On several occasions, Mia and Richard joked that a long call with Janie lasted an hour, and a short call with Janie was only 60 minutes. "I'm good, thanks," Mia said, glancing at her wristwatch. "What can I help with?"

"I've got some good news. We're nearly finished with our new batch of polymer flippers and I wanted to go over your store's order."

Mia nodded. "Ok. What do you have us down for?"

She lost track of time on the call. Pendleton Manufacturing had been a good inventory source for Snow Valley Treasures, and securing the order was too important to delay. Mia tried her best to give short answers in the hope of cutting down the call time, but as expected, it ate up another hour. Finally, with the order in place, she looked back at the puzzle. The Nutcracker clue was still blank. A crease crossed her forehead as she considered other options. "Another word for rat, maybe?" Shrugging, she typed in "THEMOUSEKING" and it fit perfectly. She'd never heard of the Rat King being called the Mouse King, but it didn't matter, the answer was a huge help. Having twelve letters across unlocked a big swath of the puzzle. Mia hurriedly scanned the Down clues that crossed with Mouse King. Within seconds, she'd tapped in the answers to four of them. She felt the sweat on her palms as she shut out the world, and focused on the puzzle.

By lunchtime, Mia had around half the answers filled in. She grabbed a quick sandwich and went back to the game. Her phone buzzed and interrupted. It was Richard. Mia tapped the decline button. Seconds later, it buzzed again; Richard was calling back. This time, Mia pressed the green "Connect" button.

"I'm busy," she said, trying her best to sound playful.

"Sorry, but there's an emergency."

"What's wrong?"

"A water pipe burst. We have a leak."

"I'm on my way." Mia grabbed her coat and dashed for the door.

Long shadows covered the floor of Snow Valley Treasures. Mia sat hunched over her phone, trying desperately to fill in the rest of the crossword. Behind her, Richard thanked the plumbers who'd responded to the leak. It wasn't a terrible mess, the leak had soaked the carpet, and dampened a few toys, but nothing was permanently damaged. Thankfully, Richard had acted quickly and shut off the water. When Mia arrived, they worked together vacuuming the water, salvaging the inventory, and cleaning the shop. Mia called an emergency plumbing service, and they were able to patch the leak. After several hours, the shop looked as good as new, and Mia was finally able to get back to the puzzle.

The puzzle proved to be as difficult as it was large. It had taken the rest of Mia's day and still wasn't complete. But it was close. Mia was only missing 43 down. The clue was 11 letters, "Reason for the Feb. season?" So far, from the words crossing 43 Down, there was a T in the second position, followed by a V, another blank and then an L. Mia knew a question mark at the end of a clue meant the answer might be ironic, or a play on words. But she was stumped by the T and V next to each other. "Blank TV, blank TV," Mia repeated to herself. "A TV? No. What is it?" She puzzled for a few seconds more, and then reread the clue. As if struck by lightning, had a realization. "Feb. is abbreviated. Of course! That means the answer is abbreviated too. Let's see. It's not A TV, it must be…" She paused and concentrated. "Saint. That's the abbreviation. It's St., so, STV…St. Valentine. Reason for the February season." While the answer had nothing to do with Christmas, Mia understood crosswords are notoriously hard to create, and not every clue can be on-topic.

She tapped the final answer into the puzzle. It fit. As soon as she pushed the last letter another animation popped up – fireworks and a "Congratulations!" banner. "Perfect! Finally!" The fireworks disappeared and a new prompt popped up. Mia read the next pop-up. "Selfie Time!" it said. "Certain squares will have circles inside of them." Mia looked at the puzzle, "Yep." She continued reading, "Every square with a circle inside of it, indicates one letter of the secret location."

"Okay."

The rules continued, "You've solved the puzzle…"

"Check," she said.

"Now unscramble the circled letters to discover the secret selfie location. Using the camera in this app, be one of the first three people to snap a selfie at the secret spot to receive one of three available points for the day."

Mia looked back down to the puzzle, she eyed the circled letters and marked them down on scratch paper. "Okay, there is A – K – R – P. That's gotta be park. What else?" She continued jotting down circled letters. "T – T – S – A – E – U." She began working it out. "Tues… no. Tas… state…state…yoo. Statue! Park statue!" She collected the final circled letters: EFRMNETO. "Fremento…no…oh, duh! Freemont! That's it. The Freemont Park statue." Freemont Park was across the street from Snow Valley Treasures, and featured a giant statue of the one of Snow Valley's founders. "Serendipity," Mia shouted. "Finally, some good luck." She raised her arms in triumph, grabbed her coat, and rushed out the door.

Mia's green car – the Lemon Lime – screeched into a parking spot. Her not-so-affectionate name for the car had stuck ever since she'd made the joke to friends a few years earlier. The Lemon Lime wasn't bad to look at. In fact, it was a late-model import. But, as Mia knew, you can't judge a book by the cover. Or, better yet, you can't put lipstick on a pig. From the moment she drove the car off the lot, it had had problems. First, it was the dashboard. When Mia turned up the radio, and the speedometer flickered. The power windows were next – either stuck up, or stuck down, and always at the wrong time. The worst though, was when the alternator went. It was Mia's most embarrassing moment. The Lemon Lime had decided to keel over at a toll bridge on the highway. Hundreds of angry drivers stuck behind her, and there was nothing she could do except wait for the tow truck. Now whenever she drove she expected the worst, and even carried an overnight bag with emergency supplies, in her trunk. Thankfully, today the car was fine.

Mia drove to the park because the statue was located on the far side, and it would have taken her longer to run. She parked in the nearest spot to the statue she could find, and jumped out. The sun had nearly set, but she could still make out several people milling around. A small congregation was not unusual for the statue, but it was a very cold day, and almost dark. That many people around the statue was a bit odd. Mia drew closer to the crowd and noticed several people were taking selfies. "This doesn't look good," she said to herself. At that moment, two joggers who looked painfully underdressed for the weather, passed her. She overheard some of their conversation.

"I can't believe the first secret location was right here, where we jog every day," said one jogger.

Her companion responded, "I know! I wish I was better at puzzles. We would've been the first two here."

Mia absorbed the information and felt a sharp pang of disappointment. Despite the ominous news, she gathered herself and continued to move toward the statue. There were nearly 20 people gathered around the monument, all of them tapping away at their phones or snapping pictures. "I've never seen so many selfies," Mia thought. "It's like I'm in middle school." But she too, removed her phone, opened the Gazette app, and took a selfie. For the picture, Mia smiled into the camera, though she didn't feel much like smiling at the time. After the picture, she tapped the "Upload" button, and wondered what would happen next. The sun had completely set and the park lights kicked on. Several of the trees on the periphery were decorated in strands of brilliant white lights which cast a golden glow across the park. Most of the people near the statue began moving away, but Mia overheard a young couple seated on a bench nearby, use the word "crossword" and she approached them.

"Sorry to bother you, but did either of you enter the Twelve Games contest?" Mia asked.

Both members of the couple smiled warmly at her. The girl answered. "Yes, we did. Did you?"

"I think so. I'm just wondering what's supposed to happen. This is the secret location, right?"

"It is. Did you upload your picture?"

As the girl asked the question, Mia's phone pinged loudly. She checked it and saw a red, number 1 in the corner of the Gazette-on-the-Go app icon. "Excuse me," she said to the couple. She clicked the icon and the app opened. A message appeared, "Thanks for entering the Twelve Games of Christmas contest! Congratulations on finding secret location 1! You are the 72nd person to do so. Daily points: 0; Total points: 0."

"Looks like you got your response," the girl said. "What place did you come in?"

"72nd," Mia admitted, somewhat embarrassedly. "How 'bout you?"

"We were in 34th, but we're gonna try a lot harder tomorrow. I think the whole town is going crazy over this."

"I'll bet. Good luck."

"You too." The couple turned away and went back to chatting between themselves. Mia read the message on her phone again and walked back to her car. She climbed into the Lemon Lime feeling dejected and cold. She started the ignition and cranked the heat – only room-temperature air spilled out. "Great. Add it to the list," she said, and pulled out her phone. She tapped Richard's name on the speed dial. The call connected.

"How'd it go?" Richard asked.

"It didn't. At least, not as well as I'd hoped."

Richard paused before responding. "That's ok. What happened? Was it not the statue?"

"It was, but 71 other people found it before me."

"Ouch."

"Yeah."

Another pause. "So, what's the plan now? Another sales promotion? I think we could mark everything 75% off and—"

Mia interrupted him. "No. I'm not done. Not by a longshot. I was distracted all day by the leak and other logistical stuff. I'm calling to tell you you're on your own for the next eleven days. That means phones, deliveries, customer service, even tornadoes. Tomorrow I'm gonna be dialed in. Think you can handle it?"

Richard sighed. "Sure. I can handle it, but are you…are you sure this is the best route to go?"

"I'm not sure about anything, Rich. But something tells me I should keep going, and it's the same feeling I had when I opened the store."

"You keep going then. You have my full support."

CHAPTER 16

Meetings and more meetings. The definition of Noah's life. He sat in the boardroom listening to another round of blathering by colleagues and partners all saying things that could've been typed into an email in minutes.

Nadine stood at the front of the room walking the group through another of her famous slide presentations. She was fierce, smart, and intense – Noah had to give her that. It was no wonder why she'd landed in the position she was in. When Noah wasn't annoyed by the late-night intrusions, he was impressed by Nadine's ability to function on no sleep. Her call the other night at 2:30 was just the tip of the iceberg. Noah had just learned Nadine had secured authorization from the company HQ to have "sleeping pods" installed on the basement floor. The pods were nothing more than camping cots, outfitted with thousand-thread-count sheets. They were installed so ambitious associates could work all night, catch a few Zs, and start the process over the next morning. She even arranged for laundry and dry-cleaning services to pick up clothes while the employees slept. Nadine had earned a reputation among the top brass as the hardest worker in the office. She'd even been nicknamed "the bat" for her relentless ability to work through the night. The nickname had first been mentioned around the water cooler and was meant as an insult, but when Nadine became aware of it, she wore it like a badge of honor.

Noah's mind was beginning to drift. Nadine appeared to be nearing the end of her presentation, which was good, then he could get back to doing real work. The mention of his name jarred him from his daze.

"Noah!" Nadine said again.

"I apologize," Noah stammered. "Can you repeat the question?"

A few of Noah's colleagues looked at each other and chortled. Nadine did not smile. "I didn't ask a question. I asked you to give us an update on the Snow Valley Treasures takeover. Where are we on that?"

Noah fumbled with papers in front of him. "What specifics did you want?"

"I want an update!" Nadine snapped. "Have you been in touch with the current owner since our last meeting with her?"

"Got it." Noah started, "I last spoke with Ms. Gallagher when she came into our offices."

Nadine looked impatient. "Nothing else?"

Noah found the paper he'd been rummaging for and felt more confident. "Here," he said, holding it up. "This is a cost breakdown of everything we'll need to do to convert the store to a modern online hybrid. The point-of-sale kiosks at every shelf will be costly, but if the data is correct, it'll be offset by a much higher customer conversion ratio than we're used to. I was able to get the schematics for the building from public records and I looked into expanding. None of the interior walls are load-bearing, meaning they can be removed at will…" Noah paused for a moment and seemed to be debating with himself about what to say next.

Nadine pressed, "And?"

"And…" he stumbled, "I mean, but, removing walls, even though it's feasible, may serve to eliminate some of the…" he paused, "character from the building. Right now, the store has several nooks and crannies, and is full of old-school aesthetic charm. If we knock down the walls, it may destroy some of that."

Nadine held up her hand for Noah to stop talking. "We'll let the design team worry about that. Continue."

"Understood. I talked with the business owner who runs the adjacent store. It's a local hardware store and he was thinking of changing locations anyway. He is willing to sell as soon as possible. Acquiring that store would give us the flexibility to double the square footage in the shop, and be more competitive with other large big-box retailers."

Nadine looked satisfied with the answer. "Good work, Noah. Have our attorneys draw up the paperwork to buy the hardware store immediately. I want to keep moving on this. Also, make contact with that little woman that owns the place, again. I want her to understand the stakes."

Noah pursed his lips and looked downward.

"Are we clear?" Nadine pressed.

"We're clear."

Noah left the meeting feeling more than a little rebuffed. He'd created a career out of being a company person, by never making waves. Now he was doing a bit of pushing back and he had the emotional bruises to show for it. Maybe it wasn't worth it. Plus, he wasn't sure what he was pushing back for. Sure, Snow Valley Treasures was cute, but it was just another store at the end of the day. Jungle had absorbed hundreds of buildings, and bought out dozens of businesses. What was so special about this one? So, Noah resolved to get more serious, and to do his job – no more kicking against the pricks.

The first stop was the 8th floor legal department. "Lawyers, blech," he thought. But he had been given strict instructions, so down he went. The legal department was like a graveyard, except graveyards are occasionally brightened by flowers. Noah was sure any flower brought to the 8th floor would wilt as soon as the elevator doors opened. He stepped off the elevator and addressed a serious-looking secretary.

"Hi. I'm Noah Caffrey. Nadine told me to come down and speak with someone here."

"Whom?" Came the reply.

"Nadine Campbell."

The secretary rolled her eyes so hard, her irises disappeared beneath her eyelids. "No..." She stated slowly, as if talking to a child. "Whom are you here to see?"

"I don't know. I was told to see someone from in-house, so I..."

"Have a seat," the secretary interrupted.

After a bit of waiting a tall, wiry man with horn rimmed glasses appeared. "Mr. Caffrey," he said. "Follow me."

The 8th floor looked nothing like the other space Jungle.com occupied. There were no glass offices, no exposed lighting, no random ping-pong tables. It was as if the 8th floor was its own entity. "So much for in-house," Noah thought as he followed the man. Near the end of the hallway the man turned toward an open door and ushered Noah inside. He found a chair and the man closed the door behind them.

"What can I do for you?" the man asked.

"I was sent by Nadine...Nadine Campbell"

"I'm aware of who Nadine is," the man said, curtly.

Noah nodded. "I was sent by her to ask you to draw up the purchase papers for a local hardware store. It's not far from here. We're planning on buying it and—"

The man interrupted again. "Already done."

"I'm sorry?"

"It's already done. I drew up the paperwork this morning." The man bent down behind his desk and produced a stack of papers in a manila file. He handed the file to Noah. "Anything else?"

Noah was confused. He'd only just told Nadine about the hardware store earlier that afternoon, unless...maybe she was monitoring his email. No. That wouldn't make much sense. But maybe she didn't trust him with the project. Perhaps she'd staffed somebody else on the deal to make sure there was follow through, to dot Is and cross Ts if Noah wouldn't. He clenched his teeth at the thought. He wasn't about to let some also-ran take his hard-earned job. Noah would do what it took. He looked at the attorney. "One more thing. I need you to draw up some purchase paperwork for an adjoining business, Snow Valley Treasures."

CHAPTER 17

Mia was up before her alarm. And in truth, she'd hardly slept at all the past night. Even when she had drifted off, she'd continually fallen into a nightmare that she missed her alarm and slept through the competition. So, for the last hour she had tossed and turned, but eventually decided coffee and a shower were better than trying to get any more shuteye. A quick breakfast – protein shake and a granola bar – and Mia was dressed and ready. The sun hadn't even come up yet. Mia looked at the clock on her phone: 6:14. The new game wouldn't go live until 7:00 AM sharp. That'd give her some time to read the paper and calm her nerves. She eased out her front door and sat down on her welcome mat to wait for the paper. After a few minutes of scrolling through her phone, Mia's neighbor Dorothy stepped out in her bathrobe. When she saw Mia she nearly jumped, and tried in vain to cover up her appearance.

"What are you doing out her so early?" Dorothy asked.

Mia smiled. "Waiting on the paperboy. Sorry if I scared you."

"That's quite all right, dear. I'm just embarrassed you have to see me in such a state. I'm lucky you aren't that handsome new neighbor of ours."

"Yeah."

"Why are you so anxious for your paper?" Dorothy asked. "Aren't you doing the Twelve Games contest?"

"I am. It doesn't start for 45 minutes though. I'm just looking for something to take my mind off things. Yesterday I was too lackadaisical. I'm taking it seriously now."

"Good for you. But don't get your hopes up. I heard half the city is trying for that prize. Apparently, it was all some publicity stunt by the paper to get more readers, and they tripled their subscriptions."

Mia looked impressed. "I didn't know there were that many people in the hunt. But that seems fair enough to me. I love the Gazette. I'm glad to hear they're doing well."

"It sounds like a scam to me," Dorothy responded. "I cancelled my subscription. Maybe you should too."

Mia smiled. Dorothy had often tried to warn her about various conspiracy theories. She was a lonely woman and spent most of her time watching TV, and cable news at that. Once, when Mia had first moved in to the condo Dorothy banged on her door and pled with her to unplug all her appliances. Dorothy had seen some exposé which claimed household appliances were being overfed electricity from the grid, and were liable to explode. Mia had invited Dorothy in, plied her with coffee and crumb cake, and gamely unplugged her appliances. The two had been friends ever since.

"I'm sorry to hear that," Mia said, "but I don't think I'll be cancelling my subscription."

"Suit yourself." Dorothy turned to head back into her condo, then paused. "Say, you haven't seen our new neighbor this morning, have you?"

"No. Thankfully."

"Why do you say that? I'm the one who should be thankful, coming outside dressed like this."

"Let's just say he's not my type."

"Your loss. More for me," Dorothy grinned.

Mia laughed and the elevator dinged. "That's my cue," Dorothy said before ducking inside. A groggy-eyed paperboy stepped off the elevator and didn't notice Mia sitting down the hallway. He dropped papers on welcome mats like he was half-asleep. Mia jogged over to him.

"I'll have one of those," she said. "I live in 2D." The paperboy looked skeptical and took on a defensive posture. "Come on," Mia said. "If I wanted to steal a paper, I could have killed you and taken the whole bag." Mia laughed but the paperboy didn't like the joke as much. After a second he seemed to realize giving a paper to Mia was easier than walking down the hallway, and he held a paper out to her. She smiled, took the paper politely, and headed back to her condo.

Inside, Mia read the day's headlines, but she couldn't concentrate. She kept checking the clock as it inched slowly toward 7:00. Finally, she gave up and folded up the paper. She brewed another pot of coffee and sat down to wait. Dawn had broken over the lake, and Mia watched as a few early morning skaters made their way onto the ice.

At last, the clock grinded its way to 6:59. There would be no interruptions this time. Mia silenced her phone, and shut her drapes. No distractions meant no distractions. Even a beautiful sunrise had the potential to take her eyes off the prize.

7:00. Mia tapped the Gazette app and a new animation danced across the screen: "On the 2nd Game of Christmas, my Daily sent to me: a logic game for puzzle points, three."

Mia had some experience with logic puzzles. In college, she'd flirted with the idea of going to law school. She'd taken a few LSAT prep courses which included some logic games. It wasn't her strongest area in the practice tests, but she'd done all right. At least she understood the basic idea.

Mia read the game setup: "Snow Valley is holding a Christmas movie festival. Only three movies – Rudolph, The Grinch, and Christmas Carol – will be screened during the festival which takes place on Thursday, Friday, and Saturday. Each movie will be shown at least once during the festival but never more than once on a given day. Each day, at least one of the movies will be shown. Movies are shown one at a time. The festival set up the following rules for the workers:

- On Thursday, The Grinch must be shown, and no

THE 12 GAMES OF CHRISTMAS

movie can be shown after it on that day.

• On Friday either Rudolph or Christmas Carol, but not both, will be shown, and no movie can be shown after it on that day.

• On Saturday either Rudolph or The Grinch, but not both, will be shown, and no other movie will be shown after it on that day."

Mia jotted down the rules on scratch paper, and looked at the first question.

"Which of the following CANNOT be true:

(A) The Grinch is the last movie shown on each day of the festival.

(B) Christmas Carol is shown on each day of the festival.

(C) Rudolph is shown second on each day of the festival.

(D) A different movie is shown first on each day of the festival.

(E) A different movie is shown last on each day of the festival."

"Okay, cannot be true," Mia thought. "So, must be false. Which answer logically has to be false." She looked through the rules and began to apply them to the answer choices. She moved to answer A. "Can The Grinch be shown last on each day of the festival? Let's see…the rules say it's shown on Thursday, with nothing coming after it. So far, so good. It can be the last on Thursday. The next rule says either Rudolph or Christmas Carol is shown on Friday, and no movie is shown after it." Mia paused. "Wait…that must be it then. 'A' must be the answer. If nothing can be shown after Rudolph or Christmas Carol on Friday, The Grinch cannot be shown last on each day." Mia clicked answer A in the app and locked it in. The app gave no indication if she was correct. She moved on to question two:

"If Christmas Carol is never shown again, once Rudolph is shown, then what is the maximum number of total movie screenings that could occur during the festival?

(A) three
(B) four

(C) five
(D) six
(E) seven

    Mia went back to her rules and worked through the answers. "Okay, we're looking for the maximum number of movie showings, and once Rudolph is shown, Christmas Carol stops being shown. That makes me think Rudolph should be near the end of the festival." Mia looked through the possibilities and, using her scratch paper, eliminated all answers but (D) six. Feeling confident she'd gotten it right, she clicked it and locked it in. If her answers were correct, she was making progress much faster than the day before.

After a few hours of work Mia nearly had the puzzle complete. She still had a few questions to figure out, but the answers she had punched in – if they were correct – gave her two guesses as to the secret location. She could feel her adrenaline pumping, but she was unsure how to continue. She simply didn't know how to solve one of the logic puzzles, and worried if she punched in the wrong answer, she'd be forced to start again on a new puzzle. She picked up her phone and called Richard.

"I need your help," she said, after the phone connected.

"Ok, shoot."

"I'm still missing three letters from the secret location, but I have it nearly figured out. It's either Jones' Christmas Tree Farm, or John's Christmas Tree Farm. Those are the only tree lots in the city starting with the letters J-O."

Richard laughed heartily. "Of course, you know all the Christmas tree farms in town."

Mia laughed too. "Laugh it up. But which do you think I should go to? What does your gut tell you?"

"Can't you just solve the puzzle and find out which one it is for sure?"

"I'm running out of time. I don't want to be the 72nd person there again."

"Go to both." Richard said, casually.

"I don't think there will be time. They're across town from

each other."

"What does your gut tell you?"

"I'm not sure."

"Then flip a coin. You said you were following your heart. Maybe fate will play a role here."

"I can't leave such an important decision to a coin flip."

"Why not," Richard pressed, "just flip it and try to convince yourself you'll go with whatever it lands on. If you're pleased by the result, you know your gut's telling you it's the right move. If you feel disappointed by the flip, you'll know to go to the opposite place. It's simple."

Mia had to admit the idea was kind of beautiful in its simplicity. "I'll try it. Thanks." She disconnected the call and retrieved a quarter from her pocket. "Ok. Heads, Jones' Farm, tails, John's Farm." She flipped the quarter end-over-end above her head. She caught it, slapped it on the backside of her hand, and revealed George Washington's shiny profile. Heads. Jones' Farm. A subtle twinge of disappointment coursed through her. Maybe that's what Richard had been talking about. She didn't know why, but subconsciously she'd been hoping the coin would have landed on tails. "I'll follow my gut, then," she thought. "John's Farm it is." Mia grabbed her coat and dashed out the door.

John's Farm was close to her condo, so it had that going for it, and Mia knew the way to boot. In fact, John's Farm was where she'd bought the tree that sat in her living room now. The drive there was inconsequential, except it seemed slow. Why, Mia wondered, did she get stuck behind leisure drivers whenever she was in a hurry? Or was it that she only noticed the slowness when she was in a hurry, and at other times she was fine plodding along? Whatever the case, it seemed painfully slow today. But after some agitation, she made it.

The parking lot was nearly empty. "This could be a really good or a really bad sign," she thought as she exited her car. John's Farm was a quaint, if cramped, tree farm. It had one entrance and one exit, and one makeshift plywood shed with a cashbox and a stool for transactions. Mia jogged toward the entrance. Nobody was standing nearby. "Here goes nothing," she thought. She pulled her cell phone from her pocket, opened the Gazette app and toggled the camera to selfie mode. She turned her back to the entrance, aimed the camera to pick up the John's Farm sign, and snapped the picture. Mia checked it. The picture was a bit crooked, and wasn't her most flattering, but it wasn't about looking pretty. She uploaded the pic. "Now I wait," she said, holding her phone tightly. To kill time, she made her way into the tree farm and wandered aimlessly. Down one of the aisles she came across a particularly delightful fir. It was tall, elegant, and extremely aromatic. Mia leaned her face toward the center of the tree to inhale the intoxicating aroma. "Ahhh. Nothing says Christmas like the smell of an evergreen," she thought. A voice startled her.

"I don't work here, but I'm pretty sure they frown on kissing their trees before buying."

Mia jumped and spun to see who was talking. Her foot wrapped around the base of the tree and she tumbled backward. As she was about to fall completely flat, a pair of arms reached out and steadied her. She regained her footing. She spoke before seeing whose arms had caught her. "Thank..." Mia looked up and saw Noah standing near her, grinning, "you!"

"Happy to help." At that moment Mia's phone pinged and vibrated in her hand. She jumped again.

"Too much coffee this morning?" Noah joked.

She didn't respond, opting instead to look at her phone. It was a ping from the Daily Gazette app. She clicked it open and read it. "Thanks for entering the Twelve Games of Christmas. We're sorry, but you didn't find the correct secret location. Currently, 7 other contestants have found today's location. Daily points: 0; Total points: 0."

"No!" Mia exclaimed, and angrily stuffed her phone in her pocket. "What a waste."

"Everything ok?" Noah asked.

Mia had forgotten he was there for a moment. She spun toward him. "For your information, no, it's not ok. I just wasted two days of my life." She paused. "I don't know why I'm even explaining this to you. Did you come here just to rub salt in my wound?"

Noah raised his eyebrows. "You're asking if I knew you were going to be at a Christmas tree lot in the middle of the day, and you were going to get some sort of text that would make you scream the word 'no' out loud, so I could make fun of you for it?"

Mia softened a bit. "It does sound a bit far-fetched when you put it that way. But still, why are you here?"

"Same reason as you. To get a tree. Unless there's some sort of tree-kissing cult you belong to, I don't know about."

"Har-dee-har-har. I wasn't kissing it. I was smelling it. Enjoying the season. Something I'm sure you know nothing about. Besides, I thought Ebenezer Scrooge didn't celebrate Christmas."

Noah laughed. "On the contrary, it was always said of Scrooge that he knew how to keep Christmas well, if any man alive possessed the knowledge."

Mia was impressed despite herself. The Christmas Carol was one of her all-time favorite books. She read it every year, and sometimes she'd even sneak a few chapters during the summer. As a little girl, she'd been scared of the spirits, especially the ghost of Christmas yet-to-come, but the happy ending was what got her through. She loved the idea that anybody can change for the better, even late in life.

"You know Dickens?" she said.

"We corporate drones don't only go around destroying people's livelihoods. We also read, from time-to-time."

"Maybe you should pick up a book on politeness."

"I thought saving you from falling was pretty polite."

"Not after causing the fall in the first place."

"Touché. Anyway, about the other day. I'm sorry for how things went down at the office. I didn't expect Nadine to say what she said – it's not what we discussed. But I still want you to reconsider selling your place."

"Not this again," Mia said.

"I mean it. We'd give you fair market, or even more than fair market value. I have the purchase offer documents in my car."

Mia turned and caught Noah's eye. "The answer is no. I love my shop, I'm not selling. If I get kicked out, so be it. So, stop asking me."

Noah raised his hands in defeat. "Fair enough. It's just business I guess. Sorry to bombard you. Can I buy you a cup of hot chocolate to make up for it?"

Mia paused and considered the olive branch. "Fine. But only because the sugar might make me feel better."

A small hot chocolate stand sat outside the tree farm, where a handful of people stood in line. Mia and Noah made their way to it. Noah tried to stir up conversation. "So, what text did you get that made you so mad?"

"Nothing you'd be interested in I'm sure."

"Try me."

"You'll just laugh at me."

"Try me," Noah insisted.

"It was about the Twelve Games of Christmas."

Noah laughed. Mia shook her head, annoyed. "I don't even know why I try, honestly," she said.

"I'm sorry, I'm sorry," Noah protested. "It's just... I've heard about it. Isn't it some sappy contest the paper does every year?"

Mia continued shaking her head. She felt personally insulted. "See? I knew you'd react this way. It's not sappy, it's festive and romantic."

Noah was still smirking. "I'm sure. It sounds very authentic too."

"You are very rude, you know that? I'm about to change my mind on hot chocolate."

"I'm sorry. No more laughing, I promise. So, why did the text make you mad?"

Mia eyed Noah, not sure whether his promise not to laugh was genuine. Hesitantly, she continued. "It's not only about the romance of the thing. For your information, there is a huge prize at the end of the contest this year."

"What's the prize?" He asked.

"A hundred grand."

Noah whistled. He looked genuinely impressed. "Whoa. I'm starting to see the appeal. Maybe I could get into this whole Christmas puzzle thing."

"Believe me, it would be lost on you. Plus, you're too late. The contest is already two days in and they've given out points. You'd never catch up."

"How many do you have?" Noah asked.

Mia was caught off guard by the straight-forward question. Her gaze hit the ground. "Er…none yet. But I will. I just got unlucky and chose the wrong place today."

As Mia was talking, the pair reached the front of the hot chocolate line. Noah paid for an order of two hot chocolates and a bag of roasted chestnuts. He held up the bag like a prize-winning trout. "See," he said, "I do get into the spirit of the season. These are chestnuts roasted by an…" He paused and looked inside the hot chocolate shack, "electric microwave, it looks like."

Mia chuckled and flashed a smile at Noah. He smiled back. She thanked him for the hot chocolate, and the pair continued walking and talking.

"I'm still a bit confused. What do you mean you chose the wrong place?" Noah inquired. "Aren't the clues supposed to lead you to where you need to go?"

"I couldn't solve one of the clues, and I wasn't sure which tree lot to go to. It was a 50-50 chance."

"And you chose wrong? Ouch. Remind me never to take you to Vegas," Noah said with a smile.

Mia chuckled again. "Tell me about it."

"Why didn't you just look up the answer online?"

"It's against the rules."

"How would they ever know? I'm sure a lot of people look up the answers."

"I'm sure you're right," Mia responded, "but I don't cheat to win. Even for that type of money."

It was Noah's turn to look impressed. He slowed his pace and shifted to look directly at Mia. "Good for you. That's rare, and really commendable."

Mia stared back at Noah waiting for the punchline, but it never came. He had an earnest look on his face. For the first time that day, she felt a bit relaxed. "Thank you." The pair locked eyes. Neither said anything.

As Mia was opening her mouth to speak, a voice rang out and shattered the silence. "Chest-nuts! Get yer' Chest-nuts!" The line at the hot chocolate shack had dwindled, and the owner was trying to drum up more business from the few people at the tree lot. Shaken from her momentary daze, Mia turned and headed off in the direction of the parking lot.

"I gotta run," she called out behind her. "Thanks for the hot chocolate."

Noah waved and yelled back, "For what it's worth, I'm glad you chose the wrong tree lot," but Mia didn't respond.

CHAPTER 18

The dust had gathered and then re-gathered on all the stuff lodged in the attic. When Noah rush-moved out of his last apartment he'd merely instructed the moving company to put anything from the attic into the crawl space in his new condo. There it would remain, neither seen nor thought about until the need for it arose. There were boxes of decorations, old high-school yearbooks, school drawings from Noah's childhood, and more. He didn't know why he held onto all of it for so long. It never got looked at. His mom had told him to hang on to the yearbooks in case his children wanted to look through them someday. There were two problems with that idea: first, Noah didn't have kids yet, and at the rate at which he was working, that possibility seemed slimmer by the day. Second, he wasn't so sure even if he'd had kids, he would want to show him any of the embarrassing inscriptions his friends had scrawled in the margins of the yearbooks. Still, he had them just in case, along with all the other junk piled on top.

The movers had stuffed the things in the crawl space while Noah had been at work, and he'd never bothered to poke his head in. He figured if the movers "forgot" to put some things in there, it was no major loss, just one less item he'd have to deal with later. But when Noah found himself in the crawl space for the first time, after returning home from the tree farm, everything seemed to be in order. The crawl space was small, and stale. Noah had had to literally crawl on all fours to squeeze through the square door. Inside, cobwebs covered nearly every surface. There were even webs on the boxes that had only been placed in the space days before. Using the light from his cell phone, Noah pawed through boxes until he found what he'd been looking for. A typewriter.

He set the typewriter on his desk next to his laptop. Noah's condo was more set up now – the bed was on a bedframe at least – though there were still boxes everywhere. The typewriter was in poor-ish condition – well-worn and the K key was missing. He pulled out a dust rag and went to work cleaning it. Despite its age, it was still a beautiful relic. Noah loved the sound of typewriters and the time and age they evoked. After a few minutes of cleaning, it became clear no amount of elbow grease would resurrect the machine. Noah pulled out his cell phone and looked up antique repair shops. He dialed one, and a woman answered.

"Kelly's Antiques."

"Hi, I have a vintage typewriter in need of some TLC. Do you guys handle that type of work?"

"Depends how damaged it is. Some things aren't salvageable."

"Great. How much would repairs cost?"

"Depends how damaged it is."

"Right. Of course."

"Why don't you bring it by? We're open 7 days a week," the woman offered.

"I'll see you in a bit."

Noah sat the typewriter on the front seat of his car. He laughed to himself that a thing which a few hours ago had been languishing in storage, was now the focus of his attention and care. As he drove, his car started an incessant beep…beep…beep, indicating the passenger was not wearing a seatbelt. "There's no one in the passenger seat," he said to nobody in particular. But the car was unrelenting. He did his best to ignore it, but after a mile or so, and driven to the point of madness, he pulled over and strapped the typewriter in the seatbelt. "Now at least if I get pulled over, the cop will think I'm a nutcase and maybe take pity on me," he thought.

The antique shop contained a mish-mash of everyday items, and only a few which looked unique. To Noah, it brought on more of a feeling of pawn shop than antique store, but that was no matter, as long as they could fix the typewriter. He lugged it to the front and set it gently on the counter. A woman in coveralls with her hair in a bun, approached. "You the typewriter guy?" she asked.

"That's me."

"I'm Kelly."

Noah stuck out his hand. "Noah. Nice to meet you."

"So where is this thing?" she asked as they shook.

Noah pointed toward the counter. Kelly glanced over and her eyes widened a bit. "What kind of typewriter is that?"

"I dunno'. I got it from my dad."

Kelly slid toward the machine to get a closer look. "Well, I'll be…" she said under her breath. "Yes, it is." Kelly turned her back to Noah and yelled into the back room. "Walt! Walt! You gotta see this."

"What is it?" Came an annoyed-sounding voice from the back.

"Come out and see fer' yerself'."

After a minute, Walter, an older man also dressed in coveralls emerged from the back room. "What is all that hollerin' about now?" Kelly pointed toward the counter. "Woo-wee. Is that an Excelsior?"

"You bet it is," Kelly said proudly, as if it were hers.

"What's an Excelsior?" Noah asked.

Kelly and Walt looked at Noah as if he had antennae growing out of his head. "An Excelsior is one of the rarest typewriters they made." Walt said. "Where'd you get this?"

"From my Dad," Noah said again. "Do you think you can fix it?"

"I think I can do you one better," Kelly said. "I'll give you five-grand right here, right now, if you let me take this baby off your hands."

Noah was awestruck. "Did you say five thousand dollars?"

"Yessir. What's it gonna be? Clock's tickin'."

Noah didn't know what to do. On the one hand, he hadn't thought about the typewriter in years, it had been stuck in storage until a few hours before, and five-grand was five-grand. On the other hand, it had a lot of sentimental value, and this woman seemed a bit too eager to offer up five thousand dollars. It made him nervous, like he was missing something. At last, he spoke. "No deal, sorry. It's a family heirloom." Kelly nodded, but she looked disappointed. "Can you fix it?" he asked.

"Sure, we can fix it. Can't we, Walt?"

"Yes, we can." Walt said with a smile.

"Excellent, how much?"

"I won't know 'til I get into it," Kelly responded, "but plan on a few hundred bucks at least."

Noah balked. He'd anticipated spending only $50-60 in repairs. But then again, he also didn't know how valuable the machine was at that time.

"Go for it." he said.

CHAPTER 19

Mia drove away from the tree farm feeling reflective. She had been surprised by Noah's mea culpa, and surprised even more at how good she felt at that moment. With the date of the balloon payment looming, and having missed two points in the Twelve Games hunt, she should have been feeling down in the dumps, but she didn't, and she wasn't sure why. Maybe it was the hot chocolate, or the Christmas spirit. Or maybe it had been Noah. He had been funny, and Mia had to admit, a bit charming too. But as quickly as the thought entered her head, she shook it off. Noah was the enemy, the roadblock. He and his company were trying to undermine everything she'd built. As she was ruminating, her phone rang. She connected the call through her car speakers, and heard Richard's voice.

"How did it go today?"

"Don't ask."

Mia thought she heard a quiet sigh. "That's ok. You'll get 'em tomorrow," he responded.

"Thanks. Anything happen at the store I should know about?"

"Nothing of consequence. Oh. A woman stopped by looking for you. Her name was…" Mia heard Richard rummage around looking for something. "Edith."

"That's interesting. Did she say what she wanted?"

"Just asked you to call her when you can." Richard recited Edith's number to Mia, who quickly committed it to memory. They ended the call with a promise to speak the following day, and Mia voice-dialed the number she'd memorized. After a few rings, Edith answered.

"Hello?"

"Hi, this is Mia from Snow Valley Treasures."

"I'm so glad you called."

"Is everything ok?"

"Yes, but I'm afraid I've done something rather silly, and I may have muddled things up."

"What happened?" Mia asked.

"I thought a lot about what you said, about just trying to call my daughter, and so, I did."

"That's fantastic. Why is that bad? Did she not take it well?"

"She was wonderful. I think she got emotional when she heard it was me, said she didn't like the way things had ended."

"Edith," Mia said, "this all sounds really positive. I'm so happy for you."

"It is. But that's the thing. She invited me to come with her to her company's Christmas party. She said I could bring someone too."

Mia pulled the car over to the side of the road, so she could better concentrate on the conversation. "That's great. This all sounds good. I still don't see how you muddled anything up."

"I'm worried about going. I'm worried about saying the wrong thing and embarrassing her. I just talked to her for the first time in two years because I said the wrong thing last time. I don't want to make the same mistake."

"I understand. But, you are a cheerful, sweet, grandmother. I'm sure you'll be just fine."

"Thank you," Edith paused. "Nevertheless, would you mind coming with me?"

Mia was shocked and not sure she'd heard right. She turned the speaker volume up on her car. "I'm sorry? What did you say?"

"Will you come with me? You could stand by me and help me out if I put my foot in my mouth."

All of the ways Mia could object raced through her mind: she was busy with the contest, she was too stressed from worrying about the store, it was Christmas. But then again, it was Christmas, and this woman was asking for her help. Besides, a work party could be fun. "I'd be glad to help," Mia said, "but I'm not sure you need any."

Edith's voice was gleeful. "Thank you, thank you! I'll call you later with the details."

"I'm so glad things worked out with your family."

"It's all because I met you. You're like my guardian angel."

Mia blushed. "I just told you what you needed to hear." They ended the call and Mia pulled her car back on the road. "Here I am dispensing advice, and I can't even get things right in my own life," she thought. She had planned to go out to eat to celebrate getting her first points in the Games. Now, exhausted and points-less, Mia pointed her car toward home.

The next morning came quietly – too quietly. Mia's alarm never went off. Fortunately, her sleep was fitful, as it had been every night of the contest so far, so she didn't miss it by much. She sat up in bed and grabbed her phone: 6:44. "How did I forget to set this?" she scolded herself. It was too late to have a nice breakfast, but still early enough to get a good jump on the puzzle. First, a lightning-fast shower, then back to her table to start on puzzle three.

Her phone clock clicked to 7:00 and Mia tapped the Gazette app. Nothing happened. She tried again. Same result. "What's going on?" she wondered, aloud. She hard-closed the app and tried opening it again. This time, a pop-up message appeared.

"We're having trouble finding you. Please check your internet connection and try again."

Mia looked at the top of her screen. Sure enough, the WiFi signal icon had a slash through it. "Not now." Rather than take the time to trouble-shoot the WiFi, Mia disconnected it from her phone to use her cellular network. She tried the Gazette app again, same error message. Her phone had one bar of service, which apparently, was not enough to power the app. Mia's pulse quickened. She wouldn't have time to wait for an internet repairman, and the time it would take to go to the nearest store would be costly. She thought about her options. "Dorothy!"

Mia crossed the hallway and knocked lightly on Dorothy's door. No answer. She knocked again, harder this time. A minute later she heard the distinct sound of a lock sliding open. Dorothy eased the door ajar.

"What you doing pounding on my door so early? Is there some emergency?"

Mia's face reddened a bit. She had forgotten how early it was. Dorothy was still in her bathrobe. "I'm sorry, Dorothy. But my internet is down, and I was hoping I could jump on your WiFi."

Dorothy stared at Mia like she was crazy. "I thought I told you I got rid of my WiFi. That's just a way for Big Brother to listen in on all of your conversations."

Mia all but slapped her palm onto her forehead. "You're right," Mia said, "I forgot. Sorry."

"That's all right. I needed to get up anyway." She poked her head out of the door and looked down the hallway. "Have you tried asking our neighbor? I'll bet he wouldn't mind."

Mia winced. The thought had crossed her mind, but she didn't want to go through the embarrassment of asking him. She knew he'd just make fun of her again for being in the competition, and probably say she owed him a favor or something. Still, it looked like her only option at this point.

"Thanks. I'll try there."

"Good luck, and put in a good word for me," Dorothy said with a wink.

Mia chuckled. "Will do."

Dorothy closed her door and Mia was alone again. She checked her watch. It was early still. Maybe Noah wouldn't be up yet. She had a flash of an idea. Since he had just moved in, his WiFi would be new, too. Maybe he hadn't gotten around to password protecting it yet. If she could get close enough, she might be able to access the signal and pull up the app without knocking on his door. She put her plan into action. Mia slipped down the hallway as quietly as she could. As she got close to Noah's door she felt her heart pounding. She knew it was silly to be so nervous about so simple a thing, but she didn't like sneaking around. She looked up and down the hallway surreptitiously and opened her WiFi settings. At the top of the list, with three full bars, was a WiFi signal called "Noah's Ark." She clicked it – no password required. Her phone connected, but now only showed one bar. Staring at her phone, she moved closer to the door. The signal jumped to two bars. She moved closer still, but tripped on Noah's welcome mat. She fell forward and banged into his front door. When she was able to steady herself, she froze and listened for movement, but heard nothing. She breathed a silent sigh of relief. Now on the mat, she looked at her phone. Three bars. "Perfect." She tapped the Gazette app. At that exact second, Noah's door swung open. He moved out into the hallway without looking and bumped right into Mia. Noah struggled to catch his balance as Mia was knocked backward. Her phone clattered to the floor. Instinctively, Noah reached down and caught her before she fell flat on her back.

"Whoa!" Noah exclaimed. "I didn't see you there. I'm sorry." Mia glanced up at him. She looked like the cat-that-swallowed-the-canary, and shrugged nonchalantly. Noah bent and picked up her phone, then paused for a second as he tried to piece things together. "Wait," he said. Mia closed her eyes knowing the jig was up. "What are you doing there? I didn't see you because you were crouched on my doorstep." He looked down at Mia's phone and saw the WiFi signal. "Apparently stealing my WiFi." he said with a wry smile.

Mia turned six shades of red, and didn't know what to say. "I...I wasn't stealing it. I was just gonna borrow it."

Noah's grin widened. "How does that work?"

Mia shook things off a bit and stood up straighter. "Fine. I was gonna steal it. But only because mine went out this morning."

He smirked at her comment. "I thought you said you didn't cheat to win."

"I didn't...this isn't...arrgh." Mia was flummoxed and embarrassed. She hated that Noah seemed to be enjoying it so much.

"I believe you," he said. "But I want to know if I'm gonna have to save you from falling every time we meet. That could get tiring for my back."

Mia felt another sting of embarrassment, but she laughed. She had fallen twice in the last two days, and admitted to herself it was kind of funny. And he didn't even know about her tripping over his mat.

"Don't worry. I won't fall for you ever again," she responded coyly. "Anyway. May I?"

"May you what?"

Mia motioned toward the phone. Noah pretended to be troubled by a torturous decision. "Well, I don't know. Now that I've caught a real, live, cat-burglar in the act, maybe I should turn you in."

For what felt like the thousandth time since she'd met him, Mia rolled her eyes. "Ha. Ha," she said, affecting a sarcastic laugh. "So?"

"I'm kidding. Of course, you can use it."

"Thank you. And sorr—"

Noah interrupted her. "On one condition."

"I knew it. It couldn't just be easy. So, what's the condition?"

"You have to let me tag along," he said with a grin.

"No way."

"C'mon. I want to see what you get out of all this sappiness."

Mia was shaking her head before he'd finished speaking. "No. I work alone. Besides, the rules specifically forbid getting help."

"Believe me, I don't intend to lift a finger"

"I'm not surprised. But the answer is still no."

Noah shrugged as if it was water off his back. "So be it. No big deal. I'll just go unplug my WiFi if you won't be needing it." Mia gritted her teeth and weighed her remaining options. Noah glanced at his watch. "It is getting late in the morning though. Good luck finding another internet source." He turned and walked back inside his door, closing it behind him.

Mia stood awkwardly on the threshold and shook her head. After a brief internal debate, she knocked on the door, loudly. Noah pulled it open and acted surprised to see her. "Oh, hi! Good to see you this morning. How can I help you?"

Mia closed her eyes and pinched the bridge of her nose. "You're a child, I swear. Fine. You've got a deal. You can tag along, but I do everything. You just keep your mouth shut and stay out of my way."

Noah laughed heartily. "You're the boss." He opened his door wide, and Mia stepped in.

CHAPTER 20

The Bagel House was alive with hubbub of the season. Holiday shoppers stopped in for carbs and caffeine refills before heading back out to brave the shopping malls; baristas buzzed filling order after order; and Christmas music played non-stop on the speakers overhead. Mia sat at a booth opposite Noah, her nose down in her phone. They had opted to rush out for a quick lunch because the bagel shop was close, it had passable Wifi, and Noah's cupboards were bare. Mia looked up from her phone and saw Noah grinning at her. She kicked herself for not having thought of The Bagel House earlier. Now she had a tag along for the day, and at this point, he was nothing but distracting.

To be fair, it hadn't been all bad. The morning had passed pleasantly enough in Noah's condo. Mia had entered the living room and selected a comfy-looking chair, one of the few not covered in open boxes, and dug in to the puzzle. For his part, Noah left her alone and typed away on his laptop. He only interrupted once, to ask if she needed anything. She didn't – too busy.

The day three puzzle was a kind Mia had never seen. Three rows of randomized letters – three on top, one in the middle, and three on bottom. The goal was to make as many words as possible using the letters available. The same letters could be used multiple times, but in every word the middle letter had to be used at least once. Each word had to consist of at least four letters. When enough words had been found, the app would reward the player with one of the circled letters from the secret location. Then new letter rows would appear and the next round would begin. The first round of letters popped up:

R-O-D
 -A-
M-P-U

Mia furiously typed in words: Road; Ramp; Pram; Puma; Ramrod," each correct word produced a satisfying chime from the app. She continued: Drama; Proud," the phone buzzed and a notification warned her she must include the middle letter in responses. She liked this game; it was fast paced and played to her strengths. She kept typing in words as fast as she could find them. After her tenth successful word, "Papa," the app revealed the first letter from the secret location: G. "Yes!" Mia shouted.

Noah looked up. "Doing well?"

"Mmm-hmm." She was already back to it. The second round of letters materialized and Mia was flying. Round two had substantially more word possibilities than the first, and required 25 correct entries before it coughed up the second clue from the secret location: D.

As the morning waned, Mia got hungry, and her mind wandered. She knew refueling was the best choice, even if it cost her some travel time. Plus, she had already put a huge dent in the puzzles and had many of the secret location's letters. B-T-G-D-R-O-I-N-E. So, they agreed to go to The Bagel House, and stuffed themselves into opposite sides of a booth.

To pass the time, Noah busied himself by scrolling through his phone. When that got old, he pulled out his laptop and made another attempt at working remotely, but he seemed bored by that too. Finally, he found another time killer: stacking coffee creamers. He built one tower after another and each would come crashing down spilling creamer cartons all over the table. Every time a tower would crash, Mia would look up annoyed, and then go back to her work. She didn't have time to play games, or even to chide Noah for playing them.

"Look! Look!" Noah called out. Mia reluctantly glanced in his direction. Noah had built a tower of creamer in front of him that resembled the Great Pyramid of Giza. Had she not been so annoyed by the distraction, she might have been impressed. "164 creamers!" Noah blurted out. "That must be a world record. Or at least a record for this bagel shop."

Mia put her phone down. "I told you this would be boring." As she finished talking the pyramid crumbled and sent creamer cartons shooting across the table and onto the floor. Noah hurriedly scooped them up.

"Actually, I'm not bored at all. Next tower will be even bigger. I'm gonna try for 200."

"If you want to stay here, there won't be a next tower. At least not at this table."

Noah frowned. "Fine." He grabbed a creamer from the pile, leaned back his head and balanced a creamer on his nose. "Hand me another one, quick."

Despite Mia's best efforts to resist, a smile crept across her face. "See? A child," she said in an attempt to cover it up. "Can't you go busy yourself with something else for a minute or two?"

Noah appeared to get the message that he was wearing out his welcome. "All right, all right," he said. "I'll give you some space." He got up from the booth and sidled over to a magazine rack to browse. Mia went back to the game.

At the same time, at the back of the shop, a man entered clutching several plastic bags. His clothes were heavily worn and bore brown and black stains. His facial hair was scraggly, and he was as skinny as though he hadn't seen a good meal in months. The man's eyes were cast downward and he slinked toward a booth. Other patrons took notice. Some immediately got up and left, and others glanced quickly in his directing then turned away just as fast. A store manager who had been sweeping behind the counter noticed the man and addressed him loudly. "Hey! Hey, buddy! You can't be in here. I've told you that before. Turn around or I'll call the police." Noah watched the scene. He looked over at Mia, but she was still engaged in her puzzle and hadn't looked up.

The man responded to the store manager. In a pleading voice he said, "Please. I'm just tryin' to get warm."

The manager was insistent. "You can't do it here. Turn around." The commotion had caused nearly everyone in the shop to watch the scene unfold. Even Mia had put down her phone to see what was happening. Her heart ached for the man, but she wasn't sure what she could do. As she wracked her brain trying to think of a solution, she saw Noah approach him. He put his arm around the man and whispered something in his ear. The man smiled and whispered back.

The store manager looked unsure of himself. "What are you two doing?"

"Marcus!" Noah shouted suddenly, and wrapped the man in a giant hug. "There you are." The man stiffened, but he hugged Noah back. "Where have you been, man? I told you we were meeting at noon. I've been waiting for a half hour."

Marcus stammered. "I'm...sorry."

Noah laughed. "Don't give me excuses. Just come on time, next time."

The store manager looked on. "You know this person?" he asked.

"Of course, I know him. I invited him here. What's the problem?"

The manager put the pieces together and figured out what was happening. He wasn't sure what to do. After considering it for a minute, all he could manage was to shake his head and say, "Fine. Whatever. No loitering."

Noah seemed pleased. "Wouldn't dream of it." He turned to the man. "Marcus, I think it's my turn to pick up the tab. What'll you have?"

Marcus walked with Noah to the counter and placed an order for a soup, sandwich, and soda. Noah doubled the order and instructed the barista to bag the second one to go. He also ordered himself a small pastry to help keep up the illusion. Once they received the food, Marcus headed toward the door without thanking Noah. Rather than feeling annoyed, Noah smiled and called after him, "Merry Christmas."

Marcus stopped, turned and said "Merry Christmas to you," before ducking back out the door into the cold.

Mia, and the rest of the bagel shop, had watched every second of what transpired. For a moment, it was quiet enough to hear a pin drop. But as soon as Marcus was gone, it was business as usual, and the din of conversation and food preparation began anew. Noah looked at Mia, who had gone back – or at least had pretended to go back – to her puzzle. He was relieved. Noah didn't like to make a spectacle of himself, and especially didn't like to show off anything charitable. That Mia hadn't seen anything suited him just fine. He made his way back to the booth and sat down with a plop. Mia didn't look up. Without saying a word, Noah went back to stacking coffee creamer.

Mia acted like she was engrossed in puzzle solving, but she couldn't get what had just happened, off her mind. She had wanted to help the man, but had felt powerless. Noah had cooly and calmly handled the situation, and now acted as if nothing at all had happened. She admired that. She debated saying something to him. But what? "How do I compliment someone for an act of kindness," she wondered. "Plus, what if he doesn't want to talk about it." Mia resolved to leave it alone, and act like she hadn't seen anything.

The rest of Noah's creamer tower came crashing down. The sound shook her from her thoughts and she noticed a barista approaching. "Great," she thought. "We're about to get yelled at for the creamer. I knew it."

Instead of yelling though, the barista appeared nervous. Noah looked at her. "Everything ok?"

"Yes," she said. "I just wanted to tell you that was really sweet what you did. My manager always kicks that guy out, and I feel bad."

Noah stole a glance at Mia who was staring at him. "Thanks for the kind words," he finally said. "It was nothing."

The barista smiled and went back to her work. Mia continued

her stare, unwavering. If someone else could bring it up, so could she.

"What?" Noah finally said, looking at Mia.

She smiled warmly. "Nothing. I'm just…impressed."

He ignored the comment. "How's the crossword coming?"

Mia lifted the phone and showed it to him. "Not a crossword, remember? But I'm getting close," she said. "I just need to figure out a few more words here.'" Noah opened his mouth, ready to speak. She cut him off. "Don't say anything! I can't get any help on this. I'm just letting you know what's left."

The store manager approached the table and caught eyes with Noah. "I know what you did there. I know you don't know Marcus or whatever his real name is. I didn't want to make a spectacle, so I let it go, but he'll be back every day now looking for handouts. If you're not here, he'll start harassing other patrons. It's not good."

Noah opened his mouth to respond, but before he could, Mia jumped in. "You know what's not good? Having a business policy that rejects people just based on the way they look. That man wasn't bothering anyone. And besides, if my friend here," Mia motioned to Noah, "told you he invited Marcus to lunch, then he invited Marcus to lunch. It's not your job to try to figure out the relationships of your customers. If you have a problem with that, I'll be glad to post your opinion on the matter to social media."

The store manager's jaw hit the floor, as did Noah's. He flashed an intimidated smile at Mia. "No, Ma'am, that won't be necessary. I suppose I guessed wrong. My apologies." He looked at Noah. "You and…Marcus are welcome anytime."

Mia looked up suddenly and stared into space over the manager's shoulder. He looked behind himself to see what had caught her gaze. Even Noah looked over to see what she was looking at. "Welcome," she said to herself. The manager squinted, looking confused. "Welcome! I think that's it."

The manager warily stepped backwards, while keeping his eyes fixed on Mia. "I'll leave you two alone. Let me know if you need anything else."

Mia ignored him, she was already tapping in "Welcome" on her phone. The app chimed. "Yes!" she shouted. "I think that was the last one."

"You should get in fights with baristas more often. Look what it does for your creative process." Noah said.

Mia smiled but she was too busy with the secret clue to engage. "Unscrambling these letters reveals…what?" She wrinkled her forehead in concentration. "Bo…tan…botanical garden. It's the botanical garden!" She slapped Noah lightly on the shoulder. "Let's go!" They jumped up, grabbed their coats, and headed out the door.

CHAPTER 21

The botanical garden was one of the gems of the city. Mia had only been there once, many years earlier, but still remembered the thick aroma of fresh flowers hanging in the air. In the summer time, the garden was a large tourist draw. The garden held various events there: wine tastings, photography classes, new art installations, and more. When Mia had attended, the garden was full of larger-than-life flower sculptures. Some depicted fantastic creatures like dragons, while others were merely ornate patterns and designs. As they drove, she wondered what kind of plants they'd have in the winter, especially with the snow. She was surprised it was even open this time of year.

As if sharing her thoughts, Noah said, "Are you sure you got the right location?"

"I'm sure. Why?"

"Just wondering what's gonna be in this garden. Surprised they'd have the location there."

Mia nodded, but didn't acknowledge the comment further. "I need positivity right now, please."

"Ok," Noah said, "I'm positive most plants can't survive in the winter." He laughed.

Mia did too. "Thanks for that," she said.

"Here to help...but also not help in any meaningful way, as per the rules." Noah said taking on faux-serious tone.

Mia pulled the Lemon Lime into a parking space, and scrambled out. The area looked deserted. "You coming?" she said to Noah who was moving at a much slower pace. He got out and followed her as she jogged toward the botanical garden's entrance. As they approached, Mia noted that they were the only two people in sight. The familiar worry she was in the wrong place crept over her. But this had to be it, she thought. Unlike yesterday, there was no other option. Unless she'd done the puzzles wrong, but she was pretty sure she hadn't. The phone had chimed at every correct answer and had given her the letters for the secret location. This had to be the place.

The gate to the garden consisted of two big, green, swinging iron gates. They were closed fast. A large padlock and chain wound itself around them, keeping any would-be trespassers out. An old sign was affixed to the gate which read, "Closed."

Mia panicked. "No. No. This can't be."

Noah looked on, concerned, but for once held his tongue. Perhaps he figured now would not be the ideal time for a joke. Mia was stressed and maybe he was worried for her. Maybe he genuinely wanted to see her do well and wanted to help, but knew Mia would forbid it, so he stayed silent.

Mia was talking to herself, weighing her options. "This could still be it. Maybe they just want us to come to the gate. I'm not in the garden, but I'm at the garden." She pulled her phone out of her pocket and positioned herself in front of the botanical garden sign.

"Want me to take that?" Noah offered.

"It says it has to be a selfie. I don't want to run the risk of disqualification for any reason." She opened the app, switched the camera to selfie mode, and snapped the picture. Then the upload process. Noah sat down on a nearby bench. Mia joined him.

"What happens now?" He asked.

"Now we wait," Mia said. As she was speaking, her phone buzzed. Noah looked at her eagerly. She was surprised. "That was quick. Do you think it's from them?"

"Open it up," he urged.

Mia clicked open the message. It was indeed a ping from the Gazette's app. The message read, "Thanks for entering the Twelve Games of Christmas contest! We're sorry, but you didn't find the correct secret location. 2 other contestants have found today's location. Daily points: 0; Total points: 0." Mia put her head in her hands.

"What's it say?" Noah queried.

"It's wrong. This isn't it. And two other people already found the location. I can't believe it."

"That's ok. At least you know you're still in the running. Aren't there three people who can get a point every day?"

"Yeah, but I don't know the location, and two people already found it." Mia held up the paper with the crossword in her hand. "I just don't get it. I could've sworn this was right." She stared at the puzzle and tried to concentrate.

At that moment, a groundskeeper in a golf cart wheeled up next to the pair; he hardly took notice of them. The man climbed down from the cart and grabbed a leaf blower that was resting in the back. The noise was loud, and Mia lost focus.

"Let's go," she said.

"Wait," Noah protested. "I wanna' ask him something." Noah walked over to the groundskeeper and waved to get his attention. The sound of the leaf blower clicked off.

"Can I help you?"

"Yeah." Noah pointed toward the garden gates. "When does this thing open?"

"If you're waitin' for the outside garden to open, you're gonna be waitin' a long time. Won't open these gates til' spring. Sorry." The man flipped the switch on his leaf blower and went back to his work. Mia started to walk away, and Noah followed. After a few seconds, the man flipped his leaf blower back off and called out to them. "But, if you're really in the mood for flowers, you can always go to the botanical garden greenhouse. It's right up that hill. Open year-round." With that, he turned his back and the sound of the leaf blower once again filled the area.

Mia caught eyes with Noah, and without a word, they sprinted up the hill toward the greenhouse.

The air was sweet with the smell of flowers, even outside the greenhouse. Mia, who was in better shape, reached the doors first. She grabbed the handle and bent over to catch her breath. Noah wasn't too far behind, but he rounded the corner, huffing and puffing.

"I didn't know this was a race," he said in between breaths.

"That's literally the whole premise of this contest. A race to be first to the secret location."

Noah laughed. "Touché." They walked into the greenhouse and a wall of warm, humid air wrapped itself around them. It felt good, especially after being stuck out by the garden gate for so long. Mia wasted no time. She pulled out her cell phone and snapped another selfie. A second later and she'd submitted it.

"Second time's the charm?" she said, hopefully.

"I've got a good feeling."

Mia held her phone and wouldn't take her eyes off the screen. She tapped her foot impatiently. "What is taking so long? They responded instantly last time."

"Be patient. Maybe it's a good sign." Noah moved farther into the botanical garden and turned to beckon Mia. "C'mere." He stopped in front of a display of white roses, and covered the name plate with his hand. "Quiz time," he said. "What are these?"

Mia chuckled. "Those would be roses."

Noah feigned being deeply impressed. "Woooow." He moved farther down the path and covered another name plate. "Ok, miss smarty pants. How 'bout these?"

Mia smiled. She liked this game, it was taking her mind off the stress of the contest and that was what she needed. She looked at the display. "Snapdragons."

"That's only half a point. What is the scientific name?"

Mia wracked her brain and tried to remember freshman year. She'd taken a botany class because it was the only thing that fit with her schedule, and part of the semester had been dedicated to memorizing scientific names for common flowers. It was coming to her. "It's…anti-something. Like anti-rhinoceros or something."

Now Noah really seemed impressed. "Antirrhinum. Very good. For that you get three quarters of a point."

Mia laughed. "Only three quarters? What do I have to say to get a full point?"

Before he could respond, Mia's phone vibrated. The familiar rush of adrenaline coursed through her. She looked at her phone and nodded to Noah. It was another push notification from the Gazette's app. Cautiously, she opened the message and read it to herself. "Thanks for entering the Twelve Games of Christmas contest! Congratulations on finding today's secret location! You are the 3rd person to do so. Daily points: 1; Total points: 1." Mia gasped.

"What's it say?" Noah asked.

Without thinking, Mia turned to Noah and wrapped her arms around him. "I got a point!" she exclaimed.

Noah laughed joyfully, and hugged her back. "Congratulations!"

The immediate rush passed, and she became aware of what she was doing. Mia yanked her arms back quickly. "Sorry," she said.

"No harm done."

"Let's get out of here."

"Wait," Noah said, "follow me." He led her down the path toward the white roses where they had stopped before. He reached over the handrail and plucked one directly from the display. Mia's face turned beet red. "What are you doing?" she demanded.

He handed her the flower. "For luck."

Still red in the face, Mia took the flower and laughed. It was cheesy, but a cute gesture – despite the criminal nature of it. "What are you doing? You're going to get us kicked out of here."

"That's only if we get caught."

As he was speaking, an angry botanical employee in a green jumpsuit approached them at a steady clip. She stopped in front of them. "Please leave the plant life alone, or you'll be asked to leave."

Mia was dying inside. She gave the woman an apologetic smile. "I'm so sorry." Then she turned to Noah. "Let's go."

"I think that's a good idea," said the employee, who turned and stormed away. Mia and Noah caught eyes and burst into laughter. Together, they hurried out of the botanical garden.

Mia and Noah rode the elevator together, which made sense because they were neighbors. They had chatted about this-and-that on the way home from the garden, but were silent now. Mia appreciated the silence. She found it exhausting when people would fill up every moment with conversation. Sometimes, she thought, it was nice just to be near people, but to be left to your own thoughts. The elevator dinged and they exited. Noah's door was first. He paused in front of it. "That was fun."

Mia nodded. "I can't believe I'm actually saying this, but yeah, it was." Noah shuffled his feet, and made no effort to go inside. Mia could see he wanted to say something, but for some reason was dancing around. "What is it?" she asked.

"Do you mind if I tag along again tomorrow? Purely for observational purposes."

Mia felt a rush of excitement. It was true she'd had fun with Noah today. Plus, when she thought she'd found the wrong place, he had made her feel better. But on the other hand, she didn't know what his game was. Why was he taking such an interest in her all of a sudden? Was this all about work and her shop? That thought made her uneasy, so she decided to demur. "I'm sure my WiFi will be working tomorrow, so there's really no need to tag along. But thanks for letting me use yours today."

Noah nodded and put his key in the door lock. "Have a good afternoon," he said, looking a bit sad. Mia was surprised she felt bad for him, and a small pang of regret hit her.

"You too," she said, and walked toward her condo without looking back.

CHAPTER 22

His phone buzzed and startled him awake. Noah had passed out on his couch for a cat-nap after his morning puzzle adventure with Mia. He rubbed the sleep out of his eyes, stretched, and looked at the screen. Two new voicemails. He clicked the first open and listened.

"Hi, this message is for Noah Caffrey. This is Kelly from Kelly's Antiques. I'm calling to tell you Walt and I were able to fix your typewriter. We got it done a little quicker than we thought, it wasn't in bad shape. It's ready for pickup whenever you want." Good news. Noah hadn't expected the machine to be ready for weeks. He tapped the redial button, and confirmed with Kelly they were still open.

The second voicemail was from Nadine. "Going into a meeting. Text me," was all it said. Noah tapped her name and a text box opened.

"Hi, Nadine, what's up?" he typed.

Her response came back quickly. "I want another update. Where are we on SVT? Have u made contact with the owner again???"

Noah considered whether to tell Nadine about the morning. "As a matter of fact, I spent the day with her. She's doing the Twelve Games of Christmas contest."

"LOL! That's hilarious, of course she is. Okay, so what intel do you have?!?!"

"She said she's not interested in selling. I don't know what more I can do."

"Well that's your job, Noah. To make her interested. It sounds like you two are buddy-buddy now. Gain her trust, and talk her into selling. It'll be better for her than a foreclosure." Noah began typing out a response, but another of Nadine's texts interrupted. "That's not a request. Act like your directorship's on the line here – because it just may be."

Noah's heart was in his throat. He didn't want to lose his job, and Nadine was probably right, selling was better than foreclosure. "Okay." He responded. Nadine never wrote back.

As he drove to the antique shop, Noah thought about the typewriter. He'd told Walt and Kelly he'd gotten it from his father, but that wasn't exactly right. Noah had never actually met his father – he had died in a car crash a week before Noah was born. Noah's mom had been strong for him. "That's the ebb and flow of life," she'd said when he was older, "one person passes, and a new one is born." But as Noah aged he recognized his father's premature death had been devastating to his mom. The matter of the typewriter was a mystery to him for the better part of his life. His father had died intestate – there was no formal will – but the typewriter had been given to Noah before he knew how to crawl. He even remembered seeing it resting on the dresser in his nursery in old baby photos. It was always there, and Noah didn't care much about it early on. In fact, in one of Noah's earliest memories, when he was about three or four, he had stuffed a pancake into the paper feed roller of the typewriter, and his mother had scolded him profusely. She took the typewriter away and told him he wasn't old enough to have it – which didn't bother him – until a few hours later when he found her holding the typewriter and gently crying. Ever since then, he had taken better care of it. At one point, during his teenage years, Noah finally got around to asking his mom about it. She told him it wasn't worth much but was one of his Dad's most prized possessions, and it reminded her of him more than any other thing, besides Noah himself. She said his Dad had planned to give Noah the typewriter when he was born, and he'd told everyone how his son was going to grow up to be a great writer – that is, if he wanted to be one. Noah always loved that story, that his dad was imagining his future while he was still in his mom's belly. From then on, Noah did all of his school work on the typewriter. His classmates, and some teachers, thought he was crazy to not use a word processor, but he wanted to be like his father, and the extra work was ok by him. When Noah went away to college, bringing along the typewriter was no longer realistic, so he left it in his mother's care. At some point after graduation she'd given him boxes of his stuff from his childhood room and the typewriter was included. There it remained, in storage, until the other day when he'd been inspired to dust it off and fix it up.

Noah pulled his car into a parking space at Kelly's Antiques, and headed into the store. A doorbell chime let workers know he had entered. After a few seconds, Kelly emerged from the back room. "Mr. Caffrey," she said, "we've got ya' all fixed up."

"That was fast."

"I know it. When Walt and I see somethin' we like, we make it the priority."

"I'm glad. Can I take a look at it?"

Kelly turned around and shifted some boxes on a shelf behind her. She hoisted the typewriter, which was covered in a small sheet, onto the countertop. "You wanna' do the honors?" she asked.

"I feel like a magician's assistant," Noah joked.

Kelly laughed. "When you see what this baby looks like, you'll know you're not far from the truth."

Noah tugged on the sheet and revealed the typewriter. It was stunning. He couldn't believe the transformation that had taken place in so little time. The sleek black steel body was shining, the K key had been reattached. Everything looked brand new. "This is incredible," he said.

Kelly was beaming. "Iddn't it? Now look, before you go falling in love with it, Walt and I talked. We're willing to give you seventy-five-hundred bucks for it. Right here, right now."

Noah looked up at Kelly in disbelief. $7,500? How much was this thing worth? He silently chided himself for not doing more research on it before coming to pick it up. Still, no matter what the price, he couldn't get rid of it. It meant too much to him, it meant too much to his mom.

"I'm sorry," he said. "No deal."

"You are a tough negotiator," she said, not giving up. She leaned forward to Noah and beckoned him closer as if she was going to whisper a secret. In a hush she said, "We'll give you ten grand. Final offer."

Noah gasped. Ten thousand dollars. That kind of money could really make a difference. But he hesitantly shook his head. "That's an amazing offer. But I just can't part with it."

"Fine by me," Kelly said, looking like it most definitely was not fine by her. "I'll just ring you up for the repairs. She retreated to a cash register and typed numbers in, rapid fire. Finally, she looked up. "That'll be $556.06."

"Five hundred and fifty-six dollars!" Noah exclaimed. "You told me it'd be a few hundred at most."

"I told you I wouldn't know how much it'd be 'til I got into it. That's the price. I don't know what to tell you. You have thirty days to pay for the labor, otherwise the property reverts to us in default."

Noah felt like he'd been bamboozled, but he wasn't about to let them get away with keeping his typewriter. He glowered at Kelly. "I'll put it on a credit card."

"Excellent choice," she said, looking a bit disappointed.

Noah carried the typewriter, and a new receipt for $556.06, to his car. Again, he placed it on the front seat and strapped it into the seatbelt. The repair price had been a bitter pill, but he had to admit, they had done a good job. The typewriter looked good as new, and he couldn't wait to use it.

The next morning came early. Noah planned it that way. Up at 6:00, showered, dressed, cup of coffee in hand and out his door by 6:30. He rode the elevator to the lobby and went in search of the door to the HVAC room. The door was slightly ajar and the lights were off. Noah pushed his way inside but couldn't find a light switch. He tapped the flashlight button on his phone and a soft, white glow poured out. The walls were bare cement, cool to the touch, and covered with all manner of pipes and cables. Noah shined his light around the maze of metal until he found his target: a cable box. He moved toward it, and felt at once, silly, apprehensive, and excited. He wondered if this is how the Watergate burglars must have felt. On the far wall, a small, plastic box labeled LightFast had several black cables splaying out of it. The cables stretched upward and disappeared behind the ceiling. Noah popped the box open. Each cable was marked by the condo to which it led. Noah scanned the cables until he found the one marked 2D. One more glance over his shoulder. The coast was clear. He unscrewed the black coaxial cable from its port and left it dangling inside the box. As soon as he'd pulled the cable free, Noah heard footsteps outside the door. He slammed the box shut.

Ramon, the building's security guard stepped into the room. "Someone there?" he said as he turned on the light. Noah squinted at the brightness. Ramon connected eyes with him, and jumped a half a foot backward. "Whoa! Mr. Caffrey, you scared me. What're you doin' in here?"

Noah stuttered, his pulse pounding in his ear. "Looking for my…rollerblades. Where's the storage room?"

Ramon moved further into the room, his eyebrows creased. "It's back over by my desk. You feelin' ok?"

"Oh yeah, duh. Sorry." Noah said, as he hurried out of the room. "Thanks." He left Ramon scratching his head, and stepped back onto the elevator. As the doors opened on his floor, he smirked and rushed inside his condo to wait. He checked the time: 6:40. The whole episode had only taken him 10 minutes.

CHAPTER 23

There would be no further morning mistakes on Mia's end, she made sure of that. After scoring a point the day before, she'd resolved to take the competition even more seriously. That meant she'd checked her internet connection, and she'd set a plug-in alarm, a battery alarm, and one alarm on her cell phone. She was going to wake up, no matter what – and she did.

The clocks all chimed at 6:15 on the dot. Mia rubbed her eyes and shut off all three alarms. With her phone in hand, she checked her WiFi connection – strong, fast, secure. "I've got this," she thought, and hurried through a shower. When she was dried, and dressed she checked her phone again: WiFi was still going strong. It was only 6:30. She still had time for a good breakfast. It was a warm bowl of oatmeal, and a fresh fruit smoothie. Finally, she grabbed some scratch paper, a pencil, and sat down at the table with her phone. It was now 6:55. Mia decided to give her WiFi one last test spin. She opened up a web browser and typed in the word "Test." Nothing happened. She tapped the search button again. After thinking for a minute, the screen went grey and the words "No internet connection," appeared. "This can't be happening again." Mia said. The WiFi icon on her phone was Xed out again. She felt like smashing her phone. "When I get a second, I'm gonna call the company and read 'em the riot act," she thought. But that didn't solve her current predicament, and besides, she had no cell signal in her condo, so calling anyone without her WiFi, was out.

Mia's mind was racing trying to think of her next move. If she borrowed Dorothy's phone to call the internet company, no doubt she'd be given an appointment next Tuesday, or the following Tuesday. It wasn't even worth the time. Her second option wasn't appealing either. The Bagel House would be slammed at this time of morning. In all likelihood, she wouldn't be able to find a booth, but even if she got lucky, the noise and chaos of the morning coffee rush would be too big a distraction. So, she was faced with option three, Noah. Another glance at her watch. It was 7:03 now. Time was ticking. Thousands of others were already knee-deep in their puzzles. Mia took a deep breath. "Fine," she said out loud, and marched down to Noah's door. She knocked lightly, almost light enough that he wouldn't hear. She was half-hoping he wouldn't answer so she could revert to option two with no regrets. But that wasn't to be. As soon as her fist left the door, she heard someone inside fiddling with the lock. Noah opened the door with an ear-to-ear grin.

"I must be having an effect on you," he said. "Two visits in two days."

"Hi," Mia said, a bit embarrassed.

"I hope you didn't come to stand outside and steal my WiFi again. It's password protected now. I had to, knowing the cat-burglar might be on the prowl again."

Mia rolled her eyes. "I'm never gonna live that down, I suppose?"

"I think that joke has still got some mileage left in it."

Mia rolled her eyes. "Great."

"Just kidding. I won't bring it up again. Cross my heart."

"Thank you."

"To what do I owe this surprise?" Noah asked.

"Well, it is about the WiFi. Mine's out again. Can I use yours?"

Noah paused and rubbed his chin as if he had a difficult

decision to make. "Of course, of course. But, remember the condition."

Mia grimaced. She figured it would come to this, and even though she'd had fun with Noah yesterday, she really wanted to concentrate on the contest. But he was insistent. "How could I forget? Yes, you can tag along." Mia stepped in to Noah's condo and found the same chair as the previous day. Nothing else seemed to have been moved. She did notice a particularly beautiful typewriter sitting on the kitchen table, but didn't have time to ask about it – the contest had started, and she was late.

Day four's puzzle was an enormous word search. In fact, it was the biggest word search Mia had ever seen. It must have had tens of thousands of letters, and was far too big to be seen on her phone screen. That meant she had to scroll around the puzzle methodically, and try to remember where she'd already looked. It was clunky, and probably not well-thought-out by the puzzle creator. Mia spent ten minutes looking for the first word, Yuletide, with no success, before deciding to switch to her tablet. She dashed across the hallway, grabbed her tablet, and linked it to Noah's WiFi. She had to re-download the app and re-login with her credentials, but it was worth the extra effort. The bigger screen was much easier to manipulate. Only five minutes later, Mia was circling her first word. She checked the list, only 29 more words to go. But her excitement gave way to panic as it dawned on her that with only 30 words to search for in such an enormous puzzle, finding each word could be like finding needles in a haystack. The app rewarded her first find by presenting the first letter of the secret location: C. Mia jotted it down on her scratch paper and went back to the puzzle.

Three hours later, Mia and Noah sat in the same booth of The Bagel House, as the day before. Mia searched and Noah listlessly scrolled through his cell phone. The store manager recognized them and approached.

"Howdy."

Noah looked up. "Can I help you?"

"Any chance your friend, Marcus, is coming to meet you again today?"

"He might," Noah said defensively. "And what if he does?"

The store manager raised his arms, palms up. "I don't mean it like that. I came over to tell you I've been thinking about what you did and...all are welcome here. From now on."

Mia smiled at Noah, he winked back. "Thanks for the update. I'm glad to hear it. But as I said, I didn't do anything except have lunch with a friend."

The manager nodded. "I get it. But I'm just saying. Next time you see your friend, tell him he's welcome here anytime."

"Will do."

As the manager retreated, Mia tapped Noah lightly on the wrist. "Look at what you did. I'm very impressed."

Noah's face flushed. "That's nice of you to say. Thank you. But anybody would have done the same. Plus, I'm sure he changed his mind more from you telling him off than from anything I did."

"I'm not so sure."

Mia bent her head back down to the puzzle in front of her. Noah went back to his cell phone for a minute, but soon locked it and set it on the table. He looked at Mia.

"I don't get it. Why go to all this trouble for some silly puzzles? I mean, besides the money?"

Mia looked up, surprised. "What do you mean, 'besides the money?' You and your company seem to know my financial situation better than me. A hundred grand would go a long way to helping save the store."

"I know. But there have to be more-productive ways to spend your time saving the store. And your chances of winning are probably pretty low."

Mia beat herself up for feeling warmth toward Noah only moments earlier. "I sure am glad you came along. Thanks for the vote of confidence," she said.

Noah shook his head in protest. "C'mon. I didn't mean it like that. I'm sorry." He looked earnest and Mia softened a bit. "I'm just saying, it's hard for anyone to win any contest like this.

Even though it's clear you're very skilled."

"For your information, it's not only about the money."

"I knew it. I'm not crazy. What else is it about?"

Mia considered her next words carefully. How much should she share? "It's...forget it."

"Please. I want to hear it."

"Fine. But promise me you won't laugh."

"I will not laugh."

"There are a lot of reasons I like this contest. Running the store is a full-time job and I don't get out much. It's nice for me to have something to look forward to, that gets me away from all everything."

"Why would I laugh at that? That seems perfectly reasonable."

"That's not all."

Noah smiled. "The plot thickens."

"When I was little, my Mom played the Twelve Games every year. She loved them. When I got old enough to participate, she taught me everything she knew about techniques and we'd play them together. It was our tradition. Of course, back then there wasn't any money involved. It was only about Christmas cheer."

Noah smiled at the story. "Does she still play them?"

"She passed, actually. Three years ago."

"I'm so sorry."

"It's okay. You didn't know. Anyway, that's why I play the Twelve Games, it helps connect me to her. When I play, I feel like she's still with me."

Noah nodded. Her story reminded him of his dad, and how he'd always felt connected to him when he used the typewriter. He smiled at her. "I know exactly what you mean."

Mia looked skeptical. "Another joke?"

"No. For your information, I didn't always want to be a..." he paused, thinking of the right words, "soulless corporate drone."

Mia arched her eyebrows. "Wow. Does it say that on your business cards?"

Noah chuckled. "I used to write. A lot. I wanted to be a

writer."

Mia was surprised. It was hard for her to picture Noah outside of his corporate boardroom, and especially hard to picture him doing creative work. But he had impressed her yesterday with Marcus, so perhaps there was a lot more to him than met the eye. "What did you write?" she asked.

"Everything. Poetry, short stories, I even wrote a novel...well, most of one."

"Wow."

"Thanks, but you can hold your applause. None of it went anywhere."

"Why not?"

"I don't know. I was too scared to do anything with it, I guess. So, after I graduated, I went for the sure thing. A nine-to-five. Which is a lot more than that actually, but the point is, I admire you for owning your own store. And for chasing your dream. However crazy it is."

Mia smiled and shook her head. "You see? You were so close to saying something nice. But you had to screw it up at the end. Are you still writing?"

"Not really. But I've been thinking about trying again. I've been feeling more inspired, recently."

"That's great."

"I even dusted off the old typewriter in anticipation."

"You use a typewriter?" Mia chuckled at the thought, and remembered seeing it on his table earlier. "Oh wait. I saw it this morning. It was beautiful."

"Yes, I do, and it so happens it's my most-prized possession. I've just forgotten about it until recently."

"Where did you find it?"

Noah told Mia the story of how he'd been given the typewriter as a baby, from his late father, and how he felt connected to him when he used it. Mia smiled as he spoke. It moved her that they'd both been through similar events with their parents. Noah also told her about fixing the typewriter, and how much the antique store offered for it.

"And you didn't sell it?" she teased.

"No. I told you. It's my favorite thing. And my Mom's, and my Dad's."

Mia was impressed again. To a lot of people, money was the be-all-end-all, but, it seemed, to Noah, intrinsic value was more important. Still, she was curious. "If they wanted to give you 10K on the spot, I'm sure it's worth a lot more at an auction. Have you looked it up?"

"I've been meaning to, but I've been too busy. Plus, I'm not sure I wanna' know. If it's worth a ton, it might make the decision to hold on to it, that much harder."

Mia nodded. "I doubt it. You seem pretty convicted, but you should still look it up, just for fun."

"I am convicted. But you're right, I'm curious too. I'll check it out." Noah pulled out his phone and navigated to a popular antique auction site. He typed in the make and model of his typewriter. Mia looked on with rapt attention. Suddenly, Noah gasped and his face went white.

"What is it?" Mia asked, anxiously.

"It's the price. They had one sell last year, same make and model, only theirs wasn't refurbished."

"And?" Mia pressed.

"It sold for $35,000!"

"My goodness! I was wrong. You should definitely sell that thing." Noah looked up to see if Mia was serious. She had a wry smile on her face. "I'm totally kidding," she laughed. "That's beautiful your dad left you such a valuable heirloom. You should hang on to it. You can give it to your kids someday." He seemed to appreciate her words. Mia tried to switch gears. "Are you going to try to sell some of your writing this time?"

"I wasn't planning on it."

"I've got an idea then. We'll make a deal. If I win the contest, you have to try to sell your work. I'll be your inspiration guinea pig."

"What a lovely way to put it," Noah laughed. "Deal."

Mia looked down at the word search. "Good. Now, can I have some peace and quiet to work on this thing?"

"By all means."

"Noah!" Mia called out. His eyes shot open. He was lying flat on the Bagel House bench, and had fallen asleep. Mia's voice called out again. "Noah, I'm done! Let's go!"

He sat up and rubbed his eyes. "You solved it?"

"Yeah, we gotta hurry."

"Where're we headed?"

"To the holiday section of the public library."

He cocked one eyebrow. "Makes sense."

Mia stood and grabbed his coat. "Let's go."

The public library was one of the oldest buildings in Snow Valley. The façade was made up of red brick and stone. One giant slab near the bottom of the building had MDCCXCIX etched into it – Roman numerals for 1799. As with most public libraries, it received the majority of its funding from the state, and had very little, if any federal backing. Mia had read articles debating the ongoing value of libraries and discussing what to do with this one if it were shuttered – they always made her melancholy. She had so many memories of being dropped off on Saturday mornings, finding a good book, and getting lost for hours in its pages. Mia loved the way books smelled, she loved how heavy and substantial they were. She didn't even mind the occasional papercut that came from flipping a page too quickly. So, when she and Noah pulled up to the library, she was filled with sense of bitter-sweet nostalgia.

They jogged up the steps and into the building. Their feet clattered on the marble floor and echoed off the walls of the entryway. A librarian looked up and furrowed her brow. They moved toward her, but slowed their pace to be quieter. "Can you point us to the holiday section, please?" Mia asked the librarian, her voice echoing off the polished marble.

"Shhh," came the response. The librarian pointed toward the back of the stacks in an adjacent room.

"Thank you." They found the section quickly. A sign hung from the ceiling indicating they were in the right place.

"This looks like it," Noah said. "Are you gonna take a

picture?"

As he spoke a librarian who had been stacking books looked at them. She put her finger to her lips. "Shhh."

Noah looked at Mia and raised his eyebrows. "Not the friendliest bunch, are they?" He said in a whisper. The librarian went back to her work.

Mia pulled her cellphone from her pocket snapped a selfie, and uploaded it in the Gazette's app. "It's the waiting that kills me," she whispered. The librarian looked over and glared. They stepped over to the next aisle and browsed book titles quietly. About a minute later, Mia's phone buzzed. She looked at Noah, her eyebrows arched. "This is it."

"Check it out," he urged.

Mia clicked open the message, and her mouth fell open.

"What does it say," Noah asked, anxiously.

Mia read the message aloud. "Thanks for entering the Twelve Games of Christmas! Congratulations on finding secret location 4! You are the 1st person to do so! Daily Points: 1; Total Points: 2; Current Standing: 11th place." Mia wrapped her arms around Noah and hugged him. He was ready this time, and embraced her too. After a second, she let him go, still overcome with joy. "Oh my goodness! I'm in 11th place!" She exclaimed.

"That's amazing! So, what does that mean?"

"It is amazing! I…"

The librarian poked her head around the corner, looking angrier than ever. "Shhh!" she said, steaming.

Mia lowered her voice to a whisper. "It is amazing. I wasn't even ranked yesterday. That means only ten people have more points than me. With some luck, I can keep finding the locations and who knows, I may have a shot at this thing."

Noah flashed Mia a warm smile. "Well, let's go celebrate! My treat."

Mia hesitated and considered her answer. The librarian rounded the corner and made a beeline for them. She looked ready to explode. "If you two can't be quiet, you'll need to leave." she said.

Noah laughed loudly. "I don't care who hears," he shouted,

"she's in 11th place!" Mia burst out laughing too, but she covered her face in embarrassment. Noah continued shouting. "I'm gonna keep yelling until you agree to let me take you out to dinner to celebrate!"

Mia was laughing but was beet red. "All right. All right," she said, "I'll go with you if you stop yelling. And I'm picking the place."

"Not The Bagel House again."

"No, not there. It's time I introduced you to the best kept secret in Snow Valley."

The librarian approached, scowling. "Please take your conversation outside! This is not the place for raucousness." she said, sternly.

Mia laughed and they headed for the exit.

CHAPTER 24

It was dusk. The sky looked darker though, due to unexpected grey clouds overhead. The weatherman on the cab's TV screen explained an arctic front was defying their models and was pushing frigid air and potential precipitation south. Noah wished he'd brought another layer. The cab dropped him off at the address Mia had given him. She was already standing by the curb, waiting. They'd opted to ride separately because after the library, Noah had gone to the office, and Mia had gone back to her condo.

When Noah climbed out of the cab, Mia couldn't stop herself from staring. He was dressed in a grey blazer with a red pocket square; slacks; and blue button-up shirt. He looked fantastic.

Noah caught notice of Mia, too, and his gaze devoured her. "You look amazing."

She was flattered. She'd chosen a short red dress – coincidentally, the same shade as Noah's pocket square – and her mother's pearls. "Thank you," she said, smiling. "You clean up pretty good yourself."

Noah took in his surroundings. They were standing on a busy road, in front of an abandoned storefront with a "For Rent" sign in the window. "Is this the restaurant?" he asked, confused.

"Follow me." Mia led him around the side of the building, down an adjacent alleyway. They stopped in front of a set of cement stairs leading to the building's basement. A tattered, maroon awning covered the staircase. The restaurant's logo was stenciled on front.

"Mama Corrieri's Bistro." Noah read, aloud.

"Yep, but it's not about the name, it's about the food. Plus, it's got a super cool vibe. Trust me."

The bistro was well-hidden – almost too well. The owners certainly weren't hoping for any accidental walk-in business. It was the kind of place where only the people who already knew how to get there could ever hope to find it.

Noah looked at the staircase. The entrance looked treacherous. The stairs were steep, and had been painted black for some reason. They led down from the alley to an all-black door. Mia led the way again. As they descended, she looked back at him, excitedly. "This was an old speakeasy during prohibition. After the passage of the 21st Amendment, the owner turned it into a restaurant. He kept it in the family, and they passed it down from generation-to-generation. It's still family owned today."

"Wow. That's amazing. How do you know so much about this place?"

Mia laughed. "Don't be too impressed. All that info is printed on their placemats. You'll see it shortly."

Noah chuckled. He was liking the place more by the second.

Mia grabbed the handle of the steel, all-black door, and swung it open. When they stepped inside, Noah's jaw fell open. They were standing in what looked like a small studio apartment. There was a bed, an old pot-belly stove, and a kitchenette that looked like it was from the 1930s. He stopped in his tracks and gave Mia a concerned glance. "Are you sure we're in the right place?"

Mia was grinning. "I told you it was cool." She strode confidently across the room and pounded her fist on the back wall. The pounding made an echo-y sound as if the wall were hollow.

A second later, a voice yelled at them through the wall. "Password?"

"Linguini," Mia said, smiling back at Noah.

Suddenly, a hidden doorway opened in the wall. Mia stepped through and beckoned Noah to follow. The door opened into a much larger room. It was a full-fledged Italian restaurant, complete with dark oak paneling, and red-and-white checkered tablecloths. The restaurant was filled with people eating and chatting, and who didn't seem the least bit surprised to see two newcomers enter. Mia approached the host stand and secured a table for two. Once they were seated, Noah allowed himself to gush. "This place is amazing! I'd heard of stuff like this, but didn't know if it really existed. How'd you find it?"

"I wish I had a cool story about how my Dad's, Dad's, Dad knew the owner or something, but honestly, this place was on the Food Channel about ten years ago. I've been coming ever since."

"But wait…is that where you learned the password?"

Mia laughed. "That's all just for show. It doesn't really matter what you say. Last time I was here with my girlfriends, a couple in front of us just said 'we don't know,' or something, and they opened the door anyway."

"What a cool place. I'm glad you brought me."

"Technically you brought me. You're buying, remember."

"Of course." Noah looked down at his placemat which, as Mia had said, told the story of the restaurant. He chuckled to himself. She had told him the story almost verbatim – a bit nerdy but extremely cute.

Mia changed the subject. "Let me ask you, do you get kicked out of every public venue you go to?"

Noah laughed. "Only with you. So, you do the math. Who's really at fault?"

A waiter approached and took their orders, he also put down a basket of garlic bread. Noah picked up a piece and took a bite – warm, slightly crispy, buttery, and just the right amount of garlic. "This melts in your mouth," he said.

Mia nodded. "Mmm-hmm. Just wait."

Noah looked over Mia's shoulder. A family was just walking through the hidden door. He looked back to Mia. "You know, I used to love coming to unique places like this, but haven't really been, since joining Jungle.com."

"Why is that?"

"I don't know. It's not really their scene. The people at Jungle are…" he paused, choosing his words carefully, "a bit stuffy."

"They wouldn't like a place like this?" Mia asked, surprised.

"I doubt it. Maybe some would, but probably not most."

Mia smirked. "Hmm. So, your corporate friends are too good for this place, but your scummy neighbor fits in perfectly, huh?"

"What? No…that's not what I…" Noah stammered.

Mia chuckled reassuringly. "I'm totally joking."

Noah breathed an inaudible sigh of relief. "I deserve that."

"The truth is, if your corporate friends wouldn't like this restaurant, it says more about them than it does about me," Mia said.

"One hundred percent. I'm glad to be away from that environment, even if it's just for a bit. Speaking of which, who is juggling the day-to-day at Snow Valley Treasures, while you're off on this adventure?

A glimmer of sadness crossed Mia's face. "My friend, Richard."

"I think I met him."

"You did. He's great. He's worked with me over eight years…" Mia put down her garlic bread and looked off into the distance. "That's why I feel so bad."

"What do you mean?"

Mia pushed her garlic bread around her plate with a fork as she thought of what to say. "I mean, if this whole thing doesn't work out, he'll have nowhere to go. He loves the store, and he's given so much to it. In fact, before this whole thing went down with the balloon payment, I was going to make him a 50-50 partner, as a Christmas present."

Noah was moved. "That's incredibly generous. I'm sure he'll appreciate it."

"Only if there's something left to give him."

The waiter returned with their soups – minestrone for Mia, and pasta e fagioli for Noah. They put the conversation on pause to take a sip. Noah's eyes widened. The warm broth danced on his tongue as every flavor took its turn to appear. "This soup is incredible!"

"I know. During the COVID lockdown I'd get their soup to-go, like, once a week."

"I'd have done the same thing." Noah took another sip and continued. "Don't worry. Things will work out for you guys."

"I hope so. And not just for Richard's sake. This may sound cheesy, but I feel like my store is part of me, you know?" Noah nodded along. "And I like to think it's a part of the community too. And I'll bet all the data you guys came up with in your pitch didn't tell you our store has more repeat customers than any other family-owned retail store in the state."

Noah was surprised. He hadn't known that, and he kicked himself for not doing more due diligence. Even if the store was struggling, if they had that kind of customer retention, changing the brand name was sure to make waves in the community. Not good for business.

Mia continued, "We have all these loyal customers, but one by one they're being picked off by…" Mia paused and looked Noah square in the eye. "well, you. Not to put too fine a point on it."

Noah winced. He hated the idea he was responsible for suffocating businesses. And there was something else which surprised him. He also hated the idea that he was hurting Mia in any way. "Look," he offered, "it was never my intention to run you out of town."

Mia nodded. "I know. It's just business."

Noah winced again. Mia was looking directly into his eyes. It was at once disarming and encouraging. She made him feel braver and more afraid, simultaneously. He decided in that moment he needed to take a stand – for Mia – but also, for himself. If he continued down his current path, he'd lose himself, maybe forever. He returned Mia's gaze. "No," he said.

"I'm gonna talk to Nadine, my boss."

"I remember her."

"I'm gonna tell her to drop the purchase idea. I think our community needs your store."

Despite her skepticism, Mia's eyes softened. "You think she'd listen to you?"

"Definitely."

Mia reached across the table and put her hand on top of Noah's. The pair locked eyes again. Mia smiled. "Thank you."

"Of course."

The main courses arrived – chicken parmesan, and chicken francese – and the conversation turned lighter. They exchanged their most embarrassing moments; talked about their childhoods; their favorite movies and favorite books. Noah admitted he'd been listening to A Christmas Carol on audiobook in his car, and that he was an English Lit major. Mia talked about why she'd opened the store and told some funny stories about clerical mistakes she'd made when she first opened – like ordering 20,000 dolls instead of 200. The conversation lasted for over two hours, but the time passed in an instant. Finally, their waiter interrupted and asked if they'd be needing anything else before leaving. Noah got the message and paid the bill. "I guess that's our cue."

After dinner, the pair exited the same door they'd come in. Mia used a different password to exit – "sono pieno" – which apparently meant "I'm full" in Italian.

Noah beamed at her. "You are just full of surprises, aren't you?"

After climbing the treacherous stairs, they made their way back down the alley to the busy street. Mia reached out her hand to hail a cab. A driver in a yellow Prius, saw her and pulled over. She grabbed the door handle, but Noah stayed put. "You coming?" she asked.

"I think I'm gonna stop by work. I've got some stuff I have to do."

"That makes sense." Mia let go of the handle and stepped closer to Noah, as he moved toward her. They stood about a foot apart. Before either could speak, the cabbie yelled out the window at them. "Let's go! I want to beat the storm!"

"What stor..." A snowflake landed gently on Mia's nose, then another on her eyelash. "It's snowing!" she said to Noah, excitedly. "I don't understand. They said no snow through Christmas."

Noah looked up and spread his arms. Thousands of large, fluffy, flakes twirled their way to the ground. He looked back at Mia. "Beautiful."

The cabbie yelled out again. "Let's get a move on. Are you coming or not?"

Mia and Noah both yelled "Hold on!" to the cabbie at the same time.

"Fine," he said, "but I'm starting the fare." He clicked a button on the meter machine on his dashboard.

"Thank you," Mia said, rolling her eyes.

At that moment, a bike messenger was pedaling down the sidewalk, quickly. He was bundled in a large puffy coat and had a scarf wrapped around his face, nearly covering his eyes. Noah was still looking at the cabbie and didn't notice the him. The biker hadn't noticed the couple either and it wasn't until he was a few feet away that he swerved. "Watch out!" he yelled, trying to steer out of the way. But it was too late, the swerve caused him to lose control and he skidded right toward them. Instinctively, Noah pushed into Mia, knocking her backward. The bike's wheels regained their traction and the biker was able to pedal past without falling. Noah had wrapped his arms around Mia to steady her, and she'd grabbed onto him as well.

"Sorry!" the biker called out over his shoulder.

Mia still clung to Noah, her adrenaline subsiding. She felt good wrapped around him. He was strong, and warm, and smelled amazing. Noah looked down at Mia and smiled. They stood face-to-face. "Are you okay?"

Mia's heart pounded in her chest. She was shaking all over – a combination of the cold; the adrenaline; and the unexpected butterflies. She didn't respond. Instead she smiled, closed her eyes, and leaned in expectantly.

HOOOONK! The cabbie's car horn ripped through the stillness. He leaned out the window. "I said I want to beat the storm. I was patient, but I am going to leave. Are you coming or not?"

The illusion had been broken. Mia let go of Noah and shook off the daze. The moment had been intoxicating, but it had passed now. She grabbed the door handle again. "I had a great time tonight," she said, as she climbed into the cab. "Thanks again."

Noah closed his eyes slowly, feeling frustrated. "Me too." He watched as the cab pulled back onto the road, and drove away.

CHAPTER 25

The next morning, Noah left his condo with a bounce in his step. He looked down the hallway at Mia's door and smiled. He was happy to think of the relief she'd feel when she woke up to her internet working. After getting home from work, the night before, Noah had crept back into the HVAC room and reinstalled Mia's coaxial cable. He felt bad about being so duplicitous, but figured it was worth it. He wouldn't have spent the day with Mia otherwise. As he screwed in the cable, he half-wished he could leave it unplugged so he could go on another field trip with her, but he'd done enough sneaking, and he had a promise to uphold.

At work, Noah headed straight for Nadine's office. It was a trip he'd taken a hundred times already, but he couldn't remember feeling more nervous about it. He knew the conversation was going to be hard, but he wasn't going in unarmed. He was prepared with the new information Mia had shared about SVT's customer retention. "That's business," he thought, "and Nadine understands business." As he approached her office, he noticed her glass walls were opaque, and that meant she didn't want to be bothered. When Jungle.com had made the decision to install all-glass offices, the executives had thrown a fit. How could they be expected to be out in the open all the time? What about privacy? Never mind the fact that all other employees were always exposed. There was so much pushback, the whole idea was almost scrapped, but Jungle's owner wouldn't give up on the idea. He insisted on an open floorplan, and transparency – literally. The negotiations turned acrimonious – the CEO threatened to resign, and the owner considered walking out because his vision was being distorted. Cooler heads prevailed though, when someone suggested they install smart glass. Smart glass uses electro-chromatic technology to allow glass walls to alternate between being completely transparent, and completely opaque. In other words, with a flick of a switch, Nadine's walls could go from clear to frosted, depending on her mood. Once the walls were installed, most executives just got used to the glass, and very few people ever switched to opaque mode. Even Nadine had to "play ball" and go along with the company culture. Her office was opaque more than others, but not always. That was how Noah knew she was not in a fabulous mood. That and the fact that as he approached her office, he could hear her barking orders at her secretary, Caroline.

"…and then take the Kominsky file and do a full background on the executive board," she said. "I want to know everything about these people. Who they're married to, what they do for fun, what they had for breakfast. Got it?"

"Yes, ma'am," came the response from Caroline's mousy voice. Noah took a deep breath and knocked.

"What is it?" called Nadine.

"It's Noah."

"Come in," Nadine offered, pleasantly enough. Noah pushed the door open. Nadine's office was fairly modest compared to others he'd been in. She had her framed diplomas on the wall, a potted plant in the corner, and pictures of various vacations she had been on: skiing in the Rockies, sightseeing in Rome, laying out on the beach somewhere. It was hard for him to picture Nadine having fun on vacation anywhere, and he imagined she had taken these pictures only to pretend she was a normal, relaxed person. He chuckled to himself as he pictured her typing away on a laptop as she skied down a mountain. Nadine's voice broke up his daydream. "What is it?" she asked, agitatedly.

"I want to talk about the Snow Valley Treasures account."

"Good. I was planning on following up with you about that today anyway. What's on your mind?"

Noah shuffled his feet. He wasn't really afraid of Nadine, in the true sense of the word, but he didn't like being overly confrontational, and this was sure to get confrontational.

"I was thinking maybe it's not the best avenue for us right now."

Nadine nodded slowly and pursed her lips. "And why in the world do you think that?"

Noah wasn't sure what to say. Should he tell her what he knew, or just try to convince her it was his intuition? "Call it a gut feeling," he finally said.

With her lips closed tightly, Nadine ran her tongue across the front of her teeth. It looked like she was seething, but trying to keep her composure. She paused and let the awkwardness hang in the room. "First, I don't do business based on gut feelings. Especially other people's gut feelings. And second…" Nadine's voice had been rising, but she paused and appeared to calm herself. "Second, this whole thing was your baby. Your idea. I don't understand all this waffling. How much must we discuss this?"

"It's not waffling. I just…I just think the store is a valuable part of the community."

Nadine frowned. "And it still will be, Noah."

He forged ahead. "As you know, I've been spending some time with the owner of Snow Valley Treasures…strictly for business purposes. And I learned a few things. Did you know they have the largest customer retention of any family-owned retail store in the state?"

"Of course, I knew that. It's my business to know that. Why do you think I'm so interested in the place? It's a perfect location with a built-in customer base. You didn't think I was chasing after it because I thought it was cute or something?"

Noah was deflated. His plan had backfired spectacularly. "No. That makes sense."

Nadine scooted her chair closer towards him. "Let me be frank: I'm disappointed in your performance, here." She let the words dangle. "You brought me this project and I thought we had a rising star. Instead, you've acted like a milquetoast ever since." Nadine grabbed a stack of papers from the corner of her desk and slid them toward Noah. "I was going to wait to tell you this, but given your new attitude, I might as well tell you now."

Noah's pulse quickened. "Ok."

"I spoke with the bank manager at Valley Mutual," Nadine continued, "he's a friend. And he told me SVT is three months in arrears on their mortgage, and has eight delinquencies in this calendar year alone."

Noah absorbed the information. "Ok."

"The bank manager also told me that according to the terms of the mortgage, SVT must use a good faith effort to repay the delinquencies, including entertaining any and all bona fide offers for market value. If they don't, the bank declares a breach based on bad faith."

Noah nodded. He understood the words, but not the significance. "What does that mean?"

"It means that because they rejected our offer without seriously considering it, they breached. The bank can call the balance due whenever they want."

Noah's felt the blood drain from his face. He wondered if he looked as pale as he felt. "The loan is already due on January 1st."

"That's the best part: the bank manager's gonna call the loan due on the day before Christmas eve now." She puffed out her chest. "And all based on my recommendation." Noah opened his mouth to respond but she was already back to gloating. "That means we won't have to wait for foreclosure, or haggle over price at an auction. The bank will take it back on the 23rd, and will sell it to us by close of business that day!" Nadine looked triumphant, as if she'd just delivered a knockout blow.

"Nadine," Noah protested, "don't you think that's bit

abrupt? Mia and…" He stopped himself at the mention of her name. He didn't want to let on his objections were personal in any way. "I mean, the people who work there are…"

Nadine squinted her eyes at Noah and then interrupted him. "The people that work there are not our concern. Unless…" the corners of her lips turned up slightly, as if she were enjoying the moment. "Unless, you're mixing business with pleasure. Do you have a thing for that girl?"

The blood came rushing back. Noah turned bright red. "I told you it was strictly business." But his protestations were too little too late.

"What an interesting development," she said. "I only asked you to gain her trust so you could talk her into selling. I didn't expect you to go and fall in love."

At the word "love," Noah's heart jumped. Was Nadine, right? Was he falling in love with Mia?

"And does she love you back?" Nadine asked, sneering.

Noah couldn't gain his composure. Nadine was relentless and his head was spinning. "I don't…I…she…"

Nadine guffawed. "This is too perfect. I didn't expect this, but it's perfect."

He tried to shake himself out of her spell. It was like being cross-examined by Matlock – he couldn't get a word in edgewise. Noah stood up, abruptly. It helped him settle a bit. "No!" he said, nearly shouting. "It's not that. It's…it's Christmas. I don't think it's right to kick someone out at Christmas."

Nadine responded matter-of-factly. "But you have no problem kicking them out at New Year's when it's going to cost us substantially more money? Christmas is arbitrary. Grow up, lover boy."

"Please," he said, desperation leaking from his voice. "This is important to me."

"Is your job important to you?"

Noah dropped his head. "Of course."

"Then I'll tell you what's going to happen. You're gonna use this cute little relationship of yours to spend time with the owner. Keep her occupied, distract her. I don't want her finding out about the bank moving up the loan's due date. They are only obligated to give her 48 hours' notice, and I instructed the bank manager to not tell them a moment sooner."

Noah stuttered again. "I…I…"

"You'll do it, or you'll find another place to work." she said, turning her chair away from him. "That's all. You're dismissed."

Noah was stunned. He felt like he was in a dream. Nadine had opened her computer and was already hard at work typing away on something. He stood there for a minute, gathering himself, and trying desperately to think of something to say, but nothing came. His mind was blank. Nadine continued to ignore him. It was as if she didn't know he was still in the room. After a minute or two, she picked up her landline and punched the key for her secretary. "Caroline, bring me the Rossman file, please." she said into the receiver, and hung up the phone. Then back to her computer. Noah looked at her with contempt. How could she be so callous? How could he have been? He resolved to think of something, some way out, and he turned to leave.

As he neared the door, Nadine called after him. "Oh, Noah, one more thing." He stopped and turned toward her, bracing himself. "Everything we discussed is considered a business secret and is therefore, privileged. If I find out any of this information is leaked to anyone at Snow Valley Treasures, I'll have no choice but to assume it was you and sue you for business and trade secret violation. Are we clear?"

Her words hung heavy in the air. They were the cherry on top of a stellar corporate-murder-sundae. Nadine's performance in their meeting was airtight; even legendary. There was no way out. Noah knew it, and Nadine knew it. His eyes were as big as saucers, and he stumbled backward out of her office. "Clear," he muttered, but Nadine was already back to work.

CHAPTER 26

Day five dawned over a winter wonderland. The night before, Mia had made sure to leave the drapes open and had fallen asleep to the beauty of snow piling on the lake. She stretched, yawned, and stared out the window. "There must be at least eight inches out there," she thought, excitedly. Her phone clock showed 6:40. She unlocked it and checked the WiFi – full signal – a twinge of sadness hit her. Maybe she could pretend it was still out, and Noah could tag along again. "That's ridiculous," she thought and shook the idea off. On her phone's contact list Richard's name glowed in red as the most recent missed call. She tapped his name and the phone connected.

"Hi, stranger!" Richard cried, cheerfully.

Mia was relieved. She'd been worried he might have been overwhelmed running things on his own. It was a lot to ask.

"Hey, Rich! Have you looked outside?"

"Excuse me, sleepyhead, but I'm already on my way in. Opening at 7:00 this morning."

Mia laughed. "Score another point for yourself. I think it's safe to say you win the trophy this year."

"You mean every year."

"Yes, that."

"So, what's up?"

"I was just calling to say make sure to put the sleds outside…oh, and the parkas. You'll probably have a lot of foot traffic today. Can you handle it alone?"

"Don't worry about me. What about you? Do you have any news?"

Mia realized she'd forgotten to update Richard about the contest. She relayed everything that had happened over the last two days – but she was careful to omit any mention of Noah.

"Wow, 11th place? I'm so proud of you. You can do this, Mia!"

"Couldn't do anything without you."

"That's true," Richard laughed. "But I won't keep you – you need to concentrate. And don't worry about me. The store's in good hands."

Mia thanked him and disconnected. It was 6:45. She rushed her morning routine. At two minutes to 7:00 she grabbed a seat at her table, wound-up like a jack-in-the-box. She felt happy, and excited, and anxious, and everything else all rolled into one. For one, it had finally snowed – and snow meant customers. Richard was going to be busy, and they needed every penny. Also, 11th place in the contest was huge. For the first time, the Twelve Games seemed real and winnable. With two points in a row, Mia was actually allowing herself to believe. But it wasn't just the snow or the contest. There was something else too: Noah. It was Noah. Despite all the chaos swirling around her with the contest, and her store, Noah had been her last thought as she drifted to sleep and her first thought that morning. She liked him. No – more than that – she was falling for him. And she felt giddy. It had been so long since Mia'd had a crush, she'd forgotten how good it felt. She daydreamed about the previous night and basked in the warmth of it. At 7:02 a text from Richard startled her. "Go get em!" it read.

"I'm late! What am I doing?" Mia scolded herself. She fired off a quick reply to Richard: "Thanks! U too!" The text snapped her out of the haze and she opened the Gazette app. The now-familiar animation danced onscreen. "On the 5th Game of

Christmas, my Daily sent to me: a word maze for puzzle points, three."

"What's a word maze?" Mia wondered. She didn't have to wait long to find out. The animation disappeared and an enormous maze populated the screen. The maze was sprinkled with letters, seemingly at random. Mia clicked on the rules: "From the maze entrance, follow the correct path to the center. Make note of all letters along the way; unscramble the words; and enter them in to the boxes provided. When all words have been successfully entered, the secret location will be revealed. Caution: should you choose the wrong path, the letters will be incorrect as well."

Mia's palms grew sweaty. "This is gonna go quick," she thought. "It's just a maze." On the screen, she zoomed in on the maze's starting point. It was hard to see. She tried dragging her finger to keep track of her place but her finger covered more than just the row she was in. Frustrated, she grabbed her tablet and opened the Gazette app from it. The maze was much more manageable on a bigger screen. She dived back in.

An hour or so later, Mia realized she'd underestimated the puzzle's difficulty. For one thing, the maze was bigger than she'd anticipated. It was multiple pages long, at least. She'd gotten to the center of the first page after about 40 minutes, but had only unscrambled one word. When she reached the center, a new maze appeared, labeled: Page Two.

Midway through the third page, Mia found her mind wandering. So much had happened recently, it was easy to float away on a daydream about winning the contest, or to think about her evening with Noah. When she'd catch herself drifting off, she'd chide herself and resume the puzzle, but soon enough she'd slip away again. She tried making a cup of coffee. She needed to concentrate and caffeine might be just the thing. As she waited for the pot to brew, her phone rang. It was Edith.

"Mia, I'm glad I caught you. You're still planning on coming to my daughter's work Christmas party, aren't you?"

"Of course, I wouldn't miss it."

"That's wonderful. It's on the 22nd at 7:00. Formal attire."

Mia glanced at a magnetic calendar she had stuck to her fridge. The evening, as with most of her evenings, was wide open.

"That sounds perfect. Where is it?"

"At my daughter's work. I'll send a car for you."

"You don't have to do that."

"I absolutely want to. You're my guest of honor. The whole thing is happening because of you."

Mia opted not to object any further. She didn't want to offend Edith, and a private car for the evening sounded fun. She'd feel like a movie star. "Then I accept," Mia said. "I'm looking forward to it."

"As am I, dear. Thank you again."

They ended the call and Mia headed toward her closet to look for the right dress. She paused as she passed her tablet, but thought, "this'll only take a second, and I need a little break anyway." A while later she emerged from her room, having selected a black cocktail dress. Mia glanced at the clock, 20 minutes had passed. She sat back in front of the puzzle and tried to get back to work. It took her a minute to find the spot she'd left off from. Soon after, though, she thought about Edith's Christmas party, and the car that would pick her up. Mia hadn't been to a party in…she couldn't remember her last party. She thought about what type of food they'd have. Would it be hor d'oeuvres, a sit-down formal, or some hybrid of the two? Would there be dancing? If so, would it be a DJ or a live band? Mia loved to dance and she loved live music. She hoped there would be dancing. Outside, a car horn blew and broke Mia from her daydream. She looked at the clock. Another 10 minutes passed. "This isn't working," she thought. "I need a change of scenery." She grabbed her coat and went out the door.

At The Bagel House, Mia sat in the same booth she and Noah had occupied on the two days prior. The store manager noticed her and smiled. She ordered herself an everything bagel and a coffee and went back to the maze. Rather than being a distraction, the cacophony in the shop helped drown out her thoughts. Mia checked her watch. The day was getting on and she kicked herself for being so lackadaisical. She finished page three, then four. Fueled with coffee, carbs, and the din of the bagel shop, she was on fire again. The puzzle wasn't particularly hard that day, it just required focus. For example, she got stuck at one point for several minutes and had to backtrack halfway out of the maze to continue down the right track. She fixed the error and again, scolded herself for being too cavalier. Finally, after a few hours of focused work, Mia reached the center of the last maze. She easily unscrambled the final letters – North Pole. She tapped them in to the empty boxes and her phone chimed. The secret location appeared on screen: Pete's Ice Cream. Mia gasped and looked out the window. "That's across the street!" She jumped up from the booth, gathered her belongings, and rushed out of the shop.

The light was already low in the sky. Mia was surprised to see how late it had gotten. Across the street, Pete's Ice Cream bustled; a line of people stretched out the door. Mia crossed the street and felt a rush of worry. "Why would there be a line for ice cream in the middle of December?" she wondered. "Maybe Pete's is always this popular." She joined the line at the back. In front of her, two teenage girls stood chatting and fiddling with their phones. Mia interrupted them. "Excuse me, are you girls here for the word maze?"

The girls looked at Mia and burst out laughing. "What's that?" one of the girls asked. She turned to her friend and whispered. "Who is this stalker?"

"We don't do mazes. We're not four," said the other. They looked at each other again and continued to laugh.

"Thanks," Mia said, halfheartedly. Despite being the butt of the joke, she was relieved to know at least two of the people in the line were there just for ice cream. She looked up and down at the other people in the line. Most, if not all of them were teenagers too. Some sported backpacks, and others wrestled, joked, and played on their phones. Mia didn't see one person taking a selfie, in or outside the store. She felt good. "School must have just let out or something," she thought. "Maybe I'm the first puzzler here again." Down the street, a bright yellow school bus with the words "Jefferson High School" emblazoned on the side, lumbered away. Mia nodded.

The ice cream line moved like molasses, but it was a small store, and Mia couldn't cut without impeding the only entryway. After an eternity of watching high school kids flirt, kiss, and even punch each other, Mia made it inside. Her phone was already queued up. She toggled the app, and snapped a selfie. The two teen girls in front of her noticed. One giggled and whispered loudly in her friend's ear.

"Did you see that old lady just took a selfie?"

"Ewww!" the other one said. "I'm surprised she even knows how to use that thing." The girls giggled and took turns stealing glances at Mia behind them. Mia shook her head, annoyed. She toyed with the idea of telling them off, but it was petty and she knew that'd only make them dig in more. Not worth it.

The Gazette app chimed indicating the picture had been uploaded successfully. While she waited for the response, Mia ordered herself a small scoop of cake batter ice cream in a waffle cone. She found a seat at one of two small, round tables in the shop. The table was a mess, covered in ice cream drippings, used napkins, and cone crumbs. But it felt good to sit inside after standing in the cold line for so long. As she neared the end of her cone, Mia's phone buzzed. She stuffed the remainder into a used cup sitting on the table, and quickly wiped her hands on a napkin. The familiar adrenaline coursed through her. "Here goes." She clicked the message. "Thanks for entering the Twelve Games of Christmas. Congratulations on finding today's secret location!" Mia's heart soared as she read the words. She was in the right spot again. She continued reading, "You are the 26th person to do so. Daily points: 0; Total points: 2. Current Standings: 16th place." She read the message in disbelief and was suddenly overcome with nausea. "16th place, 16th place," she repeated, under her breath. "What have I done?" Her thoughts ran back through the events of the day and she considered all the time she'd wasted. She was angry and blamed everyone. She listed them all in her head. First, she blamed Noah: "he distracted me even when he wasn't here." Then she blamed Edith: "If she hadn't called about that ridiculous party…" She even blamed Richard: "He's probably enjoying the snow while I'm out here doing everything I can to save the store." Mia seethed, but thinking of Richard struck a needle through her heart. Of course, she didn't really blame anyone but herself. It was her fault. She'd let herself down, but more importantly, she'd let Richard down. He was by himself handling everything, and she was daydreaming and playing dress-up.

Mia's mood was somber as she stood and headed toward the exit. The teen girls were seated at the adjacent table, and were now accompanied by several teen boys. They were all talking and joking boisterously. As Mia passed, she heard one of the girls tell the group, "There's that weird stalker lady." The group erupted with laughter. Mia gritted her teeth and stopped in her tracks. She spun toward them and the laughter ceased almost immediately.

Mia approached the table with a wide smile. "Hi girls, thanks so much for your help!" They looked at each other, confused. "My friend, Principal Boston, works at Jefferson High. Do you know him?"

The girls nodded.

"He's been looking for some students to help with community service on the weekends. I told him I'd met two of his students who were eager to give back. He's anxious to get started." The girls exchanged worried glances. Mia continued. "Here I'll just snap a pic so he knows who you are." Mia pretended to fumble with her phone. "It's the big button at the bottom, right?" She held her phone up to the group and pretended to snap a picture.

One boy stood up and puffed out his chest. "You can't take our picture without our consent!"

Mia smiled indulgently. "On the contrary, you're in a public setting so I can take your picture. But, I only took a picture of the girls, because they were the ones who volunteered. Do you want to help them with community service?" Mia held up her phone and pretended to take another shot. The group of teens all ducked and covered their faces.

"Let's dip," one of the boys said. "This lady's crazy." The

group jumped to their feet and headed toward the exit. One of the teen girls scowled at Mia as she walked by. The other, hung back until the group had walked out of the shop. She looked at Mia timidly.

"I'm sorry," she said. "Please don't send that picture to Principal Boston. My mom works with him and she'll kill me."

Mia smiled warmly at the girl. "Don't worry. I didn't actually take a picture. I don't even know Principal Boston, I just looked him up online."

The girl's shoulders relaxed and she let out a deep breath. "Thank you."

"Just try to be a little nicer next time."

"I will. I'm sorry." The girl turned and dashed out the door.

For a moment, Mia was pleased with herself. But as she went to lock her phone she saw the Gazette message staring back: "16th place." "Maybe I don't have a shot at this thing after all."

CHAPTER 27

Noah's phone jarred him awake. It was still dark outside. He looked at the clock, 6:30 A.M. "Who's calling at this hour?" he wondered aloud. He checked the caller ID on his phone. It was a number he didn't recognize. For a moment he debated about answering, but decided it was probably a robo-tele-marketer, and he pushed decline. He rolled over and shut his eyes. Just as he was falling back asleep, his phone rang again, same number. Noah grabbed it angrily and pushed the answer button. "What is it?" he barked.

Mia was on the other end of the phone. "I'm sorry," she said, "bad time?"

Noah recognized her voice and sat up straight in bed. "Mia! I'm sorry, I didn't know who it was. How'd you get this number?"

She was surprised by the question. "I hope it's all right I called. Sorry for calling so early. I got your number from the HOA directory. HOA president, remember?"

Noah tried to shake off the grogginess. "How could I forget? Of course, it's ok you called, and I'm glad you did. I've got something to tell you. I spoke to Nadine."

Mia felt a rush of relief. "That's great. I want to hear all about it, but wait. I want to tell you this first. I need your help."

Noah stood up. "Is everything ok?"

"Yes, everything's fine."

"Good. How did the Twelve Games go yesterday?"

"That's what I need your help with. I didn't get any points."

"I'm sorry to hear it. But how can I help? I thought you had to do these alone."

"That's right, but I don't need help like that," Mia said. "I just…I want you to come with me today, if you can. I think you might be my good luck charm."

Noah's heart leapt. He wanted to hug Mia through the phone, but he tried to calm himself. "I'd love to. I'm excellent at moral support."

Mia smiled. She was happy to have Noah back on the team. "With my puzzle skills, and your good luck, who knows? I just might have a chance winning. So, what happened in the meeting with Nadine? Did she listen to you?"

Noah closed his eyes and hung his head. He paused.

"You there?" Mia asked.

"Yeah, yeah, I'm here." Noah scrambled to think of what to say. "I…when I met with her…" Nadine's threat about a lawsuit echoed in his head, and he didn't want to dampen Mia's spirits "She didn't have time to talk. But I will talk to her soon," he lied.

Mia was a bit deflated. "Thanks for trying. I appreciate it. So, listen, I'm on my way to The Bagel Shop. Get ready and meet me there. There's not a moment to lose."

Noah's head was still down, his eyes clenched tight. He'd just lied to Mia and didn't know how to tell her the truth. "Mia…"

"Yes?"

"I'll see you soon."

They met at what had become their usual spot, The Bagel House booth. When Noah arrived, he found Mia typing busily on a puzzle. He took a seat across from her, and she paused to smile and thank him for coming. The morning passed uneventfully, they talked a bit, and laughed a bit. Noah beat his previous coffee creamer tower record by two whole creamers – a fact he interrupted Mia to celebrate. By mid-morning, Mia had most of the puzzle solved. She held it up to show Noah. The secret location was only missing a few letters. "I think it's the airport," she said. "Let's go now and I'll solve the rest on the way. If I'm wrong, we still have time to double back, but I'm pretty sure that's it."

Noah and Mia piled into the Lemon Lime and headed toward the airport. It was located on the outskirts of town which meant it would be about a 20-minute ride. Noah drove so Mia could concentrate on finishing the puzzle. "Do you mind if I turn on some music?" he asked.

"Not at all."

"What channel plays Christmas music in Snow Valley?"

Mia bit her upper lip. "Ummm…try 96.4 FM."

Noah tuned the dial and Burl Ives' "Rudolph the Red Nosed Reindeer," crackled over the speakers. He reached for the volume knob and turned it up. Suddenly, all of the dashboard lights went dark, and the speedometer dropped to 0. Noah panicked. "What happened? What's going on?"

Mia hadn't seen it, but she looked up from her phone and understood immediately. She laughed. "Did you break my car?"

Noah relaxed. "You know about this?"

"Yes, unfortunately. Why do you think I call it the Lemon Lime?"

When they arrived at the airport Noah found a close spot and they ran inside. Mia positioned herself in front of a sign welcoming people to the international airport, and snapped a selfie. She uploaded it to the Gazette app. While they waited for the response, they walked through the lobby and talked. Noah noticed one flight was headed to the United Kingdom.

"Oh, London," he said. "I've never been, but I'd love to go."

"Are you a big traveler?"

"I love traveling. I used to go on trips all the time with my family, but since I've grown up, I haven't done it as much. Do you travel much?"

Mia shook her head. "Not much. I went to Paris once, and it was magical. But…" she paused.

"But what?"

"But I don't really have anyone to go with."

Noah stopped and smiled at her. "Let's make another deal, then. If you win the contest, I'll go with you on a trip. Anywhere in the world."

Mia's butterflies kicked in again. The idea of a trip and of extended time with Noah was intoxicating. "Wait," she smirked, "you're saying if I win, you'll fall on your sword and let me pay for a trip around the world for you? How chivalrous."

Noah laughed. "Of course not. You need the money for SVT. If you win, I'll pay for the trip. It'd be my pleasure. You can buy us gelato or something."

"Oooh, so you're saying we're going to Italy? What about London?"

"Oops, I mean, you can buy us fish and chips, mate." Noah said in an awful attempt at a British accent. "Or why not go to both?"

Mia laughed as her phone pinged. It was a push notification from the Gazette app. She felt the icy chill of stress in her veins, and tapped it open. "Thanks for entering the Twelve Games of Christmas, day 6. Congratulations on finding today's secret location!" You are the 2nd person to do so. Daily points: 1; Total points: 3. Current Standings: 13th place."

Mia wrapped her arms around Noah. "See? You are my good luck charm. Better brush up on your Italian."

The following day, Mia and Noah became a well-oiled machine. Noah woke up, got ready, and met Mia outside her door at exactly 6:35. Then it was on to The Bagel House. They assumed their positions at "their" booth, and Mia went about her business. After an hour or so, the store manager approached. "I've never seen either of you before, and now all of a sudden you're my most loyal regulars. What's the story?"

Mia looked up, but Noah put up his hand as if to say, "I'll handle it." She went back the puzzle. "Nothin', we just like the vibe here."

"Sounds good. Happy to have you." The manager produced two plates with sticky buns on them. He laid them on the table.

"On the house. For my new regulars."

They both thanked him. "What was that about?" Noah asked Mia as the manager walked away.

"I think it's just his way of apologizing. Or saying thank you for what you did the other day."

Noah stuffed the sticky bun in his mouth. "Ofd…rane…mmmf…ummph."

Mia laughed. "Why don't you finish chewing, and then tell me."

Noah took a sip of water and swallowed. "I said, I'll take that kind of apology any day."

"Me too," she said, and took a bite.

Mia worked for the next several hours. Noah intermittently got up to make phone calls, scrolled through is phone, typed on his laptop, and even read from a novel. Finally, Mia announced she'd finished the puzzle.

"Where to?" he asked.

"The fairgrounds. Let's step on it."

When they got out of the car at the fairgrounds, Mia felt a sense of déjà vu, and she liked it. The whole thing was starting to feel routine, but not in a bad way. It was a sense of comfort, as if she were completely herself and could let her guard down with Noah. She snapped her selfie and they walked around the fairgrounds while she waited for the response. At one point, Noah's hand brushed hers. He apologized, but she got the goosebumps and wished he would reach out and hold her hand. She felt a bit foolish, but like a 7th grader with a crush, she stuck her hand out away from her side, in an attempt to make it more likely he'd brush by again. "Why isn't he grabbing my hand?" she thought. Her phone pinged and ruined the moment, but only momentarily. It was good news. Another point and she'd jumped up to 10th place.

"First again," Noah beamed as he wrapped Mia in the now-traditional after-message hug. "You really are good at these puzzles."

"No," she demurred, "it's only thanks to my good luck charm."

Game days eight and nine had similar results. Mia scored points on both days, finding the secret locations first and third respectively. On day eight, the location was the local ice-skating rink and they stayed after to skate together. Her point total moved her into 6th place overall. Day nine's location was the public pool, which Mia thought was a weird place for a clue to lead. She was so bewildered by the location she was sure she'd done the puzzle wrong. Rather than rushing off to the pool, she'd stayed an hour longer at the bagel shop ensuring her answer was right. As a result, she was barely the third person there, and almost missed out on a point that day, completely. But it worked out, and she was happy. Her point total yielded a standing of 3rd place, and she and Noah were overjoyed. Yet, despite her Twelve Games successes, something was bothering her. She and Noah had an obvious and palpable connection, but Noah still hadn't made a move of any kind. He hadn't even held her hand. And there was something else. He had been acting a bit distant too, as if something were bothering him, but he never said what it was.

CHAPTER 28

Noah's conscience was eating him alive. He had fallen for Mia, and it felt fantastic. She was smart, beautiful, and witty, and everything he'd ever wanted in a partner. But he couldn't move forward because he'd told her a lie. A huge lie. A lie that would affect her business and her very future. The longer he waited to tell her the truth, the worse things became. Noah knew when Mia found out he'd had kept the bank's date change a secret from her, and worse still, when she discovered he had in fact spoken with Nadine, she would never trust him again, and she'd be justified in that too. He woke feeling a bit melancholy. On the one hand, he was spending every day with a girl for whom he was falling fast, and on the other, his lie was spending every day undermining that relationship. "I'm gonna tell her today," he resolved with himself.

Later, he met Mia in the condo hallway. She wore her hair down and it bounced on her shoulders. She was stunning.

"Ready to kick some puzzle butt?" she said cheerfully.

He paused, and struggled to gather strength. "Listen, Mia. There's something I need to talk to you about. It's important."

"What is it? Is everything ok?"

As he opened his mouth to speak, they heard a shriek from Dorothy's condo. "Help!" She yelled. "Heeeelp!" Dorothy's door swung open in a flurry and she sprang from the condo wearing her bathrobe. She saw Mia and relief crossed her face. "Oh, Mia! Thank heavens. I need help."

Mia and Noah shared a concerned look. "Is everything ok?"

"No, everything is not ok. Why do you think I'm asking for help?" Dorothy answered. "Come in here. Look" Dorothy walked over to her open door and beckoned them to follow. The inside of her condo was neat, but in need of updating. Her carpeting was a heavily-worn orange shag from the 70s. Probably the original from when the building was put up. There were green curtains hanging on the widows and a sparkly-yellow flower pattern covered the kitchen countertop. Dorothy led them to the living room. She gestured towards the coffee table. "See?" she said.

"See what?" Mia asked.

"I've been robbed."

Mia, whose adrenaline had been on overdrive began to relax. Noah cocked an eyebrow and looked at Mia who shook her head reassuringly.

"What is missing?" Mia asked.

"My remote control. I'll bet it was those newspaper people. They're still mad I cancelled."

"No, I don't think so," Mia said, patiently. "Have you had a look around the house?"

"I've looked everywhere. It's not here. That's how I know I had a break-in."

Noah was still confused, and tried to weigh in. "Was anything else of value taken, Dorothy?"

Mia surreptitiously raised her hand palm up to Noah to stop further questions. But it was too late. Dorothy was already concerned.

"I don't know," she said, "I didn't think to check my jewelry. Do you think they took that too?"

"I don't think anyone broke in here. I'll bet if we give this place a good once-over we can find it," Mia said, reassuringly.

Dorothy shook her head as if Mia were wasting her time. "Be my guest, but you won't ever find it. I've looked."

Mia bent down and searched the living room. As she did so, Dorothy sidled up next to Noah. "How're you settling in? You liking it?"

Noah looked at Mia crawling around the ground, searching for a remote. He smiled. "Honestly? I'm in love."

Dorothy pinched his arm lightly. "I know just how you feel. I love Snow Valley too. Do you have a girlfriend? Or are you single and ready to mingle?" She flashed him a wide smile. At the mention of the word girlfriend Noah shot a glance at Mia who looked back. They caught eyes for a second. "Well?" Dorothy pressed.

"I'm single," Noah said, finally.

"Good. So am I!"

Noah laughed gamely. "I'll keep that in mind."

On all fours, Mia held up the remote control triumphantly. "Got it!" she shouted.

Dorothy looked a bit embarrassed. "Good. No break-in this time. But I'm tellin' ya'. Those newspaper people are sneaky." She grabbed the remote from Mia. "Thank you." She invited the pair to stay, but they promised a raincheck. Mia explained that she needed to get to the puzzle. As they made their way down the hallway toward the elevator, Noah turned to Mia. "What's her story? Do you know her very well? Is she ok?"

"Who Dorothy? Oh yeah, she's fine. She doesn't have dementia or anything, she's just a conspiracy theorist. Always assumes 'big brother' or some nefarious corporation is out to get her. But she's always been like that. As long as I've known her."

"Really?"

"Yeah. A few years ago, when I first moved in, she told me the security guy was a plant and was just casing the building for a robbery. It's nothing new, and nothing to be worried about. Just a quirk. I think she's just lonely."

Noah nodded sympathetically. "I understand. We should visit her, when this is all over."

Mia smiled. "She'd like that." They reached the elevator and climbed aboard. Mia checked her watch. At the same time, Noah turned toward her determined to tell her the truth. "Anyway, Mia, I have to talk to you—"

Mia's head was down looking at her phone. "That can't be the time!" she exclaimed. "Oh no. Oh no, oh no. The puzzle's going live in one minute. How did that take so long?" She was flummoxed, but became aware Noah had been trying to get her attention. "I'm sorry, what were you saying?"

"I was saying I have something I need to talk to you about."

The elevator dinged and Mia checked her watch again. "Can it wait until after The Bagel House? I have to open the app in, like, 30 seconds. Hopefully I'll have cell service on the drive over."

Noah nodded. "Of course."

The Bagel House was full, and their booth already had someone sitting in it. "You think that's bad luck?" Mia asked Noah.

"Definitely. We're gettin' that booth." Noah walked over to the table and pulled out his wallet, sliding a $20 bill into his hand. A woman sat sipping coffee and reading a romance novel. Noah cleared his throat and the woman looked up. "Excuse me, Ma'am," he said through a toothy smile. He pointed to Mia and continued, "My fiancé and I sat here on our first date one year ago today and we wanted to come back to… reminisce." Noah set the $20 on the table and slid it toward the woman. "We would consider it a great courtesy if you would be so kind as to choose another booth."

The woman looked down at the money and laughed. "I'll change seats. And you don't have to pay me. Congratulations on your engagement!"

Noah pushed the money closer to her. "Please, coffee's on me today."

The woman smiled and reluctantly picked up the cash. "Well thank you. And Merry Christmas." She gathered her things and retreated to a different spot. Noah grinned at Mia. "See? Lucky spot."

Mia laughed and slid into the booth. "You are a good liar.

Too good. Remind me never to get on your bad side."

The words hit Noah like a dagger. He closed his eyes and let the words wash over him. "Why didn't you just tell her when you had the chance?" he berated himself. It was too late now, plus Mia had asked him to wait.

She looked down and dived into the puzzle. Only a few hours later her head popped up. "I'm done."

"Already?"

"Yeah. I can't tell if today's was just easy, or if I'm just really dialed in."

"I'd say it's the latter. So, what's the location?"

"It's the post office. And I'm sure it's right."

Noah looked confused. "Which post office? There are a million. Does it say which one?"

Mia shook her head. "It doesn't, that's the weird thing. But none of the clues have been super on-point. I'll bet it's the old-timey one in downtown."

"Why do you think that?"

"Just 'cause. It makes sense it would be a beautiful, historic one rather than some random one in a strip-mall next to an MMA dojo where the MMA master gets mad if you look in his windows, even though he ostensibly wants people to come in and sign up for classes."

Noah laughed. "That was weirdly specific. I'm assuming that's based on experience?"

"Don't ask."

"Okay. Let's go."

Noah climbed into the passenger seat of the Lemon Lime. Mia sat in the driver's seat and turned the key. Nothing. She turned it again. Still nothing. "Uh-oh," she said. "Not now, please."

"What's happening?"

"This is the Lemon Lime, remember? But it always works eventually." Mia took the key out of the ignition, took a deep breath and tried again." There was a soft clicking noise but the engine did not turn over. A bright red light flashed on the dashboard. It looked like a picture of the battery. Mia could feel her stress level rising rapidly. Why was this happening today? She looked over at Noah. "Please tell me you know something about cars."

Noah grimaced. "I'm sorry. I know nothing. Or next-to-nothing. I think your battery's dead. Do you have jumper cables?"

"No, do you?" Noah was shaking his head before Mia could even ask the question. "What am I gonna do?" she groaned. Then, like a bolt of lightning, the obvious answer struck her.

"Why don't we take your car?"

"I rode with you, remember?"

Mia had already considered that. "I know. But we're not that far from the condo. We could run back and grab your car. I'll come back and have this jumped later."

Noah nodded. The idea had merit. After all, they were really only a couple blocks from where they lived, as the crow flew. "Let's do it," he said.

The run wasn't easy, but Mia was tough. The ice-cold air made it difficult to breathe deeply, and she wasn't dressed for athletics at all. Still, she was doing better than Noah. He was dragging behind her like a crashed water skier who forgot to let go of the tow cable. Whenever Mia would get a few hundred feet ahead she'd stop and wait for Noah to catch up. By the time they reached the parking garage of their condo, Noah was green. Mia felt bad she'd pushed him so hard. "Do you need to take a break?" she asked.

"No," he said, gasping, "I'll catch my breath in the car."

Mia smiled. Noah was a trooper. Even though he looked like he wanted to vomit, he was still willing to push on to help her. He tossed her the keys and collapsed in the front seat. Mia opened the driver's side and the smell of fresh leather engulfed her. "Wow. I'm starting to see why you like your job."

"Just wait till you try the built-in back massager."

"This I have to see."

Mia tried to drive the speed limit, but it was hard. For one, she was trying to win a race, and for two, she had 400 horses under her right foot. The back massagers were a nice touch, too.

They helped relieve the tension she'd been holding.

The post office was a tall, elegant, granite structure. The entrance was marked by several pillars, and the front steps were guarded by two stone lions. It looked more like a grand entrance to a palace than a municipal building. Mia eased the car into a parking space.

"You ready for the ball, Cinderella?" Noah teased.

"I just hope this car doesn't turn into a pumpkin."

They climbed the steps of the post office two at a time, and pulled on the door. It was locked fast. They tried another, same result. Mia gritted her teeth. "Not again. I swear this contest is aging me."

"What day is it?" Noah queried to no one in particular.

Mia thought about the question. "It's...It's Sunday. No wonder it isn't open."

"You sure this is the right spot?"

"A hundred percent."

"So, what do we do?"

Mia was frustrated, and a bit short-tempered. "I don't know. I guess we just wait for some leaf-blowing groundskeeper to come along and tell us there's a back entrance."

Despite the snark, Noah chuckled.

"I guess I have no choice but to try taking the pic' here," she said. She turned her back to the post office sign, snapped a selfie, and uploaded it to the app. Noah sat down on one of the concrete steps and Mia joined him.

"I guess we'll know if you're right in a couple of minutes."

"Guess so." She paused. "I'm sorry I was so crazy today. Just stressed about everything and the car was the straw that broke the camel's back. I just can't handle any more bad news right now."

"I get it. Don't apologize."

"What was it you wanted to talk to me about?"

Noah sucked in a breath of cold air. It was now or never, he knew that. He had to tell her the truth. Maybe she'd say she hated him and walk away, but maybe not. Maybe instead she'd be understanding and know he'd been stuck between a rock and a hard place. As he opened his mouth to speak, Mia's phone pinged. "You've gotta be kidding," he said aloud.

Mia slid her phone into her pocket. "No. I'm done putting the Twelve Games first. What did you want to say?" But even as the words spilled from her tongue, she subtly glanced at the phone in her pocket. Noah knew her mind would be elsewhere, and he hated to spoil the moment.

"No," he insisted. "It's me who's sorry. Let's talk tonight, over dinner. We don't have a moment to lose with the Games."

"Are you sure?"

"Just check it."

Mia pulled her phone back out and unlocked it. Sure enough, it was a Gazette push notification. She read it aloud. "Thanks for entering the Twelve Games of Christmas, day 10. Congratulations on finding today's secret location!" You are the 1st person to do so! Daily points: 1; Total points: 7. Current Standings: 1st place." Mia paused for a minute, stunned. "First place! You hear that? I'm in first! I'm gonna win this thing!"

Noah beamed. He was truly happy for her, but inside his joy was mitigated by his confliction and the conversation he had to have tonight. Mia wrapped her arms around him and kissed him on the cheek. His heart fluttered with excitement and he hugged her back.

CHAPTER 29

On the way home from the post office, Noah drove, having fully recovered from his unexpected morning calisthenics. Mia cranked the stereo with Christmas music and she and Noah sang along joyfully. Noah's singing voice was, in a word, awful, but his effort and earnestness were off the charts. Mia found it endearing he wasn't embarrassed to belt out "Rockin' Around the Christmas Tree," even though his version sounded more like the Wicked Witch of the West being boiled by water. He parked in his usual spot and Mia hopped out. "I'll see you tonight?" she asked.

"Definitely."

Back home, Mia arranged for a tow truck to pick up the Lemon Lime from The Bagel House and drop it off at a nearby mechanic. It was still early afternoon, but when she disconnected, weariness washed over her and she barely made it to her bed before crashing. The contest had her burning the candle on both ends for days, and that coupled with the stress from the balloon payment had taken its toll. She passed out and didn't wake up for hours. When she finally did open her eyes, it was early evening and had gotten dark outside. Her phone was buzzing on the side table next to the bed. Still half asleep, Mia clicked the answer button without checking the caller ID. "Hi, Noah," she said, groggily.

Richard sounded confused. "Who's Noah?"

Mia sat up quickly in a thick cloud of embarrassment. "Rich, hi. Sorry, I didn't know that was you."

Richard was laughing, "I can tell. Who's Noah?"

Mia scolded herself. She was awake now and regaining her composure. "Nobody you need to be concerned with. What's up?"

"What's up? You asking me that? I haven't heard from you in days."

"I'm sorry I haven't checked in more. I have been so crazy-busy with this contest. Tell me everything. How's it been going? Did the snow bring anybody in?"

"Mia, it's been bananas!"

"What do you mean?"

"I mean any minute now, I'm expecting Jadyn — our new seasonal employee — to walk through the door."

"No way. You had to hire help?"

"Yep. He's a college kid from my neighborhood — back for the holidays and looking to pick up some work till the next semester starts. Really nice guy."

"That sounds perfect."

"Just about. But we're getting low on inventory. Especially the exclusives from Zhang Wei."

"Have you ordered more?"

"That's the weird thing: I haven't been able to get ahold of him."

Mia chewed on the news for a moment, but shrugged it off. "Maybe he's just on vacation or something."

"Yeah, maybe."

"I'll shoot him an email; see what's up."

"Are you sure? I don't want to distract you."

"It's fine. It'll only take a second."

"Thanks." Richard switched gears. "So? Spill…"

Mia smiled to herself and decided to slow-roll him. She took on a faux somber-sounding tone. "About that…" she paused for dramatic effect.

"What? Is it bad?"

She wanted to drag things out further but was too excited. "I wouldn't say that…I'm in first place!" she screamed.

"Shut up!"

"I promise!"

"No way. Are you messing with me?"

"I promise, Rich! I think I'm gonna do this thing."

Mia could hear Richard getting choked up on the other end of the phone. "That's…so…good!" he struggled to say, as his emotions took hold. "I'm so happy for you."

"For us."

"Yeah, for us. This has been such hard week without you, and I'm so glad you're out there making it worthwhile." Mia felt another pang of sadness. Richard had really carried a heavy burden for her, and he was exhausted. "So, you really might win this thing, huh?" he asked.

"Yes, I really might. The Gazette app posts all the standings at the end of the day. I'm in first place with seven points and the three next closest people have six. That means if I can score points the next two days, I am guaranteed to win the contest – no ties."

Richard let out a whoop on the other end. "I'm so happy. I'm not ready to say goodbye to this place."

Mia nodded. "There's something else."

"What? Is it bad?"

Mia laughed. "Not at all. I have a surprise for you."

"Ok…"

"I was gonna wait till Christmas, but you should hear this now: I'm making you a fifty percent partner." The line went dead. At least, it sounded like it was dead. "Hello? You there?" After a few seconds Mia heard muffled crying.

"Thank…you." Richard finally said between tears. On her end, Mia teared up too.

"You deserve it," she said softly.

Richard sniffled and seemed to get ahold of himself. "Wow.

Now you just have to win that contest so I have something to split. I don't want fifty percent of nothing."

Mia laughed. "That's the plan."

Mia still had a few hours before her celebration date with Noah. That left her enough time to get to the bottom of the inventory issue. She opened her phone and tapped the email icon. After clicking open a new draft she typed "ZH" into the address bar. The phone suggested Zhang_Wei34@superfuncoolgifts.com, and Mia tapped it into place. She typed out a quick email:

"Hi Zhang,

My colleague Richard said he's been trying to get in touch but hasn't heard from you. We'd like to make another order – potentially bigger than last time – please respond as able."

Mia pushed send and heard the satisfying "whoosh" sound that meant an email was successfully sent. She got up to go get ready for her date.

When she got out of the shower, she noticed a red "1" on her email app. She clicked it open and was pleased to see it was from Zhang. She clicked his name and the full popped up on screen.

"Hi Mia,

My apologies for not following-up with Richard. I've been approached by a large corporation who's offered me more money for my exclusive inventory. My company and I will no longer be available to service Snow Valley Treasures.

Regards."

The email was cold, short, and to the point. Mia ruminated on the problem. Zhang had been one of her biggest suppliers, and was by far her biggest exclusive. She didn't know how to replace the loss of his inventory. After staring out her window, lost in thought, she remembered her date. This is why she'd wanted Richard to handle all logistics during the contest. The stress was all-consuming. But Mia still had her date – and the Twelve Games. She tried to put her stress in a boat and push it out to sea. The inventory issue could be solved later. Tonight, it was time for a little celebration.

CHAPTER 30

It was still a half hour before the time they'd agreed to meet, but Mia was too excited to wait. First place in the contest, and a date with Noah. "I can sneak over there a little bit early," she thought. She grabbed a bottle of sauvignon blanc, two glasses, and snuck out her door. Something smelled amazing. As she drew near Noah's door she could tell the smell was emanating from his condo. She felt like a cartoon character floating toward the smoky smell of something delicious. "And he can cook?" she thought, excitedly, "a man of many talents." As Mia was about to knock on the door, she heard Noah's voice inside. She paused. Maybe Noah had a guest. But no, there was only his voice. He must be on the phone, she figured. Again, she raised her fist to knock, but stopped when she heard her name.

"Her name is Mia," Noah said.

Mia smiled. She felt bad about eavesdropping, but the conversation was about her after all, so maybe it was ok. "Maybe he's telling his mom about me," she thought. She continued listening.

"Yes, I've met with her several times." A pause. "Every day since we talked. We spend the whole day together." Another pause. "No, we never stopped by her store. I don't know if she's thinking about it."

Mia was confused. If he were talking to his mom, this would be an odd setup. Why would his mom care about her store? Plus, Noah sounded exasperated, not happy.

After a few seconds, he spoke again. "I don't know what else you want me to do. I've told you everything I know." Another pause. "As I said, we worked on the Twelve Games of Christmas every day. Nothing out of the ordinary happened today other than us using my car, which I already told you about." Noah let out a long sigh. "I'm done with these updates. I've told you everything I know."

He disconnected the call, and Mia knocked loudly on his door. She covered the peep hole so he wouldn't know who or what to expect. A second later the door swung open. When he saw Mia, his mouth fell open, and his face flushed. He stood there in an apron with a phone in one hand and a wooden cooking spoon in the other. He stammered. "I...Hi! I thought we had planned to meet at 7:00."

Mia didn't engage with the false niceties. "Told who everything you know?" She demanded.

"You heard that?"

"I heard enough. Who did you tell everything you know about me?"

"I didn't want you to find out this way, but in a way, it's good this happened."

"Find out what? You still haven't told me who you were talking to." Mia's tone was accusatory.

"I was talking to Nadine."

Mia closed her eyes and absorbed the information. She was at once deeply hurt and deeply angry. Only a few seconds before, she had been foolish enough to believe Noah was telling his mom about her. She wanted to turn and run away, but her desire to know what was happening was even stronger. "You were telling Nadine about me? About my store? What is this, some kind of corporate reconnaissance mission?"

Noah was shaking his head and waving his hands palms up. "No, no, that's not it."

"What is it then? Are you just hanging out with me to get

information?"

Noah was back on his heels. "No. I've loved spending time with you. And you asked me to hang out, remember? You wanted me to be your good luck charm, right?"

The words hit her hard. It was true, Mia had asked him to be moral support for the Games. But still, why was he informing his boss about their activities. Something didn't add up. She was tired of having the conversation in the hallway where others could hear. She shoved her way into the door. "May I," she said, as she entered.

"Of course," Noah said, but her abrupt entrance caused him to stumble backward, and his phone slipped from his grip. In slow motion, Noah dropped the spoon and tried to catch the phone before it crashed to the floor. He swiped his hand at it, and his finger inadvertently brushed the camera app. The catch proved too difficult, and the phone clattered to the ground near Mia's feet. She bent down to pick it up and inspected the screen – no damage. When she reached forward to hand it to Noah, something caught her eye. On screen, there was a picture of a calendar, and Zhang Wei's contact information. Mia retracted her arm and looked closer. She was confused.

"How do know Zhang?" She looked at Noah who was ashen-faced, then back to the phone. The pieces fell into place in her mind. "Is this…is this my calendar?" she asked, calmly.

Noah looked panicked. "Mia, please, let me explain."

"Did you take a picture of my work calendar, yes or no?"

Noah hung his head. "Yes, but it was before I met you. I never meant—"

Mia put her hand up. "Wait." She'd just remembered the email from Zhang earlier that night. "You called Zhang, didn't you? It was you, all along. You sabotaged my inventory source. You used me, lied to me, and now you're feeding all your little spy info to your boss." Mia felt dizzy.

Noah had given up trying to protest. "Yes, I called Zhang. But that was before I met you, before I knew what you and SVT meant to this community – to me."

Mia felt tears welling in her eyes, but she held her composure.

"Save it," she said, and shook her head in disbelief. "This whole time I was under the delusion that you…" she struggled to find the right words, "that you, liked me."

"I do." Noah tried to interject, but Mia continued.

"The worst part is, I liked you too. A lot. But now I find out this is all some sort of…of…" she paused, "espionage or something!"

Noah frantically tried to stop the bleeding. "You don't understand."

"I think I understand quite well, thank you. Would you believe when I first heard you talking to Nadine I thought you might have been telling your mother about me?" Mia bit her lip and muttered almost to herself, "I must look pretty stupid."

The words stung Noah, but he was fighting a losing battle. "Mia, please. Just listen."

"This is crazy. What are you gonna tell me next you knocked out my internet so I'd be forced to come crawling to you asking for help?"

Noah bit his lip and looked down. "It sounds weird when you put it that way, but I just wanted an excuse to see you."

Mia's comment had been intended sarcastically. The horror it was real, began to wash over her. "What? You didn't really, right?" She looked into his eyes and he nodded. "What a weird, twisted, toxic thing to do. How did you even…never mind. I don't even want to know."

"Mia, please. Just give me a chance to explain."

Mia gave him a cold gaze. "I think I'm done listening, actually." She put the bottle of wine in his hands. "I brought this for us to celebrate. I guess you can still celebrate successfully fooling me, but you probably only need one glass." Mia tried to hand Noah one of the wine glasses but he refused to take hold. "Unless Nadine is coming by to have a laugh too. On second thought, here, have both." Mia put both wine glasses on the ground, just inside Noah's door, and turned to leave. She managed to keep her composure at least until the hallway. When she crossed the threshold, tears filled her eyes. Noah followed her out the door, but she kept her back to him. She would never show him weakness again. She rushed toward her condo.

Noah called after her. "Wait!"

"Please leave me alone," she said softly, without turning around.

CHAPTER 31

Mia allowed herself to cry that night – she deserved a good cry after everything she'd been through – but promised herself not to throw good energy after bad, in the morning. She still had a job to do, and do it she would. She got up early, which wasn't too hard because she didn't feel like sleeping anyway. There were no issues with her internet, and the app opened as it should.

Mia sat down at her kitchen table to begin, but it was too quiet. Her thoughts kept gravitating to the night before. Her phone buzzed with a text and she checked it. It was Richard wishing her good luck.

She tapped out a quick reply, "Tks."

She tried again, but couldn't focus on the puzzle – she hadn't even read through the rules – and decided she needed to get out of her condo. She considered going back to The Bagel House, but realized that would only remind her of Noah. She crept out her front door and tip-toed down the hallway past his door. "Why can't my condo have an emergency fire escape?" She jammed the elevator button repeatedly like it was a pinball machine, and kept looking over her shoulder at Noah's door. But when the pain and awkwardness of a potential run-in with him, grew too intense, she took the stairs.

Mia looked for the Lemon Lime in the parking lot; it was nowhere to be found. A shot of adrenaline momentarily coursed through her, until she recalled arranging for the tow truck the night before. "Perfect," she muttered, wrapping her scarf around her face, "great start to the day." Mia called a car, which took her to the mechanic, who informed her she owed them $347 bucks. She forked over the money without a word of question or complaint. She was in a foul mood. What was a few hundred dollars more?

The Lemon Lime coughed and choked but fired up okay. The clock on her phone read 9:28, and she hadn't even begun puzzle 11. "What a waste!" she thought, as she grabbed her phone and typed another text to Richard: "On my way in."

"R u sure??? Everything ok?!"

Mia didn't bother responding. She jammed the car into gear and took off.

"Well look what the cat dragged in," Richard joked as Mia pushed her way into the store. "Feels good to see your face around here." But when he saw her expression, his smile drooped. He'd known her long enough to see she was deeply upset. But, to be fair, anyone would have known. It was painted all over her face. "What is it? Did you not find the location today?"

Mia shook her head. "I haven't even started."

A flash of concern. "Why not?" he asked. Mia walked toward him, tears welling once again, and he embraced her in a warm bear hug. "What's wrong?"

Mia apologized for crying, grabbed a tissue, and gathered herself. Then she told Richard the whole story – about the picture of her calendar; about Noah's conversation with Nadine; about sabotaging her internet; everything. Well, almost everything. Again, she left out the part about falling for him. She couched the story in a way that painted Noah only as a would-be new friend. But Richard could read between the lines. He let her vent, and only nodded and "mmm-hmm-ed" where appropriate.

When she finished the story, he paused to consider it. "A

corporate spy, huh?" he said, grinning. "I didn't know they really existed. I feel like we're in a mob movie or something. Hopefully he doesn't come back and..." Richard switched his voice to a stereotypical New York Italian accent, "make us an offer we can't refuse." Mia laughed through her tears. It felt good to be back. It was nice to see Richard and nice to be at her home away from home. "What's the plan now?" he asked.

"The plan is the same. I've gotta win the money. I just have to focus." Mia held up her phone.

"Well, what are you talkin' to me for? Get it done!" As Richard spoke, the temporary employee, Jadyn, ambled out of the back room carrying a box. He was tall, and lanky, and wore a sheepish grin. He came over and introduced himself. Mia liked him immediately.

The front door chimed and several customers walked through at the same time. Richard looked at Jadyn. "Can you go help them, please?" Jadyn smiled and bounced in the customers' direction. Richard looked back to Mia. "As I was saying." He gestured toward the back office, but Mia shook her head.

"I like the din of a busy place. I'll work out here." She found a seat at a kid's table and opened the app. Richard grabbed a chair across from her, his back to the door. The day's puzzle was a series of word jumbles. "Ok, the first one is eight-letters and the category is Christmas songs."

Richard nodded, knowing he couldn't help, but interested to see the process play out. Mia paused, then suddenly shouted, "Nadine!"

Richard looked over at her, quizzically. "I know I'm not supposed to help, but that doesn't sound right. And it's not even eight letters."

Mia pointed to the window. "Nadine." As she spoke, the bells on the door jingled and Nadine entered the shop. She scanned the room and her gaze found Richard's.

"Is Mia in?" Nadine hadn't noticed Mia sitting behind him.

"I'm here," she said. "What do you want?"

Nadine walked toward them. "I've just come to talk. You'll want to hear what I have to say. Is there someplace private..."

She noticed Mia and Richard were at a kid's table, "someplace private that's not made for children."

"This whole place is made for kids. Maybe that's why you've never understood it."

"Indeed."

Mia stood up and told Nadine to follow her. She led her to the lone office in the back. Mia moved behind the desk, taking the leather office chair herself, and leaving the rolly chair for Nadine. "I'm in a hurry. What is it?" Mia asked.

"I'm afraid I have some bad news."

"I'm not surprised."

"Well you may be when you hear it. I know you don't trust me, but believe it or not, I have come to help you."

"I don't believe it," Mia said, matter-of-factly, "but go ahead. You've piqued my curiosity."

Nadine tried to appear taken aback by Mia's brusqueness, apparently not used to pushback. "I've spoken to your bank. They are calling the balloon loan due on the 23rd."

Mia smirked. "Nice try. Is that the best you've got?"

"I wish it were a joke. You can call the manager yourself to verify. And I suggest you do."

Mia looked carefully at Nadine, she didn't appear to be joking. In fact, she looked deadly serious. "I would never want to play poker against this woman if this is a bluff," Mia thought. She was unnerved. "I don't know what game this is, but I don't appreciate it," Mia said, finally.

Nadine put her hands in the air, palms forward. "No games. I assure you this is happening."

"I'll bite. Let's say the date is moved up. You said you were here to help?"

"I'm here to offer you a chance to sell the store to Jungle, one last time. We are willing to pay you fair market value, right here, right now. But the offer is getting lower by the second."

Mia nodded and clicked her tongue on her teeth. "There it is."

"You can sell to us now, or suffer major losses in foreclosure. The choice is obvious."

Mia took a breath to slow the conversation down. "I don't believe the loan is moved up. This is clearly a desperate ploy to cheat me out of my business. It won't work. I have a plan to save the store. I'm sure your spy told you all about it."

Nadine cackled. "That little crossword contest? Yes, he told me. We had a good laugh too." Mia looked horrified and it showed on her face. Nadine noticed. "Oh, does that make you sad?" she said, mockingly. "Don't tell me you thought he actually liked you."

Mia's mouth fell open. Nadine twisted the knife further. "You did! That is so adorably naïve. Noah likes his job. He likes money. Actually, it was Noah's idea to move the loan date up. I tried to tell him it was cruel, but when he sees something he wants, he goes after it."

Mia was stunned and speechless. She felt like she couldn't breathe.

"So, how 'bout it?" Nadine asked with a sneer. "Sell to me now and save yourself any more embarrassment."

Time felt like it slowed to a crawl. Mia could hear Nadine speaking but couldn't make sense of the words. Had Noah really lied to her about everything? How could she have trusted him? Out of the corner of her eye, she saw Richard's shadow outside the door. "Richard!" she thought. "I can still help him." He had been so loyal to Mia over the years, giving up other career opportunities to help her grow the store. If she sold the store to Jungle now, at least she'd have half of something to split with him. He would have a nice nest egg to live on while he searched for another job. And maybe Nadine was right. Going through a foreclosure would be costly both in terms of time and money. Nadine was nasty, but at least she brought a viable offer. An offer which could give them both a start on a new life. "Ok," Mia said, after a long pause, "let's make a deal."

Nadine all but licked her chops. "Glad to see you came to your senses. It really is better this way. You'll feel better in the long run." She rifled through her briefcase. The paperwork included a standard sales contract with "boilerplate legalese" and a "more-than-fair" price offer, at least according to the way

Nadine explained it. As Nadine quickly ticked through the high points of the offer, Mia felt like she was on autopilot, nodding and "uh-huh-ing," along. She felt numb, but at least she was helping Richard. That was something. At last Nadine finished and slid the contract across the table toward Mia. "I just need your autograph here," she said, pointing to a signature line at the bottom.

Mia picked up a pen and clicked it open. As the pen was nearing the paper, Richard burst into the room. "Stop!" He shouted. Mia jumped. "Don't sign that."

"I have to," Mia said.

"You don't have to. You're saving this store." Richard moved around the desk and took the pen out of Mia's hand. He handed it to Nadine who scowled at him. "I've heard every word you've said," he told Nadine, "and I don't know if you're lying, if you're serious, or if this is some sick joke, but she…" Richard pointed to Mia, "we, are never selling! Especially not to you."

"You don't have a vote here," Nadine responded.

Mia was looking at Richard, awestruck. His words emboldened her. "Oh yes he does. He's right. I couldn't sell to you if I wanted. He is a fifty-fifty owner."

"That's not what it says on the deed," Nadine sneered.

Mia smiled at Richard. "Looks like your information's wrong." She stood up and moved to the door. "I think that's about enough of this. If you'll excuse us."

Nadine snatched the contract off the desk and stood up in a huff. "You'll be foreclosed on in two days. You'll regret this. We'll swoop in when this place is dead and we'll pick its bones."

"You can leave now." Richard shouted. Nadine marched for the door without saying another word.

Mia's phone pinged with the sound of an incoming text. It was from Noah. "Mia," it said, "I'm so sorry for how things happened. I wanted to tell you. Please give me a chance to explain."

Mia typed out a quick response, "Don't worry. Your boss Nadine just told me everything. Thanks." Almost as soon as she pressed send Noah called her. She pushed decline. A second or so later her phone buzzed again. Declined.

Finally, another message came through, "I don't know what she said but please give me a chance to explain for myself."

Mia began typing a reply but thought better of it and pocketed her phone. When Nadine was all the way out of sight, Richard turned to her. "What were you thinking?"

"I don't know. You think she was telling the truth about the loan?"

Richard held up the phone. "Only one way to find out."

CHAPTER 32

Mia sat in the lobby of the bank bouncing her knees and fidgeting with her purse zipper. When she'd spoken with the bank manager all he would tell her over the phone was that there was a matter of importance they needed to discuss in-person. She had the Gazette app open on her lap, but couldn't concentrate on it. She was still a long way from finishing. She looked at her watch. It was already late morning. Usually by this point she'd have half of the puzzle done, if not be nearing completion. That realization made her feel physically sick. She snatched a grape flavored lollipop from the bowl next to her, hoping the sugar would settle her stomach and improve her mood. It didn't. At last, the bank manager called her name. "Ms. Gallagher?"

"That's me," she said as cheerfully as she could manage, as if her demeanor would have an outcome on the meeting.

The bank manager did not return her cheeriness. "Follow me," he said, morosely. He led her into his office and motioned for her to have a seat. "Ms. Gallagher, the reason I called you in today…"

Mia cut him off. "I was told my balloon payment had been moved up to the 23rd. Is that right?"

"Unfortunately, that is what happened, yes."

Mia's temper shot to 100. "What are you talking about?" she asked. "You can't just do that!"

"The terms of the loan are clear, Ma'am."

"Move it back to the first."

"I'm afraid I can't do that. Unless…" Mia's spirit lifted a bit at the word 'unless.'

"Unless what?"

"Unless you can cover a quarter of the amount due. As a bridge collateral."

Mia was flattened. How much more bad news could she take? "You're asking if I have 25 Grand on me?"

"Not quite that much, but essentially, yes."

"I don't."

"In that case, I'm afraid there's not much else we can do." The bank manager stood up as if the meeting was over. "I'm sorry."

"When do I have to come up with the money?"

The manager paused and looked at his calendar. "It's due by close of business on the 23rd, so you have 'til tomorrow at 5:00."

Mia thought about the contest. Even if she won, it was hard to picture her getting a check; getting it to the bank; and getting it cleared in time to pay her bill by 5:00 tomorrow. Some days, she didn't even snap the selfie until that time. Plus, tomorrow was the last day. It could be a hard puzzle, and probably would be. She needed more time. A few more hours at least. "Can I please have 'til midnight tomorrow?"

"The bank closes at 5:00, Ma'am."

"Tomorrow at 11:59 pm is still the 23rd. As long as I get the money by then, I should be ok, right? Can't someone meet me here? I'll be depositing a check for $100,000. I can't do that online. Isn't that good for your bank? Can't you make an exception?"

The manager thought about the proposal. "Where would you be getting this money?"

"It doesn't matter. I can get it. Can you meet me or not?"

The bank manager looked over Mia's shoulder. She turned to see what caught his eye, and saw a man standing just outside the office. "Who is that?" she asked. "Is that your boss? Can he make an exception?"

"That is the branch manager, and he does not have time to…"

Mia jumped out of her seat and left the office to plead her case to him. The branch manager smiled as Mia approached.

"I'm told you're in charge here," she started. "I'm a small business owner and I need a few hours extension on my balloon loan tomorrow. I'll be depositing a substantial sum, but won't have it by five pm. Can you or somebody please make an exception to meet me here after hours?"

"Ms. Gallagher, I presume?"

"Yes."

"From Snow Valley Treasures?"

"Yes."

"I don't see why that would be a problem."

Mia couldn't help herself. She leaned over and hugged the man. He laughed and pulled out his wallet. "Here's my card. Call me when you're ready to make the transaction."

"Thank you so much!" Mia exclaimed.

"My pleasure. Oh, and keep up the good work at your store. My grandkids love it."

"I'm trying."

The bank manager watched the goings-on from his office window. Mia couldn't be sure but she thought she saw him shaking his head in disapproval.

CHAPTER 33

When a pitcher is on his way to throwing a no-hitter – a rare baseball game in which nobody from the opposing team gets a base hit – the pitcher's team will start to become aware something special is happening and leave the pitcher alone. They won't sit near him in the dugout, they won't talk to him, or congratulate him. The pitcher is left in his own little world in order to keep the spell alive. That's how Richard felt about Mia. Noon rolled by, then 1:00, and 2:00. The shop doorbell chimed repeatedly with last-minute shoppers and Mia never looked up. By 3:00, she had made a substantial dent in the puzzle, and by 4:00 she was nearly done. "If only I could have done it this quickly in the morning," she thought. Throughout the day, Richard left Mia completely alone. He didn't want to mess with her concentration. There were moments when he needed or wanted to ask her things, but resisted the urge. She was his pitcher, and he needed her to pitch the perfect game. As the sun began to hang low in the sky, Mia finally looked up. "Done," she said.

"What's the location?"

"It says 'mall Santa.'"

"What're you waiting for?" he asked.

Mia looked up at Richard and smiled. "I…thanks for

everything, Rich."

"Yeah, yeah. We can do this after you win the money. Get outta here." Mia laughed. She was on her feet and out the door a few seconds later.

At the mall, the Santa's Village wasn't located in the "North Pole." The sign hanging above the display indicated this village was supposed to depict Hawaii. "Santa's on Vacation," it read. As she drew near, Mia could see plastic palm trees, a surfing polar bear, and Santa wearing green board shorts and a red Hawaiian shirt featuring hula dancing elves. "Now that is odd," Mia thought. "Probably some corporate mall flunky's idea of a way to draw more customers." It seemed to be working though. The mall was packed. A line of cute kids trying to relay last-minute wishes to Santa, wrapped circuitously through the area. Mia smiled at a few as she positioned herself in front of the Santa sign and snapped a selfie. Now the dreaded wait. She noticed several others taking selfies by the sign and she her pulse quickened. But after the small moment of panic, realized most of the people taking pictures had small children in tow.

Mia busied herself by browsing through books at a cart in the center of the hallway. "Maybe I'll be able to read more when they foreclose on me," Mia thought, darkly, and smirked at the joke. She picked up a copy of The Wind in the Willows and thumbed through it. Mia had seen the cartoon once, but had never read the book. "How much?" she asked the teenage worker.

"Everything's five bucks."

Mia pulled a five-dollar bill out of her pocket and handed it to the kid. She held up the book. "I'm getting this one," she said.

The teen took the money and looked wholly uninterested in what she had to say. Her phone vibrated and she froze. It was a push notification. She swallowed hard. It was late in the day, she knew that, but was it too late? She pressed the open button lightly with her thumb and the message popped up. "Thanks for entering the Twelve Games of Christmas, day 11," it read. "Congratulations on finding today's secret location!" You are the 4th person to do so! Daily points: 0; Total points: 7. Current

Standings: Tied 1st place." Mia flinched when she read it. She couldn't believe it. So close to shoring up a guaranteed victory. But she was still tied for the lead, and that was big. Tomorrow would be a race to the finish. "First one there wins," she thought. "Tomorrow I'll be ready."

CHAPTER 34

The bank manager sat in his office, brooding. He didn't like people going over his head, and he certainly didn't like being contradicted by the branch manager. Nevertheless, he debated about whether or not to tell Nadine about what happened for three reasons: first, she might think of him as incompetent; second, he was kind of scared of her; and third, he wasn't sure the extra few hours would make that much of a difference in the long run. In the end, his fear won out and he decided calling was better than nothing. Plus, even if she were mad, he'd at least get to hear her voice. He picked up his phone and dialed.

"Hi, Nadine. It's me, Robby…" he paused to listen for signs of recognition. There was silence on the other end. "You know, from the bank."

"Yes, Robby. What do you need?"

"I wanted to give you the heads-up. The branch manager gave that Snow Valley Treasures lady an extension on her timeline 'til tomorrow at midnight."

"What?" Nadine hissed. "How did you let this happen?"

"It wasn't my call. The branch manager overruled me. I just follow orders."

Nadine shut her eyes and pinched the bridge of her nose.

"Fine. Who's staying at the bank to keep it open?"

"The branch manager himself."

"I want you to stay too," she ordered. "Make sure to lock those doors at 12:00 sharp."

"Of course, Ma'am."

Nadine slammed the phone onto its cradle. "Incompetence all around me." She yelled for her assistant. Caroline rushed into the room frantically.

"How can I help?"

"What do you know about that puzzle contest from the paper? How did it go today?"

Caroline consulted a tablet computer she was holding. "The entrants are all anonymous but it says there are four people tied for first place with seven points apiece."

"I think it's safe to assume one of the four is the toy store lady, don't you?"

Caroline looked a bit unsure. "I think so, Ma'am, yes. You said she seemed confident about her chances of winning. According to this article, there are only four people who can win the contest now. It says the first person to reach the location from among the four that are tied will win tomorrow. If she's one of the four, I'm sure she knows she is in the running."

Nadine looked behind Caroline and motioned for her to shut the door. She leaned forward across her desk. "As you know, we have a lot of money invested in this thing. I can't have it go sideways because of some silly contest. Are you with me?"

"I think so, Ma'am," Caroline said, timidly.

"I want you to make sure the gift shop woman does not win tomorrow. Distract her or something. Is that clear?"

"Crystal…" Caroline shuffled her feet as if deciding whether or not to proceed. "But how much time do you want me to spend on this? Just 'cuz the Christmas party is tonight and…"

Nadine held her hand up to silence Caroline. "I don't care about any Christmas parties. I want you to do your job, for as long as it takes. Believe me, if you do things to my satisfaction you'll have the best Christmas of your life."

———

Mia drove home from the mall feeling sorry for herself. She'd had a chance to outpace the competition but she spent the day at the mechanic's, fighting with Nadine, and having it out with the bank. On the other hand, Nadine had come to intimidate her, but all she'd ended up doing was tipping Mia off that the bank loan was moved up. A tactical error on her part. If Nadine hadn't said anything, Mia wouldn't have known to ask for an extension, so in a weird way, it was a win. She kept thinking about how depressing it would be to have won the money but to find out it was too late to deposit it. She shuddered at the thought.

Mia's phone buzzed. In her regular life, she liked to hear the ping of a text or the buzz of a phone call. But now, with her nerves so jacked-up about the contest, and her emotions so raw about Noah, any phone buzzing just brought on an ocean of stress. She checked the screen. It was a voicemail from Edith. Her blood ran cold. Was the party tonight? She pushed the "Listen" button and the voicemail played through her car speakers.

"Hi, Mia. I just wanted to let you know the car will be outside your place at 6:30. The driver's name is Sal. Tell him hi from me. I'm looking forward to seeing you!" Mia felt like throwing her phone out the window — all it did these days was add anxiety to her life. She checked the clock. 5:45. That would be enough time to get ready, if she could hurry. "Thank goodness I already laid out my outfit," she thought.

At home, there was time for a quick shower, hair and makeup. Mia checked herself out in the mirror. Not bad, considering she only had about 40 minutes to get completely ready. At 6:31 she bounded down the stairs and found Sal, holding a placard with her last name on it. Sal was nice. It was no wonder Edith had wanted Mia to send her regards. He was a first-generation immigrant from Italy. Got his driver's license at 21, and started his own car service at 26. He was half-retired now, but would still drive VIPs and friends whenever the occasion arose. Edith had asked him as a special favor to take Mia to and from the party. Mia felt like royalty. Sal opened the door for her, and offered her some champagne and light crudité – both of which she accepted happily. By the time they were nearing their destination Mia was beginning to relax. The champagne was working its magic and Mia was having fun chatting with Sal. She had been on such high alert the past week and a half, it was nice to do something to take her mind off the pressure.

The car slowed to a stop and for the first time on the trip, Mia glanced out the window. She recognized her surroundings. "Oh no," she said. "This can't be it."

"This is it," Sal laughed, through his thick Italian accent. "I've been doing this a long time."

"Maybe it's in a different building," Mia thought. "Which business is it?" she asked Sal.

"It's for that internet company everyone uses. Jungle somethin'." He glanced at a clipboard beside him. "Yeah, Jungle.com."

Mia froze, not sure what to do. At first, she thought of running, but it was way too cold, and she wouldn't make it far in her heels. Then she thought of asking Sal to take her back, but what would Edith say? She was relying on Mia, and Mia would be there for her, by hook or by crook. She had no choice. Mia bid her temporary goodbyes to Sal – who promised to be right there whenever she was ready to leave – and climbed out of the car.

For her own "office" Christmas party last year, Mia took Richard out to a bowling alley. They'd split a pitcher of beer, bowled two games, she crushed him at air hockey, and then it was off to a restaurant. Finally, they'd decided to spread Christmas cheer by going caroling door-to-door. It was a great evening, and anything but a traditional office Christmas party – at least by Jungle.com's standards. Mia exited the elevator on floor 70, and her jaw fell all the way back to one. She had never seen anything like it. The party theme seemed to be a carnival, circus, and winter wonderland, all rolled into one. As the elevator doors opened, two fire breathers blasted crisscrossing flames in front of her. A butler in a black tux immediately took her coat and welcomed her inside. They were on the top floor of the building; a completely open floor plan. It looked big enough to land a jumbo jet inside. The ceilings were 50-60 feet high, as if there were supposed to be two or three extra stories of the building that had simply just vanished. Above her, dangling from the ceiling were ribbon dancers and trapeze artists, all spinning and swinging elegantly above the commotion. Across the room, a giant ice sculpture carved to look exactly like the building they were in, glowed in an ethereal blue light. As Mia stepped deeper into the room she was stunned by a mid-sized ferris-wheel, spinning happy party goers round and round. In one corner, there were carnival games: ring toss, darts, knock-the-cans; and the prizes were insane: tablets, smart watches, gift cards, top-of-the-line headphones. In another, was the petting zoo featuring two predators: a Bengal tiger, and a large aquarium with a shark. Dancers, acrobats, sword swallowers, and other performers mixed and mingled and entertained the crowd. It was excess unlike anything Mia had ever seen, and it was intoxicating – at least at first.

Mia moved through the crowd looking for Edith, and noticed the party seemed to be devoid of anything related to Christmas. There were no lights, no Christmas trees, no carols being played or sung. Those were some of Mia's favorite things about the holiday, and she wondered why they had been omitted here. Edith saw Mia first and approached her with a wide smile. They hugged. "This place is amazing," Mia said.

"I know it. They go all out here. How was the ride in?"

"Sal is the best!"

"I'm glad you enjoyed it."

"Where's your daughter?" Mia asked. "I'm looking forward to meeting her."

Edith looked pained. "She told me she couldn't be here tonight. She's busy finishing up with some things at work. But she sends her regards and told me to tell you she hopes you'll take her up on a raincheck."

"I'm sorry to hear that. Of course, I'd love a raincheck."

Edith smiled. "But don't worry, we can still enjoy the fun."

She turned toward the bar. "Want a drink?"

"Sure. I'll take a rosé, please." Edith ordered the drink, and one for herself, then turned back to Mia. "How have things been going? With your daughter, I mean," Mia asked.

"Wonderful. I will be forever grateful to you."

"I didn't do anything."

"Pish-posh. It's all thanks to you. If you hadn't given me the advice when you did, I might never have called Nadine to make up."

Mia was sipping her wine as Edith spoke and almost choked on it. Wine shot up her nose, her eyes went wide, and her face pale. She began coughing.

"Are you ok, dear?" Edith asked.

After a minute, Mia got ahold of herself. "I'm ok. I'm sorry, did you say your daughter was Nadine? Is it Nadine Campbell?"

Edith looked shocked. "Do you know her?"

Mia was too bewildered to answer coherently. The past few days' roller coaster of emotions and surprises was nearly unbearable. "I don't...I think...we may have crossed paths."

"How wonderful! I'll have to tell her."

"No! Don't!" Mia exclaimed, a bit too forcefully. Edith furrowed her brow, confused. "I just think it will be a nicer surprise when we get together."

Edith looked unconvinced, but acquiesced nevertheless. "That sounds good too."

Mia excused herself from Edith momentarily and retreated inside her head. How could she have been so foolish, she scolded herself. This is what she deserved for trying to do the right thing. No good deed goes unpunished. She began thinking up excuses to leave that wouldn't hurt Edith: she'd left the stove on, her cat was stuck in a tree, she had the measles, her cat had the measles, anything would work at this point. As she steeled herself to break the bad news to her host, an emcee stood at the front of the room with a microphone. "Everyone, it's time to take your seats for dinner, please."

Edith grabbed Mia's hand with a grin. "Wait 'til you see what they've got on the menu. Follow me!"

Reluctantly, Mia trailed behind her over to her table. Despite being wrapped up in her own thoughts, Mia noticed even the place settings here were impressive. Each table had a centerpiece tower made from glasses of champagne. There was a single glass on top with three underneath it, and six underneath those, and so on. The top glass was overflowing with bubbling champagne which poured down onto those underneath it. They each spilled down onto the ones below, like a fountain. Mia couldn't immediately see how they pulled off the illusion. There were no wires or cables running to the centerpiece. But a quick peek under the table revealed a well-hidden wire running from a hole in the center of the table to an outlet underneath. The whole presentation was a sight to behold, and Mia wished she could have enjoyed it under different circumstances.

The waiters brought the appetizers first, squid ink pasta with shrimp and scallops. Weird, but surprisingly tasty. Next, the main course was cannoli with ricotta, and leeks, flambéed. Also, odd, but beautiful and delicious. Edith and Mia chatted throughout dinner. They talked about Edith's granddaughter – "beautiful, smart, and lucky enough to get the family's red hair" – Edith's Christmas plans – "spending time with Nadine and Renee" – and about the weather – "so happy to finally have some snow." Overall, it was a pleasant meal, and again, Mia began to relax. After all, Nadine wouldn't be joining them and it seemed Edith truly didn't know about their connection to each other. Before the dessert course was served, an executive at another table clinked his glass with a knife. Someone from the audio-visual team rushed a wireless microphone over to him. "Merry Christmas," he began. Loud cheers and applause came from the captive audience. "I know everyone wants to dive back in to dessert, so I'll be brief. This has been a good year." More cheers. "This has been a great year." Another round of applause. "So, I wanted to take a moment and thank everyone for their hard work. If I had time, I'd thank you all individually, but then we'd never get out of here and we'd be forced to party in this room forever." That got the biggest cheer of all. "But I do want to call out a few people who went over and above the call of duty." The executive scanned the tables looking for someone. "Nadine?" he yelled into the microphone. Mia held her breath. "Nadine? Is Nadine here?"

"She's not here!" someone yelled from a table near the back.

"I'm told she's not here. Probably still working." He scanned the audience again and Mia finally exhaled. "Who else is from her team?" The executive asked, almost to himself. "Oh, Noah. Noah Caffrey!" Mia's blood turned to ice. She heard a familiar voice behind her but didn't dare turn around.

"I'm here," Noah shouted from another table. Another cheer from the audience.

"Noah," the executive said, "come over here and tell these people what you're working on right now. That exciting project you and Nadine have cooked up."

Noah navigated his way around the maze of tables and grabbed the mic from his colleague. "Hello everyone," he said. He had to hold his hand over his eyes to block the light from a spotlight that had been shined down from some unseen audio-visual worker. "I'm…I'm Noah. I transferred from the Sun Valley office not too long ago…" more cheers. "I wasn't prepared for a speech, thanks a lot, Gary." The audience chortled. "But yes, Nadine and I have been working together on an acquisition project to expand into brick-and-mortar buildings. Thank you." There was a smattering of applause. Most people looked surprised by the abrupt ending. Noah handed the microphone back to the executive, Gary.

"Oh no you don't," Gary said, "You don't get off that easy. Tell 'em about the place you're buying." He put the mic back in Noah's hand.

"All right. It's a hardware store we are turning into retail space." More cheers.

"The other store," Gary urged.

Noah looked tentative. "Um…the other store is a gift boutique. We were trying to buy it, but…" He halted, "I don't know if…"

Gary looked impatient and leaned into the mic. "Don't worry, folks. We didn't transfer him for his public speaking ability." The audience erupted, it was the biggest laugh of the night so far. Gary smiled at the reaction and took the mic out of Noah's hand. "What he was saying is they are taking over an antiquated little boutique store. Gonna completely gut the place and push it into the 21st century. It will be the first all-digital, slash, physical retail store in the world. And Nadine and Noah here are responsible for it all." Noah smiled awkwardly. Another round of applause from the audience. Noah tried to slip back to his seat. "Wait," Gary said, stopping him. "Tell 'em about the bank thing. How you moved up their mortgage so we'd be the only company that could put an offer on the place." The audience laughed, whooped, and cheered. Gary turned to them, hamming it up. "You have to hear this. It's genius. The owner had no idea what happened." Gary tried to shove the microphone back into Noah's hands. Noah shuffled backward toward his seat.

Mia had heard enough. She was boiling over from anger, sadness, and betrayal. She struggled to fight back tears. "I'm sorry," she said quickly to Edith, "I have to go."

"Is everything ok? You'll miss dessert."

"I'm sorry," was all she could muster, as she scrambled out of her seat and made her way toward the exit. Noah was now in full retreat from the spotlight and could not see where he was going. He was still shielding his eyes as he made his way around the table. At the same time, Mia was rushing away from Edith's table with her eyes on the ground. They collided. Hard. Both fell all the way to the floor. The audience gasped and several people nearby jumped to their feet to help.

"I'm sorry," Noah said without looking up. "I didn't see you."

"It's my fau…" Mia picked herself up off the floor and saw who it was that bumped into her. "Noah," she mumbled.

Noah heard her voice and recognized Mia. He gasped. "Mia! What are you… How…"

She looked at him for a half a second. It was the look on her face that stuck with him. For the second time since he'd known her, she gave him a look that cut to his core. She didn't look angry or sad – just confused. For a moment, the pair locked eyes and Mia said just one word: "Why?" The next second, she was on her feet running to the exit.

Noah was still on the floor in shock. He felt like he was in a dream. The dazzling lights above him, the cacophony of chatter around him all spun into a dizzying blur. What had just happened? Why was Mia here? He felt hands grab him and lift him to his feet. Someone dusted off his shoulders. He muttered a quick "thank you," and an "I'm ok," before stumbling to the exit, himself. Behind him, Gary was still vamping on the microphone. "As the world turns…" he said gleefully. The audience was in stitches.

CHAPTER 35

A grey light crept through Mia's window and cast a dreary glow in the room. She was asleep on top of her bedspread, still wearing the black cocktail dress from the night before. She had managed to take off her heels and her mother's pearls before crashing, but only just. When she woke, her hair was matted and last night's makeup was smudged. "I look like Alice Cooper got electrocuted," she thought as she assessed herself in the mirror. After a coffee and a hot shower, Mia felt, and looked, much more like herself. She glanced at the calendar on her fridge. December 23rd. The last day of the competition. It was 6:25 am, she sat down at her kitchen table with a bagel, to wait. She took a bite and her thoughts rushed back to Noah and the events of the night before. She tried to push the thoughts from her head; she needed to focus. Despite all that had happened, she needed to focus.

Mia flipped on some Christmas tunes on the radio and forced herself to sing along. That made her feel a bit better. To kill time, she went outside to grab her paper. Down the hallway, a technician was pulling on some wires. Mia noticed, and approached him. "Quit messing with the internet lines. I'm tired of it breaking down every other day," she snapped.

The electrician was more than a bit confused. "What are you

talkin' about?" he said. "I'm not a cable guy."

Mia looked at his uniform: SV Electric and Gas. A wave of embarrassment washed over her. Still, she was in a sour mood and wanted someone to blame. "Just make sure you don't pull the wrong wire."

The electrician glowered at her. "Whatever you say, lady."

Mia turned and walked briskly toward the elevator.

The Bagel House was emptier than usual, and Mia didn't like it. She wasn't particularly superstitious, but the change in energy couldn't have been a good omen. Nevertheless, she plopped herself down at her regular booth. The store manager smiled at her. "Where's your friend?"

Mia played dumb. "Marcus? I don't know. He might be in later." She looked down at her phone in hopes of ending the conversation. It worked. Mia unlocked the phone just as it began vibrating. It was a text from Noah. She considered pressing delete without reading it, but curiosity overcame her. She clicked it open: "Hi Mia, there is so much that needs to be said. If u feel up to it, I'd love a few min of ur time. If not, I understand, but I'll be ready to talk whenever ur ready. In any case, GOOD LUCK TODAY! I know you've got this." Mia swiped left to delete, and did not respond.

The introductory animation for puzzle 12 was the most elaborate yet: "On the 12th Game of Christmas, my Daily sent to me: one final push for all the money." The words bounced on screen and looked like they might pop out right onto the table. The animation dissolved and revealed the final puzzle: a crossword. "So, it ends how it began," Mia thought. She pinched her fingers on the screen to zoom out and get a better look. The puzzle was big, but not by much more than the first day's. It still seemed daunting, though. Or maybe Mia was just tired. Rather than excitement, she felt overwhelmed. The prospect of solving another enormous puzzle, with all the world's pressure on her, was hard to bear. She hadn't gotten a late start, but it felt like it. She was on edge and felt like she was slogging through mud. "Why can't you concentrate," she chastised herself. "Just focus." Maybe she needed more caffeine. She ordered another coffee from the barista. Then another. Nothing seemed to help. The morning was rolling by and she was struggling. She kicked herself for coming back to The Bagel House. It only served to remind her of Noah, which was both painful and distracting – a double whammy. She decided she needed a change of scenery. Minutes later, she was in her car scowling.

When Mia pushed the gift shop's door open, Richard looked up, worried. "What happened? Did somebody already find the last location?"

"Nothing happened. I came here to finish the crossword."

Richard checked his watch. "You haven't finished yet? It's after 1:00."

"I'm perfectly aware of what time it is, thank you."

Mia noticed Richard was carefully choosing his words. Perhaps he could see he was on thin ice. "I meant no offense. Just saying. Do you need any help?"

She glowered at him. "I've told you before, I can't get help with this or I'll be disqualified. I just need peace and quiet." Richard's eyebrows shot skyward. Mia had rarely, if ever, treated him so poorly. But she quickly justified it in her mind. "He can't fault me for it," she thought. "The entire business and both of our careers rest on me finishing first at a crossword scavenger hunt. No pressure."

"I'll give you peace and quiet," Richard said, and went about his work.

Richard looked hurt, and Mia felt sorry. He was blameless. Truly, she was mad at herself, but she let the opportunity to apologize pass, and strode into the back office. Slowly she began to properly focus. "Ok, a six-letter word for hope. Starts with a D…" she paused and thought it out. "Desire." She penciled in the answer and moved on to the next clue, then the next, and the next. She moved at a steady clip. Within an hour, she'd completed nearly the whole puzzle and had enough of it done to guess the secret location. "The Daily Gazette," she said aloud. "They must mean their headquarters." Mia moved quickly now. She jumped from her chair and jogged toward the door.

On her way out, Mia glanced at Richard, and for a moment,

thought he'd been crying. But she doubted he would have cried over how she treated him. He was tough. "I'll talk to him once I've won the contest," she reasoned, and yanked the door open.

Her phone automatically connected to the Bluetooth in the Lemon Lime and she heard her ringtone through the speakers. Richard was calling her. "Not now," she thought, and declined the call. A few minutes later, Richard's name popped up on her caller ID again. "What does he want?" Mia wondered, but she iced him again. She wanted to stay focused on her task. By the third call, Mia was steaming. She pushed the green "Connect" button on the steering wheel. "What is it?" she shouted. Richard didn't immediately respond, but she could tell the line hadn't gone dead. She felt a pit in her stomach. "Hello," she said, this time softer. It sounded like Richard sniffling. "Richard, is everything ok? You're scaring me."

Finally, he spoke. "I'm so sorry."

Mia's pulse was pumping now. Something must have been wrong. She pulled her car over to the side of the road. "What is it, Rich?"

There was a long pause. "The contest. It's over."

The words didn't immediately register. "What do you mean, it's over?"

Richard sobbed gently. "I'm sorry. I know how hard you've worked. You deserved it."

"Please, Richard. Tell me what's going on?"

He took a moment, probably to gather himself. "It's all over social media. Someone already found the location. Someone won the money."

At once everything flashed through Mia's mind. She remembered planning her business, and getting the bank loan; she remembered telling her parents; and remembered how proud they'd been of her. She thought about her first customer, and hiring Richard. And she especially thought about the last two weeks and nearly killing herself to keep the place afloat. "No," she whispered, "it can't be." Mia heard the jingle of the SVT door in the background.

"A customer just walked in. I'll call you right back."

Mia hardly heard the words, and didn't respond. The call disconnected. A second later, her phone buzzed again. It was a push notification from the Gazette app. Mia blinked and clicked it open, "Thanks for entering the Twelve Crosswords of Christmas contest! We're sorry, but our winner has been found. Better luck next year!" As she read the words, her phone slipped from her grasp and fell between the seats. She stuck her hand down to grab it and her fingers struck something unusual. It was the rose Noah had plucked for her at the botanical garden. She lifted it up and looked at it. What was once a beautiful, vibrant white, was now a wilted, brownish grey. It was a fitting image. Angrily, she snapped the stem and threw the rose onto her floorboard. After several deep breaths, she dropped her head and wept.

It was evening. The lights were on inside Snow Valley Treasures, and a sign on the door was flipped to "open." Mia eased inside and found Richard dutifully unpacking a box of toys and displaying them on the shelf. That made her tear up again. He was still doing his job, even to the last second. When he saw her, he gave her a sympathetic smile. She walked over to him and wrapped him in a bear hug. "I'm so sorry, Rich. I was so rude today…every day, really. I left you holding the bag while I ran off on a treasure hunt. Please forgive me."

Richard smiled and hugged her back. "There's nothing to forgive."

Mia pointed to the box he was unpacking and chuckled through her tears. "You know we're out of here tonight. No need to unbox anything."

Richard shook his head. "I always unbox at 4:00, and I will until they drag me out of here."

Mia's heart ached. Never was there a more loyal friend. "Then I'll help you," she said. The two spent the next hour unboxing their most recent shipment of toys. They dusted, and vacuumed, and made sure everything was ship shape, as if the store would open the following morning. As the clock neared

5:00, the landline phone rang.

"Think it's the bank wanting to extend the loan?" Richard joked.

Mia picked it up. "Snow Valley Treasures."

A voice on the other end sounded confused. "Sorry. Maybe I have the wrong number. I'm calling from Beds n' Linens. Is there a Richard there?"

"Sure," Mia said, "one moment." Richard overheard the conversation and picked up the call, Mia listened for a few seconds.

"This is Richard."

"Hi, Richard. I'm calling in regard to the job application you sent in," the voice said. Mia smiled softly and hung the phone on the cradle. A few minutes later, Richard found her in the back office. He looked embarrassed. "I'm sorry I didn't tell you, Mia. I just…I was worried that if…"

Mia cut him off. "You have nothing to be sorry for." She smiled warmly. "I'm glad you're seeking other opportunities. How did it go?"

Richard was relieved. "Good. I have an interview on January second."

"That's great. Linens, huh?"

"I figured if I can sell toys, I can sell bedsheets."

"I guess that makes sense." They both laughed and continued sprucing up the store one final time.

CHAPTER 36

The smart glass was opaque. Nadine didn't want to be heard or seen. But perhaps by accident, her door was open a slight crack. A miscalculation by her assistant Caroline who now stood in front of Nadine's desk, giving a report. Noah approached the office and overheard the two talking.

"Excellent work with the contest, Caroline. I was just told that it's all over," Nadine said.

Caroline beamed. This was the first time in her year-and-a-half working for Nadine that she'd received any sort of praise. "That's right, Ma'am. And needless to say, the Snow Valley Treasures lady did not win."

Nadine nodded. "I heard that too. So, who did?"

"That's the best part. Nobody."

"What do you mean?"

"Well when you said we had to stop her from winning the contest, I was really stuck as to how. But then I ran into a guy from IT who was bragging about being the best hacker in the city…"

Nadine shifted uncomfortably in her seat.

Caroline continued, "I asked him if he thought he could hack the Daily Gazette app. He was like…" Caroline affected a lower voice to sound like a boy, '"Yeah I could do it, but I don't wanna get fired.' So, when I told him you wanted it done, he was all about it."

Outside the door, Noah bristled. It took every ounce of strength he had not to burst through the door, right then and there.

Nadine looked surprised and displeased. "You said I wanted it done?"

Caroline was still smiling. "Yeah, so anyway, he used some sort of firewall busting software or something and that let him become the administrator for the Gazette's app. I think they kicked us out now. They'll probably double their security."

Nadine stared at Caroline without saying a word. Caroline appeared nervous, but she pressed on. "So…uh…then once he hacked in, I told him to send out the message the last clue had been found. 'Cause I knew that way, the Snow Valley Treasures lady would stop looking. And the deadline for the payment would expire." Caroline finished her story looking pleased with herself. Nadine said nothing. After a few seconds of awkward silence, Caroline fished for more praise. "What do you think?" she said, smiling.

Finally, Nadine spoke. "What have you done, Caroline?"

The smile melted off her face. Noah leaned in closer. "About what?" she asked.

"I mean what were you thinking? You hacked the Daily Gazette? Do you have any idea how crazy that is?"

Caroline was bewildered. "But I thought…didn't you say to do whatever it takes?"

"Within the confines of the law!" Nadine shouted. "Distract her, lie to her, toilet paper her house. I certainly didn't say to commit, what I think might be a felony, on the company's behalf. And I definitely didn't want you telling some IT guy I condoned the hack myself!" Nadine was trembling with anger. Caroline was trembling with fright.

"I…I'm sorry."

"Do you realize how serious this is? We could go to jail over this. I have a little girl, Caroline. You know that? I don't need to go to jail. When I said do whatever it takes I didn't mean to involve yourself in a criminal enterprise."

Caroline burst into tears and began sobbing uncontrollably.

Nadine softened a bit. "Calm down. You didn't steal any money, did you?"

"What?"

"The hack. It didn't win the contest's money, did it?"

Caroline shook her head rapidly. "No. No. No. It was only a fake message," she said between sobs. "We didn't break into their bank account or use fake any identities or anything."

Nadine breathed a sigh of relief. "That's good. Let's just hope they figure it was kids messing around and don't investigate it further."

Noah had heard enough. He smashed his shoulder into the door and burst into the room. Both Caroline and Nadine jumped. They were caught off guard and both had guilty looks on their faces. "You cheated her!" Noah shouted. "You cheated her and you used me to do it."

Nadine regained some of her composure. "I don't remember you knocking."

"The door was open."

"What did you hear?"

"Enough."

Nadine pursed her lips. "This is business, Noah. Calm down."

"That's not business. That's fraud."

When he said the word, Nadine flinched and looked past him to see if anyone in the hallway was listening. There was no one else around. Nadine scowled. She didn't seem to appreciate being pushed around. "Careful, Noah. I'm still your boss. And it's not fraud. There was no money taken. Nothing stolen. Just kids being kids. All we did was delay the contest a bit. No harm, no foul. There was no benefit to the company."

"No benefit? What about cheating a person out of a hundred K, so we can swoop in and buy the property for cheap."

"You have no proof."

"I have my testimony," Noah seethed.

Nadine dug her heels in. "Are you threatening me?"

"Just letting you know I'm going to make this right."

"It's too late to intervene."

"We'll see about that." Noah spun himself toward the door to storm out. As he pulled it open he turned back and shouted. "Oh, and I quit!"

Noah jumped in his car and raced back to his condo. On the way, he dialed the bank and had a chat with the branch manager. He checked the clock, 4:07. "There's still time," he said to himself. As he drove he rehearsed and re-rehearsed the conversation with Nadine. He couldn't believe she'd stooped so low. He ran through all the pithy things he wished he would have thought to say at the time, and kicked himself for not coming up with them. Still, he'd jumped in and threatened his boss. It wasn't nothing. But it would mean nothing if he couldn't help Mia. Noah parked his car illegally right outside the building entrance. He bounded up the stairs three-by-three, and reached his condo in about 30 seconds. Frantically, he burst through his door and ran into his bedroom. There, sitting on the desk was his shiny, refurbished, typewriter. He snatched it and sprinted back to his car.

Kelly was wearing the same pair of coveralls along with the same smirk, when Noah burst through her door. "Well, well. You brought the Excelsior home, I see."

"Yes, I did. You wanted it, you got it. But I can't sell it for less than $25,000."

Kelly whistled. "No deal."

"C'mon. I looked it up. It's worth more than that at auction. It says $35,000 online."

Kelly looked at him as if he were a child who understood nothing. "That's best-case scenario, bub. You know how often an item gets best-case scenario at auction?"

"No."

"Well let's just say if that typewriter don't have some graffiti by Banksy underneath it, it ain't gettin' no 35 thousand. I told you we'll give you the ten. That offer's still on the table."

Noah paused considering it. It was too much of a bath. He knew he was being taken advantage of at that price. Plus, that amount wouldn't come close to covering the bridge collateral. "No. 20."

"Fifteen final offer. Take it or leave it."

Noah closed his mouth and flicked his tongue against his teeth. Of course, they'd meet in the middle at $15,000. It was basic negotiating. If he'd started at $25,000 they would have met at a more reasonable sum. But the clock was ticking and Noah had no other choice. He tried one last, desperate counter. "Please. I need this for a bridge collateral payment. I just quit my job. $17,000, or I walk out this door right now, and go to a different antique dealer." He put his hands on the typewriter as if he were ready to walk at the slightest hint of pushback.

"Walt!" Kelly cried. "Waaaalt. Get out here." Walt lumbered out from the back room, also dressed in his blue coveralls.

"What's this now?" he said.

"Do we want this Excelsior for $17,000?" Kelly asked him.

Noah watched him closely, and could have sworn he saw the corners of Walt's mouth turn up slightly. Walt walked over to the machine and feigned a close inspection of it. Never mind that he and Kelly had been the ones to fix it up only days earlier. "I suppose that'd be ok," came his eventual reply. Noah breathed a sigh of relief. They conducted the transaction and paid Noah in one hundred and seventy, crisp, hundred dollar bills. The stack was so thick, Noah was worried he'd look like a drug dealer. He took one last, long look at his Dad's typewriter and shook his head. "This is more important." When everything was signed over, he thanked them and dashed from the store. As soon as the door shut behind him, he heard what he thought was boisterous laughter.

CHAPTER 37

Mia and Richard stood side-by-side as she prepared to flip the "open" sign to "closed" for the very last time. The gift shop was sparkling clean, with everything in its proper place. It looked more like it was ready for a huge sale on Black Friday, than a shop being shuttered. Earlier when they had been cleaning the place, a few last-minute shoppers had stopped in. One had never been there before and remarked how beautiful it was. She'd asked if they were going to be open on Christmas Eve, and Mia and Richard shared a pained glance. They told her no, and didn't bother explaining why. The customer replied she thought it was nice they were taking off time for the holidays. "Little does she know how much time we're taking off," Mia had thought.

The flipped the sign together. A tear dropped down Mia's cheek. "I can't believe that's the last time we'll ever do that," she said. She smiled sweetly and looked at Richard. "But we had a good run, didn't we?"

"That we did." Mia flicked out the lights and place went dark. Richard held out his arm. "Shall we?"

"Let's do it." Richard grabbed the door handle and the familiar chime of the bells hit their ears one more time. Mia took his arm. But just as she did so, she was startled by the phone ringing. Instinctively, Mia glanced at her watch 5:07.

Richard looked at the ringing phone and called out, playfully, "We're closed! Permanently. Call back, never." He laughed.

Mia moved back into the store towards the phone. "What do you think," she said to him. "One more call, for old time's sake?" She picked up the receiver.

"Hi, Mia. I'm glad I caught you."

"Who is this?"

"This is the branch manager. From the bank. We spoke yesterday."

Mia flinched. She'd forgotten to call the manager and he'd probably been sitting around waiting for her. "I'm so sorry. I should have called. I'm not going to be able to get the money by tonight. But thank you so much for being willing to standby. Go enjoy your Christmas."

"It was my pleasure, but that's not why I'm calling."

Mia arched her eyebrows. "I'm listening."

"I just wanted to confirm with you that your bridge collateral was successfully processed. The balance is no longer due until January 1st."

Mia's heart pounded. "What are you talking about?"

"Your balloon payment. The collateral has been taken care of. You now have until January 1st."

"There must be some mistake. I didn't pay any…"

The branch manager cut her off. "There is no mistake, Ma'am. The amount has been covered and it was made explicitly for your account. I handled the transaction myself."

Mia was stammering. "You're telling me someone paid you $25,000 on my behalf? Who?"

"That's right, Ma'am. And I'm not at liberty to disclose that kind of information over the phone. My apologies."

Mia's head was spinning. "I don't know what to say."

"I do. Merry Christmas." He paused. "Will there be anything else this evening?"

"I…no. Merry Christmas to you, too."

The branch manager disconnected the call, and Mia stared ahead, shell-shocked. Richard looked concerned. "What is it?

Everything ok?" Mia said nothing. "Mia!"

She snapped out of it. "That was the branch manager from the bank. He said someone paid the bridge collateral."

"Are you kidding? Who?"

"I don't know. He wouldn't say."

"You don't think it was No—"

Mia cut him off. She'd had the same thought, but wouldn't permit herself to go there. "No, I don't know."

"What does this mean?"

Mia grinned. Suddenly she stood up and marched over to the door. She flipped the "closed" sign back over to "open." "It means, we're not done yet!"

Richard whooped. "Yeah!" He paused, then continued. "There is just one, teensy, tiny hiccup though."

"What's that?"

"Where are we gonna find $75,000 in seven days?"

"Don't bother me with the details. I don't know how, but we're gonna do it. Like we always have."

At that moment Mia's cell phone buzzed wildly. Several messages came through, one after another. She glanced at the screen, they were from the Daily Gazette. Mia clicked the first one open. "Our deepest apologies," it said, "on our security breach earlier today. To be clear, no one's personal information was compromised. The breach has been closed and we are working with IT to ensure such an aberration never occurs again."

"What is that?" Richard asked.

"Looks like the Gazette got hacked." Mia clicked open the second message. "This message is to alert you that you are still in the running for the Daily Gazette's grand prize of $100,000. As a result of the security breach earlier today our system incorrectly informed our readers a winner had been found. THERE HAS NOT YET BEEN A WINNER DECLARED." Mia read the words and shook. She almost dropped her phone. The message continued. "The final day of the contest will now officially commence tomorrow (12/24). NOTE: the secret location will not be the same as today's, nor will the puzzles.

Best of luck!" Mia trembled and looked like she'd seen a ghost.

Richard looked over, concerned. "Everything ok?"

"I swear my heart's gonna give out over these ups and downs."

"What is it?" Richard insisted.

Mia burst into laughter and turned to Richard. "There was no winner today. It was a fake, a hack. They're doing the final day tomorrow. We're back, baby!"

The good news was tempered a bit when the Lemon Lime refused to start. Mia tried everything she could, even popping the hood and jiggling wires and cables, but the car wouldn't budge. She glanced at her watch. No mechanic's shops would still be open, so she decided to leave her car at work and walk home. The fresh air would do her good, and she needed to think. It had been a weird, 48 hours. Only an hour earlier she had gone through the emotional hemorrhage of shutting down her shop for the last time, and now, suddenly, it was reopened. The day had been a see-saw and Mia was woozy. She strode past the diner where she'd met Edith, and smiled. It seemed like months ago now. Next, she passed The Bagel House where the majority of her Twelve Games work had been completed. She thought about Noah and all the fun they'd had there together, her heart ached a bit. The weather was temperate, so she skipped the turn for her block and continued walking. The exercise felt good, and she wandered aimlessly.

An hour or so later, the temperature dropped. Mia was far from home, and didn't feel like walking all the way back. She pulled out her phone to order a Rydeshare and her phone went black. Dead battery. Mia spun in a circle looking for a payphone. "Do they even exist anymore?" she wondered. There were none in sight. She was in a mostly-residential area – a place she recognized but was not completely familiar with. Across the street, Kelly's Antiques still had its lights on. Mia crossed the street and climbed the steps to the front door. A sign out front said "closed" and indicated Mia was way past the store's opening hours. But there was a warm glow from inside. Mia peered through the glass and saw a woman's pony tail poking out from around the corner. She rapped lightly on the glass. The woman leaned around the corner, noticed Mia, and shook her head. It was the owner, Kelly.

"We're closed," she mouthed, and turned back to whatever she'd been doing. Mia knocked harder. Kelly looked annoyed, but came to the door. "What is it?" she demanded.

"I'm sorry," Mia said. "My phone battery died and I need to call a cab. Can I use yours please?"

Kelly suspiciously eyed Mia up and down as if she might rob her. At last she said, "Go ahead. Phone's right over here." Kelly led Mia to the counter and pulled an old rotary phone out from under the desk.

"This phone is fantastic," Mia said, admiringly. She dialed the number of a cab company and told them her location. "20 minutes they said," she told Kelly after she'd hung up the phone. "Thank you very much." Mia moved toward the door to wait outside, but Kelly took pity on her.

"You can wait in here if you want. Where it's warm."

"I'm in your debt again. Thank you."

"It's Christmas, after all. C'mon." Kelly beckoned Mia to follow her to the back room. There, Walt sat over a plate of cookies and a glass of wine. When he saw Mia, he stood.

"You didn't tell me we was gon' have guests, Kel," he said. "I'm Walt." He reached his hand out and Mia shook it.

"She's just waitin' on a cab."

"Welcome. Help yourself to any wine or cookies you want."

Mia smiled. "Thank you both for your generosity." She poured herself a small glass of red, and picked a wreath-shaped sugar cookie. The cookies and wine were an odd pairing, but then again, nothing about Mia's life had been normal lately, and she had to admit, it tasted pretty good. Mia chatted with Kelly and Walt and browsed some of the antiques they had for sale: a grandfather clock, a globe that opened to reveal a wet bar, a violin. Then she noticed a shiny, black typewriter. "This is a beautiful piece," Mia commented.

Kelly chuckled. "Iddn't it? We just got it in this afternoon. Excelsior. That's what they call 'em."

Mia's interest was piqued. "How did you get it?"

"Like I say, we just got it this afternoon. Some young guy came runnin' in all in a panic and sold it to us."

Walt grinned and piped in, "Yeah at a third of what it's worth, too."

"Poor guy didn't know what hit him," Kelly continued. "But he was desperate for the cash so we made the deal. That's how it happens with a lot of this stuff. Especially around the holidays."

Mia nodded, but her wheels were spinning. "Did he say why he needed the money?"

"Prolly' just to buy Christmas presents," Walt offered.

"No, no. He said somethin'." Kelly corrected Walt. "He said it was for a bridge or somethin'. I don't really know. I wasn't listenin' that close on account-a I was tryin' to wheel and deal."

"That's how it is in this business." Walt added. "Ya' gotta have a thick skin 'cuz everybody comes in with one sob story or another, and ya' never know who's tryin' to pull the wool over your eyes."

Mia could feel her pulse quicken. "Did he say it was for a bridge collateral, by chance?"

Kelly slapped her hand on the desk. "That's it! Bridge collateral payment. How'd you know that?"

"Did he say anything else?" Mia implored.

Kelly was a bit confused by Mia's sudden interest in one customer, but she tried to answer. "I don't know. Yeah. He said he just quit his job and he needed the money for a bridge whatchamacallit. I didn't ask anything else."

"Had you ever seen him before?" Mia asked.

"Yep. That was the strange thing. He had us fix it up for him a few days before he sold it." Kelly shrugged. "I don't know. People do weird things. What can ya' do?"

Mia felt like the wind had been knocked out of her. The Excelsior was Noah's most prized possession. He was going to use it to become a writer, and instead he'd pawned it to two people who cared little about it and toasted to taking advantage of his desperation. "Thanks for your hospitality," Mia said. "I'm going to wait outside. I don't want to miss my cab." She put her drink down and walked away.

"See?" Kelly said to Walt, "weird things."

Outside, Mia felt like crying for multiple reasons. On the one hand, she wanted to cry tears of sadness for Noah's loss. The thing he loved the most was now stashed on a shelf in some dusty antique store, with people who were ambivalent about its sentimentality. On the other hand, she wanted to cry tears of gratitude. Noah had done something so selfless for Mia, she couldn't believe it. He'd sacrificed not only money – and it was a lot of money – and not only his favorite possession, but his very dream of writing on his dad's typewriter, for her. Finally, she wanted to cry tears of happiness. Happiness that Noah must have had real feelings for her; happiness in her recognition she loved him back; happiness in knowing his intentions had been pure and that she wasn't being used by him.

And what was this about him quitting his job? She needed to talk to him, to get to the bottom of it. To tell him how she felt. Mia pulled her cell phone out of her pocket to call Noah, and remembered the phone was dead. "Stupid battery," she muttered, and paced back and forth waiting for the cab. Finally, it arrived and climbed aboard to head home. The cab ride was one of the longest of her life – at least it felt that way. She couldn't wait to get to her condo and go right to Noah's door to straighten things out. At home, she paid her fare and ran inside. Mia tapped the elevator button repeatedly, but it was too slow. She'd take the stairs.

At the same moment, directly above her, Noah was holding the elevator door open for Dorothy, who was a bit slow getting on. Dorothy was heading out to pick up some late Christmas gifts, and Noah had some business to attend to.

Just as the elevator doors finished closing, Mia burst through the stairwell door onto her floor. The hallway was empty, and quiet. Mia dashed to Noah's door and knocked. No answer. She knocked again, louder. Nothing. Mia's heart sank, but then she thought of her phone. She could plug it in and call him. The agony of waiting for her phone to power up was almost unbearable. Mia sat near her counter where her phone was charging, for three lifetimes. Finally, the icon glowed brightly and the phone sprang to life. Mia wasted no time. She dialed Noah's number, but the call went straight to voicemail. She tried again. Same result. "Why is his phone off?" she wondered. She tried firing off a text, "Hi, we need to talk. Please call me," it read. But it bounced back as undelivered. Mia bowed her forehead onto her fridge in frustration. What else could she do? As she stood back up, one of the sticky notes on her fridge stuck in her hair. "That's it," she thought. She grabbed a pad of yellow sticky notes and jotted a quick sentence, "Noah, I'd love to talk to you. Please call me when you get this. –M." She ran down her hallway and stuck the note to the center of Noah's door, but not before knocking one more time, just to check. Satisfied she'd done everything she could, she turned her phone volume all the way up, set all three alarms, and went to bed.

CHAPTER 38

Noah bid goodbye to Dorothy after exiting the elevator. Outside, a cab was sitting by the curb. The cabbie was messing with the meter. "That's good luck," Noah thought. "There are never cabs out here." He jogged outside and put his hand up. The cabbie rolled down the window. "You on duty?" Noah asked.

"Hop in."

"Glad you're here. I'm in a hurry."

"Just dropped someone off here that was in a hurry too. I guess it's always rush-rush around the holidays." The cabbie opined.

"Guess so." Noah told the driver his destination and cab pulled away. When they arrived, Noah paid the fare and moved to climb out.

The cabbie turned back to him. "You sure this is it? Place looks closed down."

"Yeah this is the place. The Daily Gazette. Thanks again." Noah left a healthy tip and the cab was on its way. Inside, Noah found himself in a large, darkly lit office. He crossed the room and shook hands with Mr. DuPonte, the paper's owner. "Thanks for meeting me so late." Noah said.

"Happy to. Sorry things didn't work out at Jungle. I was

excited to have you around for a while."

"I know. Me too."

The words hung in the air. Mr. DuPonte smiled and spread his arms. "You said you needed help. What can I do?"

Noah pulled a folded piece of paper out of his pocket and handed it across the desk. He checked his watch. "I know you're almost at the deadline, but I wrote something I'd like you to print. If that's all right."

Mr. DuPonte grabbed the paper and opened it cautiously. His forehead creased. "Is this true?"

"Every word."

Mr. DuPonte nodded, his look softened. "Good. I trust you. I'll get this off to the team right away."

"Thanks."

"I'm glad to see you're writing again. Your mom will be happy." Mr. DuPonte grabbed two glasses and a bottle of something brown. He poured Noah a drink. They clinked glasses.

"Yeah, I guess."

Mr. DuPonte paused and savored a slow sip from his drink. "So where're you off to?"

"New York. My plane leaves tomorrow night."

"New York's nice," Mr. DuPonte mused. "Just make sure you're running towards what you want and not away from it."

Noah nodded and finished his drink. "Will do."

Mr. DuPonte extended his hand. Noah grasped it and pulled him in for a hug. "Thanks, Grandpa. Merry Christmas."

CHAPTER 39

BANG! BANG! BANG! Mia jumped, delirious. It was still dark outside. BANG! She checked her clocks, 5:30 A.M. "What in the world is happening?" she thought, panicked. It took her a second to get her bearings and process what was happening. BANG! It was her door. At first, she thought it might be Noah, but quickly dismissed the idea. Why would he pound on her door so early? Then, adrenaline hit her. "It must be an emergency," she thought. It was the only explanation. Mia jumped from bed, threw on a robe, and raced to the door. Without checking the peep hole, she yanked it open. There, also in a bathrobe, stood Dorothy with a newspaper, two coffees, and a grin from ear-to-ear.

"Is everything ok?" Mia asked.

Dorothy let out a hearty laugh. "Merry Christmas neighbor," she said, way too boisterously for that time of the morning. "Now you know how it feels to have someone bang on your door and roust you from bed."

Mia was still trying to piece together what was happening. "What...I..." Dorothy handed her the paper. "What's happening?"

"Sounds like you need this." She shoved one of the coffees into Mia's hand. "You still in the contest or not?"

"I am."

"Good, then my efforts weren't wasted. I want you to bright eyed, and bushy tailed. So, turn that brain on."

"I don't know what to say."

"Start with thank you, and then say you'll win that contest."

"Thank you," Mia laughed. "But wait," she held up her to-go coffee, "I thought you didn't like to go to these places. Identity theft."

"I thought about that. But then I figured, what the heck. You've been scratching other people's backs for so long, it's time you let someone else scratch yours."

Mia wrapped Dorothy in a warm hug and thanked her again. "This means a lot."

"Yeah, yeah, yeah," Dorothy smiled. "I gotta go check on the cat. You go out there and win this thing now. I'll be watching." She crossed the hall and disappeared inside her condo.

Mia was off to the races. She showered in seconds – the way people do when the hot water runs out – and dressed even quicker. The day was dawning. Outside, the sun reflected brilliantly off the newly-fallen snow and filled the room with warm light. BANG! BANG! BANG! Mia jumped again. More pounding on her door. "Dorothy!" she chuckled, and jogged to her door. "Hang on." For the second time that day, she was surprised. She swung the door open and found Richard standing on her mat with a familiar woman.

"Good. You're ready." He was all business. Richard was holding a granola bar, a fruit plate, a yogurt, and a cheese Danish. He handed the food to Mia. "Eat up. You'll need the energy. There's no time to cook today."

Mia raised her eyebrows and subtly nodded toward his guest.

"Sorry," he said. "You remember Harmony?"

Mia looked at the woman and her memory clicked into place. Harmony was the mother of the little girl who'd donated her two dollars to the Children's Hospital – Mia had given her the CityBot engineering toy. "Yes. Hi Harmony. I'm Mia," she said warmly, extending her hand.

Harmony shook it vigorously. "Hi. I want to thank you for what you did. My girl Tess, she loves that Robot thing. Carries it with her everywhere."

"I'm happy to hear that." Mia surreptitiously shot a "what's-going-on?" look at Richard.

He interjected. "Mia, I noticed your car was left in the lot last night. Harmony offered to chauffer you around town today – while you solve the puzzle."

Mia was nonplussed. "That's so nice of you!" She set the tray of food on her counter and told Harmony to help herself. "Excuse me for a minute," she said, and pinched Richard on his side to get his attention. Richard excused himself, and followed Mia. When they were out of earshot, Mia whispered, exasperatedly, "What is going on right now, Rich?"

"What? We're just here to help."

"I can see that. Why? How?" Richard was smirking. "What did you do?" she asked.

"It wasn't me. Have you seen the paper?"

"I have it. I haven't read it yet. Why?"

Richard went back into the kitchen and grabbed Mia's paper. He plopped it down in front of her. "I think you'd better take a look at this. This is why she's here."

Mia looked at the paper and didn't see anything out of the ordinary. "Rich, what…" Then it caught her eye. There on the bottom, right of the front page, was a picture of Snow Valley Treasures. Mia's blood ran cold. "Why is the store in the paper?"

"I'll leave you alone a minute." Rich said, and joined Harmony in the other room. Mia picked up the paper to begin reading.

****

Got Same-day Delivery? You Have Me to Thank. Your Business Belly Up? That's My Fault, Too

In our frenetic, fast-paced society, convenience is a valuable commodity, but it may come at too high a price. During the pandemic, we all relied on contactless delivery, and more-convenient shopping experiences to stay safe – to stay away from people. Now that the threat has abated, however, our habits have become entrenched, and we still remain distant. Our relationships suffer, as do our local small businesses.

I worked for a giant online retailer for ten years. I helped feed it as its appetite grew. It devoured business-after-business, growing bigger and more powerful by the day. As an executive in charge of corporate acquisitions, I found targets for the hostile acquisitions and cleared the paths so the smaller businesses were unable to resist. My team and I stooped to any low to provide fodder for the giant – we misled business owners; applied pressure to their banks and lenders; absorbed their inventory suppliers; and even engaged in corporate espionage. And we did it all under the guise of "helping" the businesses. We offered them deals, and told them we were on their side. We weren't. We hurt businesses, and more importantly, we hurt people. It is the regret of my life.

Snow Valley Treasures is one such victim. But SVT is unique. It's still fighting the giant – it has refused to be eaten. SVT has served this community for over ten years, striving to create one-of-a-kind shopping experiences for one-of-a-kind gifts. It is beloved. Nevertheless, the giant's jaws are still unhinged, trying desperately to subject it to its insatiable ravenousness. Something must be done.

If the giant cannot be stopped, the potential victims must be protected. We need to arm the victims, not with sword and shield, but with positive exposure and patronage. Today is Christmas Eve, one of our own – Snow Valley Treasures – is in the fight of its life. Let us come together to spread the word, shop local, and fight alongside SVT and other local businesses to slay the giant.

****

Mia's heart was pounding, the chills washed over her and goosebumps popped out. She frantically scanned the article for the author's name: Anonymous. Mia sprang out of her seat and rushed into the living room. She hardly noticed Richard and Harmony as she passed. She yanked her front door open and ran down the hallway. It was her turn to pound on a door. BANG! BANG! BANG! She stopped and listened closely.

There was no movement inside. Next, she pulled out her phone and pressed Noah's name – straight to voicemail. Finally, she tapped out another text: "I saw the article. Was that you? Did you write it? Please call me."

Down the hallway, Richard's head poked out of her door. Mia had been so absorbed in Noah and the article, she'd nearly forgotten about the contest. Richard stepped out and walked toward her. "What d'ya think?"

"I don't know what to say."

Richard grinned. "I know. I was floored too. The Gazette posted the article online last night. Harmony saw it and sent a message to our social media page asking to help. She wasn't the only one. You should see how many people are asking to help. It was like It's a Wonderful Life."

Mia bit her bottom lip, gratitude welling. Richard worried he'd gone too far. "I asked her to come along. Is that ok? I can tell her you don't need the help."

She hugged him. "It is a wonderful life, with friends like you. No. I'd be happy to have the help. Now let's get some food and get going."

They smiled at Harmony as they reentered the condo, and the three of them devoured the tray of food. On the way to Harmony's car Mia paused again in front of Noah's door. The sticky note she'd left the night before was still there, and appeared to be untouched. Mia's heart ached, but she didn't have time to dwell on her feelings now.

In the parking garage, Richard hugged Mia and bid her goodbye and good luck. He was headed to open the store for the last shopping day of the season. Mia climbed in shotgun. "Where to?" asked her new chauffer.

"The Bagel House," Mia said proudly. "That place is lucky."

The Bagel House line stretched out the door. It was the busiest Mia had ever seen it. Harmony opted to wait in the car – she had some business she was going to do on her phone – while Mia completed the puzzle. They exchanged numbers so Mia could call her when she was ready. The puzzle hadn't gone live yet, so Mia had some time. Despite already feeling jittery, she wanted more coffee, and joined the back of the line. From a distance, the store manager caught eyes with her and came running over. "My regular!" he said, excitedly. "You never told me were the Snow Valley Treasures lady. I saw the article on my social media feed. My kids love that place."

"I didn't know you'd been there."

"You don't wait in this line," he said. "Follow me." The manager ushered Mia past the line into the warmth of the shop. Mia glanced around quickly, every table was full and every seat taken. Every one, that is, except her regular booth. It had yellow caution tape stretched across it and a large "Reserved" sign sitting on top of the table. The manager led her over to the booth. He tore down the caution tape and removed the sign. "Your chariot awaits."

"You saved this for me?" Mia asked, genuinely moved. She plopped herself down in the familiar, comfy seat.

The manager crouched down to her level and lowered his voice. "What you and your friend did for me was way more than I could do for you. I will always be grateful to you for that. Speaking of which, will he be joining us this morning?"

For the second time that morning, Mia felt an ache in her heart. "I don't think so."

"That's too bad," the store manager said. "I was beginning to like those coffee creamer towers." Mia laughed. "What can I get you?"

"I'll take a tall coffee and a plain bagel with cream cheese, please." Mia pulled out her purse and rifled through it for her wallet.

The manager put up his hand and shook his head. "Your money is no good here. One tall coffee and bagel coming up." He turned and headed to the kitchen. Mia smiled, pulled out her cell phone, and opened the Daily Gazette app one more time.

CHAPTER 40

Edith stood in her living room examining things. Everything looked in order, but only a close inspection would be enough. After a minute, she walked to the coffee table and adjusted a book called "Bridges of the World," that was a little crooked. "There," she said, "ready." A moment later her doorbell rang. Nadine and her daughter, Renee, shivered on the doorstep. Edith opened it with a grin. "Merry Christmas Eve," she sang out. Nadine was typing rapidly into her phone, scowling. She looked like she was in a foul mood. Edith couldn't be sure, but it looked like Nadine's eyes were puffy, as if she'd been crying.

Renee jumped into her grandma's arms. "Do I get a present now, Grandma?" she asked.

"Not 'til tomorrow. But it's getting close. Go over by the tree and count how many boxes are wrapped up." Renee was off like a shot and slid down on her knees to count. The tree was fake, but it was beautiful. All white lights, with only red ornaments. Still, Edith looked at it and couldn't help but feel some regret. It was a tree for grown-ups: no whimsical ornaments, no Santa, no tinsel. She felt sad she hadn't had time to get the old family ornaments from storage. But then again, she didn't know she'd be spending Christmas with these two until a few days ago.

Nadine finally looked up from her phone. "What are you two going to do today?"

Edith was confused. "Won't you be joining us?"

"Maybe tonight. Something came up."

"On Christmas Eve? But you already worked through your work's Christmas party."

Nadine looked annoyed. "You don't think I know that? I said, something came up!"

Edith was worried she had pushed too far. She had to tread lightly. "That's ok. We'll have lots of fun when you get back." Then an idea struck her. "Renee, how would you like to help me get the old tree out of the attic? It has all your mom's old Christmas ornaments. The ones she made at school when she was your age." Edith looked at Nadine who was frowning. "If, that's ok with your Mom."

"Please Mom?" Renee pleaded. "Can I? Please?"

"The attic stairs are dangerous," Nadine said. "Make sure you stay close to Grandma and hold on tight to the handrail when you go up and down."

Edith nodded solemnly. "Your Mom took quite a spill down those steps when she was a little girl. She's right. You have to be very careful."

Renee jumped and giggled. "I will! Can we go up there now? Please, please, please, please, pretty please?"

"Once I leave, you can go up there with Grandma."

"Noooooooo. I want you to come too, mom! It's your tree. Please. You're always working. Just stay for a little bit. Then you can go."

Nadine checked her watch, and she checked her phone. Finally, she let out a long sigh. "I'll go up there for a little bit." The three generations of women all climbed the stairs to the second floor. From there, the attic could be accessed by a pull-down trap door that was built into the ceiling. The string was too high for Edith to reach so Nadine did the honors. The trap door swung down with a screech and the stairs slid into place. Renee's eyes were filled with wonder and excitement. She had never seen anything like it. "Who knew an attic could be so fun?

I should start charging the neighborhood kids to come see this," Edith joked.

Nadine had been right. The stairs were borderline treacherous. Little slats of wood about ¾ of an inch thick and two inches wide. Each step felt like it was going to snap. Nadine held her breath as her mom climbed up in front of her. The steps were bowing and she was sure one would break and her mom would come tumbling down. But nothing happened. Edith made it safely to the top. Then it was Renee's turn. She hopped up the slats as easily as a bunny on a hillside. "These are cool stairs," she said. "I wish all the stairs in your house were like this, grandma."

Edith laughed. "That makes one of us." Finally, Nadine clambered up the stairs, also without incident. The smell of the attic was at once familiar and foreign. Nadine was brought instantly back to her childhood. The smell was intoxicating and powerful. It was like time travel. She hadn't been to the attic, probably since she was 16 or 17 years old. Yet, as a little girl she had spent so much time here. She remembered playing dress-up with her father using old clothes that were stored in trunks. She and her mom had played pirate ship and had navigated the attic looking for buried treasure. Countless games of hide-and-seek had ended up there too. When she was older, and wanted to be alone, she would go into the attic to think. Sometimes she had stretched her phone, cord and all, all the way up there to talk to her friends about boys. Nadine paused at the top of the stairs and drank in the memories. It was all so familiar, but it felt like a lifetime ago. The emotional weight of her childhood rested heavily on her heart.

Across the attic, Renee was already digging through boxes looking for one marked "ornaments." "Found it," she shouted, triumphantly. Seconds later the lid was off and she was elbow-deep in the contents.

"Slow down, sweetheart," Edith said. "A lot of those are fragile."

"I wanna see my mom's stuff," Renee grinned, undeterred.

Nadine and Edith found seats on old, sturdy trunks and

gathered around the box. "Let me show you," Edith said. She reached into the box and produced a small, transparent, ornament. Inside was a hospital bracelet and a tiny knit cap. "This is what your Mommy wore at the hospital the day she was born," Edith explained. "Look how small that little hat is. Isn't it cute?"

"Why did you wear a hat at the hospital, mommy?"

Nadine smiled. "They put hats on babies to help keep them warm. Babies like to be nice and warm when they're first born."

"Can I hang this one up?" Renee asked.

"Of course."

Next, Edith pulled a small, hard wreath-shaped ornament out of the box. When Nadine saw it, she laughed. Edith snuck a surreptitious look at Nadine, pleased to see she was having fun. "What's funny about this one?" Edith asked.

"I never told you this story?"

"Not that I remember."

"Listen Ren," Nadine said. "You're gonna like this too. I made this ornament for Grandma when I was in second grade. And the day we were making them I had a stomach bug, but I didn't want to go home and miss out on making it. I didn't tell anyone and stayed in my seat."

Renee giggled. "Then what?"

"I got sick and threw up a little bit on the ornament."

Renee covered her mouth and laughed. "Ewww!"

"I know, gross. I was so sad. My ornament was wrecked. And I had worked so hard on it."

"What did you do?"

"I took it into the hand dryer in the bathroom, dried it off as best I could, and then painted over it."

Renee belly laughed. Edith did too. "Is this true?"

"Yes, it is."

"C'mon."

"I promise."

"Eww!" Renee said again. "And you never knew, Grandma?"

Edith was still chuckling. "I most certainly did not!" The three of them continued laughing. Edith proceeded to pull many more ornaments out of the box, each with a special or funny story. Nadine, who had said she had to rush off to work, ended up staying in the attic for hours with her mom and daughter. Finally, it was nap time. They carried the box downstairs and tucked Renee into one of the guest beds. Nadine got ready to leave. As she was gathering her things, she was feeling introspective and nostalgic. She looked at her mother. "Thanks for watching her. I'll be back this evening."

"There's nothing I'd rather do in this world."

Nadine smiled. It was nice to have her mother back, rather than some random babysitter. "Thanks Mom." Nadine paused for a second, chewing on her words. Then said, "I'm glad you called me the other day."

"I am too."

"Out of curiosity, what made you do it? I thought about calling you from time-to-time, but the longer I was away, the less I thought I could."

"It's not what made me, but who."

"Someone told you to call?"

"Yes. My guardian angel."

"Who is it? Do I know her?" Nadine asked.

"I'm not sure. I think you might though. Her name is Mia. She owns that cute little gift shop near here. Snow Valley Treasures."

Nadine lost the color in her face. She felt dizzy.

"Is everything ok?" Edith asked, concerned.

Nadine felt weak in the knees. "I'm sorry, Mom. I gotta run. I'll see you later tonight." She pushed her way out the door. Edith looked on, confused.

CHAPTER 41

The Gazette app sprang to life and music poured from the phone speakers: "On the 13th Game of Christmas, my Daily sent to me: 13 words to search for; 12 to unscramble; 11 rebus puzzles; 10 spot the difference; 9 hidden pictures; 8 stacked-row-challenge; 7 mixed-up riddles; 6 letter mazes – 5 logic games – 4 puzzle blocks; 3 Guess When's; 2 Sudoku; and a crossword to win the whole thing." Mia reread the words. "Wow," she said out loud. "They threw in the whole kitchen sink."

Doing 13 puzzles in one day sounded impossible. Especially considering every other day there had only been one. But on closer inspection, Mia discovered the puzzles were truncated. The word search, for example, only had 13 words to find, as opposed to the 30 from the previous puzzle. More importantly, the search box itself was considerably smaller – hundreds of letters as opposed to tens of thousands – so it was much more manageable. Mia found the first two words within seconds, and only 15 minutes later she crossed "13 words to search for" off her list. The 12 scrambled words were easy, too. All Christmas themed, and all very straightforward – YADCN NECA – can only stump someone for so long. By 7:30 Mia was moving on to 11 Rebus puzzles. She loved rebus puzzles and had never seen them in the Twelve Games before. She scrolled to the first one: it had the word "ROADS" written both vertically and horizontally, and they intersected in the middle. "Crossroads," she said, and typed in the answer. The second was a picture of the word "UP" resting on the roof of a house. Mia didn't hesitate. "Up on the Housetop." She tapped in the words.

The puzzles were almost too easy and Mia was flying through them. She thought about her competitors. Somewhere in Snow Valley, three other people were crouched over their phones, sweating away, as nervous as she was now. The thought made her uneasy. The other three competitors were easily as good as her. She knew the challenge was essentially a coin flip.

Mia solved another simple rebus – a cartoon knight covered in holes – and filled in the answer. Her phone buzzed. It was Richard. A cacophony of noise poured out from Richard's end of the phone. "Rich?" Mia shouted. "It sounds loud. Are you there?"

"Sorry to interrupt, but you need to hear this. It's pandemonium!"

"Where are you?"

"Where do you think? Snow Valley Treasures. People are lined up, Mia! The line goes down the block. This is insane!"

Mia laughed out loud. "Is Jadyn there to help?"

"Are you kidding? The guy's been working his tail off!"

Mia laughed out loud even as her stomach flip-flopped. She almost couldn't stand to be hit with any more emotional news today, good or bad. "That's amazing."

"I know. Now it's up to you. The whole city's behind you, Mia, but you gotta go save this thing." Mia nodded solemnly. Richard was right. The rush of new business was welcome, and would certainly help, but even a few banner days would not be enough to save the store. It was up to her now. Mia thanked Richard, and disconnected.

After working at the puzzle for a couple hours straight, she needed to take a five-minute break. Mia had finished the word search, the unscramble, the rebus puzzles, spot the difference, and the hidden pictures. She needed to stretch her legs, so she went outside for some air. Her phone showed no missed calls. Mia tapped Noah's contact – straight to voicemail again. "What is happening," she wondered. "I hope he's ok." It was weird, in that day an age to have a cell phone turned off for 24 hours. Weirder still was the fact that Noah had not touched the note Mia had left. Even if he'd seen it and wanted to ignore it, she had to think he would've taken it off the door. But she was getting side-tracked again. Right now, the puzzle was the most important thing. She ducked back inside and went back to work.

About an hour later Mia's phone buzzed again. A tick of adrenaline. Maybe it was Noah. She picked it up. "Hello?"

"Hi, Mia. This is Harmony, your driver."

"Is everything ok?"

"Everything's fine. But…" Her voice trailed off as if she had something to say, but was too afraid to say it. "The thing is, I've been out of work for a while, and I have sent off a bunch of resumés. A company just called me and asked if I could do an interview today."

Mia was happy for her. "That's so great."

"But I don't want to leave you high and dry, so I told them I'd get back to them."

Mia didn't hesitate for a second. "You call them back right now and tell them you'll be there as soon as possible. You have already been a ton of help today. I'll be fine. I'll figure out the car thing."

Harmony sounded relieved. "Are you sure?"

"Of course, I'm sure."

Harmony thanked her and disconnected the call. Mia smiled and buried her nose back in the puzzle. She was making headway, and as long as things were correct, she was making good time. Mia placed a quick call to Richard and let him know she would be car-less for the rest of the day. "Ok," he said. "Let me work on it and I'll get back to you."

A few more hours ticked by and Mia was nearing completion of the games. She checked her watch, it was noon now. The stress was piling on. One of the other four competitors may have already completed everything. It struck Mia that the competition was particularly difficult because the competitors never knew where they stood. In other competitions – like sports – the teams know the score and the time. But Mia had to fly blind until she reached the location and got the good (or bad) news via push notifications. To add to the stress, in previous days, she only had to finish in one of the top three positions to receive a point. But today, she had to be first, and that meant she had to be perfect.

It was 1:02, when Mia set her phone down. "Done." she said. Her palms we're sweaty, and her back ached. But she was done. Every puzzle complete, every box filled in. A wave of relief washed over her, but there was still the matter of unscrambling the letters: ARTEDSEAPHOER. Thirteen days, thirteen puzzles, thirteen letters in the secret location. "Why'd it have to be lucky 13?" Mia thought. It was incredibly difficult to unscramble. Mia tried several different permutations, none of which made sense. "This could be anything," she thought, her desperation rising. She stared at the letters for a few minutes more, but her head was spinning, she was getting nowhere. "Maybe a change of scenery," she thought, but remembered she didn't have her car. She made the decision to try to solve the puzzle as she walked back Lemon Lime which was still parked at work from the night before. If it didn't start up, she could borrow Richard's. Mia pulled out a twenty-dollar bill, scribbled "Thank you, and Merry Christmas," onto a note, left them on the table, and rushed out.

CHAPTER 42

It was a brisk day and the bright sun had been replaced by snow clouds. Mia clutched her jacket close to prevent the breeze from going through her button holes. Despite the cold, there were a lot of people on the street: last-minute shoppers, people headed to parties, even some Victorian-era-dressed carolers singing "God Rest Ye Merry Gentlemen." Mia felt like she was in a Christmas movie. She trudged past them smiling, but was tied in knots. She'd gotten nowhere unscrambling the puzzle. If anything, thanks to all the new distractions, it was now more difficult. She considered doubling back to the warmth of The Bagel House, but at that moment, a sleek, black, late-model SUV pulled up alongside her. The passenger window rolled down the driver leaned over and called out to her. "Mia!"

Mia was startled. She didn't recognize the car. She squinted, and ventured closer, peering into the open window. It was Nadine. Mia's temper ignited. "Why is she haunting me?" Mia thought. Without a word, she backed away from the car and continued quickly down the street. The SUV followed and pulled alongside her again.

"Mia, wait," came Nadine's voice from inside.

Mia stopped and turned toward the car. "I can't do this right now. I'm in a hurry." She continued moving down the block and yelled over her shoulder. "It's Christmas. Don't you ever take a break?"

Again, Nadine pulled the SUV alongside Mia who quickened her stride. The SUV kept pace beside her. "Please Mia, I want to talk to you. It's not about your store, I promise."

Mia stopped suddenly and glanced at her watch. 1:47. It was getting late now. She closed her eyes slowly, clenched her jaw, and turned towards the car. "What?" she shouted, a bit too loudly. A few pedestrians looked over to see what was happening. Mia waved her hand apologetically. "What?" she said again, this time softer.

Nadine stopped the car and put it in park. She climbed out and approached Mia on the sidewalk. A meter maid was standing nearby writing tickets for illegally parked cars. She saw the SUV and approached them. "You can't park there."

"It's just for a second. I'm just picking up my friend," Nadine said.

Mia's eyes almost popped out of her head. She didn't know what game this was, but the only way she was getting in Nadine's car was if she were tied up in the trunk.

The meter maid looked impatient, and sighed. "Look, lady. The only reason I didn't give you a ticket already is because it's Christmas. Move the car now."

Mia couldn't help it, but she kind of liked hearing the meter maid tell Nadine off.

"Go ahead and ticket me," Nadine said. "I have to talk to my friend now."

Mia felt like she was in the twilight zone. Nadine kept calling her 'friend,' she wasn't sure what was happening, but she kept her guard up. The meter maid furrowed her brow as if she too were confused. "If you say so." She proceeded to type Nadine's license plate number into her ticket machine. She printed it and slipped it under the windshield wiper. "I'm going to come back by here in 15 minutes, Ma'am. If this thing is still here, I'll be forced to give you another ticket."

Nadine shrugged as the meter maid walked away. She leaned

close to Mia and whispered, "Company car."

"There it is." Mia thought. "What do you want?" Mia demanded again.

And then something peculiar happened – at least from Mia's perspective. Nadine hugged her. Mia's arms were pinned at her side and she didn't know whether to run, to yell for help, or to hug Nadine back. She finally decided to just stand there and wait for it to end. At last Nadine loosened her grasp and looked at Mia. "I'm sorry," she said.

Mia didn't know what to feel. The past 48 hours had been the most emotional of her life. A lump lodged in her throat. "For what?" she managed.

"For everything. You didn't deserve anything I did to you."

"Is this some kind of trick?"

"No tricks. No games. I'm sorry for how I treated you. I justified it by believing 'all's fair in love and war.'" It's not, and I'm sorry."

Mia was still unsure. Nadine had been crueler to her than almost anyone in her life. "Why the sudden change of heart?"

Nadine looked at the ground. "I lost my job today. This morning actually. Right before I dropped my daughter off at her grandma's. Nobody knows yet. You're the first person I've told."

Despite everything, Mia pitied Nadine. She knew the feelings of loss from saying goodbye to her gift shop, and Mia didn't have a child to support. "I'm sorry," she said.

Nadine shuffled her feet. "Who knows. Maybe it's for the best." Mia nodded, not sure what else to say. Nadine continued, "So, listen. I spoke with my mom this morning."

"Edith?"

"Yes. And she told me what you did for her. For us."

"It was nothing. She's very sweet."

"It wasn't nothing. It meant the world to her and to my daughter. I didn't know how to contact her, didn't know what to say. I was absorbed in my own world. If you hadn't stepped in, my daughter would probably have grown up without her grandma."

Mia smiled at Nadine. "I'm happy for them."

Nadine smiled back. "Anyway, are you still in the running for that contest?"

"Uh-huh."

"I want to help in any way I can. I called the store looking for you and spoke with your associate. He told me where to find you. Said you didn't have a car." Mia nodded. "Let me be your driver. I'll take you wherever you need to go."

"That's very kind, but I don't know where I need to go. I haven't unscrambled the puzzle yet."

Nadine considered the conundrum. "Then let me drive you to lunch. You can solve it on the way. My treat."

Mia had been too involved with the puzzle to consider lunch. But she was hungry. "Nadine, thanks for what you said."

"No, thank you. Now let's go before that meter maid gets me again.

CHAPTER 43

The SUV was gorgeous. Mia didn't know much about cars, but this was impressive. Brown leather interior, seat heaters and seat coolers – not that those would be needed today – separate climate control, Bluetooth, automatic everything, and even driver assisted parking "Beautiful car," she said as she strapped herself into the passenger seat.

"I know. Shame I have to give it back. But business is closed 'til the 26th, so I figure I can put a few more miles on it."

"I hope you don't mind my asking," Mia said as Nadine pulled the SUV back onto the road. "Why were you laid off?"

"I wasn't laid off. I was fired. Axed outright." Nadine was being surprisingly forthcoming. She paused and considered her words. "Let's just say I was involved in some…how do I put this…extra-legal corporate misdeeds. No theft or anything, but, if I'm honest, I would've fired me too." Mia arched her eyebrows, but nodded conciliatorily. "Noah quit when he found out about it," Nadine mused, almost to herself. "Who knows. He may've been the whistle blower."

Mia felt butterflies at the mention of his name. She was relieved to hear he wasn't mixed up in whatever it was Nadine had ensnared herself in. "How is he? Do you know?"

"I called around looking for him, even called his grandpa."

"Who's his grandpa? How'd you get his number?"

Nadine shrugged. "I just looked it up. He owns the Daily Gazette."

"What?" Mia's head was swimming. If Noah's grandpa owned the Gazette, that meant Noah was probably responsible for the op-ed that morning. She was overcome with emotion, but took a breath. "And did his grandpa tell you anything?"

Nadine was matter-of-fact. "Yeah. I think he said Noah's moving to New York."

Everything moved in slow motion again. Mia felt like her world was upside down, and nothing made sense anymore. Nadine, Mia's enemy only hours earlier, now seemed like the nicest, most honest person alive. And Noah, whom she'd fallen for, was leaving. Mia could feel her heart banging inside of her chest. "Excuse me for a minute," she said, and pulled out her cell phone. She dialed Noah's number. Voicemail. Mia slammed the lock button and stuffed the phone away.

Nadine had been watching out of the corner of her eye. "Everything ok?" she asked.

"Just stressed."

Nadine cocked her head sideways as if to say, "I know how that feels." "Do you want me to turn on some music? That always helps me calm down."

"Sure."

Nadine flipped on the radio. "What do you like?"

"I'm fine with anything."

Nadine navigated to a channel featuring "The best hits from the 80s 90s and today." A Bruce Springsteen song was just finishing. Mia tried to take a deep breath and relax. The music was a nice suggestion. The pair rode along in silence for a bit. Mia tried to think about unscrambling the puzzle. It was daunting, but someone was going to do it. She pulled out her phone and checked the Daily Gazette app. No winner yet, as far as she could tell. That was good. She looked over at Nadine, and took a deep breath. The ride was pleasant, as was the help. It was nice to have so many people come to her aid. "No matter what happens with the store," she thought, "I've got some good people around me." The next song clicked on the radio. It was a song from an 80s hair-band, Poison. Mia had heard it countless times in her younger years. She recognized Brett Michaels' voice as the lyrics oozed out of the speakers: We both lie silently still in the dead of night... Mia closed her eyes and tried to clear her mind. It was nice to be at rest for a moment. The song continued and reached the chorus, Nadine was humming along:

Every rose has its thorn
Just like every night has its dawn
Just like every cowboy, sings his sad, sad song
Every rose has its thorn

"Every rose has its thorn," Mia hummed too. "Every rose has its thorn...Wait!" Suddenly Mia's eyes shot open and she abruptly sat up in her seat.

Nadine jumped and pushed on the brakes. "What is it?"

"The Rose Parade!" she shouted. "I think that's it! That's the answer to the puzzle! Do you have a pen?" Mia frantically opened glove compartments and visors to look around.

Nadine was excited. "Right here." She handed a pen to Mia who immediately went to work writing out the letters. "This is it!" Mia spun towards Nadine in her seat. "Forget lunch! I know what to do.

CHAPTER 44

The Christmas Rose Parade was an annual tradition that dated back almost 100 years to when the town was much more agrarian. Clever local farmers who couldn't grow or sell crops in the snowy winter, began growing flowers – but mostly roses – in their greenhouses to sell for the holidays. As the practice caught on, it created an oversaturation of roses in the city and farmers struggled to make ends meet. Legislators put their heads together and decided to sponsor an annual rose parade where farmers could sell their flowers to the municipality. The legislators hoped the parade would be a boon to tourism and pay the back the city's burden of purchasing flowers. The gamble paid off, and every year the parade got bigger and more elaborate, and attracted visitors from all across the country. The city's restaurants and bars were always flooded in the days leading up to the parade. In 1919, they had used candles to light the floats, but now the parade highlighted an electric display that was the biggest in the state. Sometimes TV crews would even broadcast the parade nationwide. Not to be outdone, the rose displays were also breathtaking. Floats, sometimes two stories high, decked with roses of every color and type would drive down the street delighting children and adults alike. Mia had loved the parade for as long as she could remember.

The SUV barreled through the crowded city streets in the direction of the parade. Mia was in full-on panic mode. She didn't know what was more stressful, Noah leaving, the Twelve Games contest, or Nadine's driving. They blew through a stoplight and Mia grabbed the handle above her head. "That was red!"

"Looked green to me." Nadine laughed, a bit too maniacally. At last, they rounded the corner of main street and Mia saw the park where the parade launched from. Nadine screeched on her brakes. The street had been barricaded off to traffic in preparation. The sidewalks were already beginning to fill with parade-goers setting out camping chairs and blankets. There was nowhere to park. "Can you make it from here?" Nadine said.

"Yes." Mia paused and touched Nadine's shoulder. "Thank you. And Merry Christmas!"

Nadine smiled. "Go get 'em."

A second later, Mia was out of the car pushing her way past the barricade. A police officer came jogged. "This area's closed to the public."

"Please," Mia pleaded. "I'm in the Twelve Games contest. I need to get over there."

The cop looked over his shoulder to see if his superiors were watching. They were consumed by something on their phones and didn't look up. He stepped out of the way and motioned with his head for Mia to pass. She gave him a sincere look of gratitude. "Thank you." She ran across the icy ground, her feet aching and her heart pounding. She was exhausted, but nothing would stop her now. She crossed the several-hundred-yard expanse of the park and arrived out-of-breath at the parade staging area. There was hardly a soul around. Not for the first time, Mia wondered if she'd made a miscalculation in one of the puzzles somewhere. Or more likely, she had unscrambled the words incorrectly. Still, she was here and it was worth a shot. Mia reached into her pocket and pulled out her cell phone. In a routine that had become overly familiar she flicked it open to selfie mode and positioned herself to showcase the parade behind her. The shutter clicked. She checked the picture, it was fine, not blurry. As quickly as she could, she uploaded the picture to the Daily Gazette app.

Mia looked up and took a deep breath. For the first time in weeks she was standing around with nothing to do and no pressure to hurry anywhere. She gazed at the parade floats lined up in the road. They were impressive. The one nearest, depicted Santa on a rooftop and was made entirely of roses. There were red roses for the suit, white roses for his beard, and even some dyed-black for his boots. He held a sack of toys and had his finger on the side of his nose. "I could use a little more of that Christmas magic, Santa," she said to the float. "If you have any left for me."

As if on cue, her phone buzzed. She froze, her heart was beating wildly. She didn't dare look. A few seconds later it buzzed again, a second reminder a message was waiting, as if she needed it. Carefully, methodically, Mia raised the phone to her eye level and tapped the message. "Thanks for entering the Twelve Games of Christmas! Congratulations on finding location 13!" Mia let out a huge sigh of relief and felt tears well in her eyes. She'd found it. No matter what, she had found it and had done all she could.

But something was wrong.

That was the end of the message. She tried to scroll further down the page, but there was nothing else written. Hands shaking, she hard-closed the app and reopened it, but no other message appeared. The panicky feeling Mia had become so familiar with of late, set in. Maybe that message was the whole thing. Maybe she didn't win. Or worse, maybe there was supposed to be more to the message but it didn't get sent all the way through and got lost in cyberspace. Or, maybe this was only one leg of the final puzzle and she was missing something. Maybe, maybe, maybe. "Stop," she told herself. "Breathe." She followed her own advice and took a deep breath. It helped. Mia continued to breathe mindfully. She thought about things that made her happy. She thought about how much help she'd received today. She thought about Richard and about Edith. She thought about Harmony and about Nadine. And of course, she thought about Noah. So many people in her life who cared and wanted her to succeed. "You're only as successful as the company you keep," she thought to herself. "If that's true, I've already won."

BOOM! The sound of an explosion right behind Mia caused her to jump so high, she nearly dropped her phone. She turned to see confetti raining down from one of the floats. Several more confetti cannons unleashed their attack. Suddenly, speakers on the floats blasted an instrumental version of The 12 Days of Christmas song. The music continued to swell. Across the way, parade-goers were on their feet gawking, wondering if the parade had started early this year. At the same moment, from a building behind one of the floats, a group of people, all dressed in business attire, emerged. They were applauding. The group was accompanied by a camera crew who traded off filming them approach Mia, and filming Mia watch them approach. Mia caught a glimpse one of the men in front, carrying what looked like a giant, Styrofoam check. Across the street, the onlookers had begun to bunch up, staring at the spectacle. An elderly gentleman in a three-piece-suit reached Mia first. The music volume softened, and the man spoke. "Mia Gallagher?"

Mia's heart was racing. "Yes?"

"My name is Alan DuPonte. On behalf of the Daily Gazette, its affiliates, and all of its readers, I want to be the first to formally congratulate you and tell you that you are winner of the Twelve Games of Christmas contest!"

Mia felt like she was going to pass out. Her knees were buckling. Tears filled her eyes as the realization of what she'd accomplished set in. She had saved her store, and saved Richard's job. Snow Valley Treasures would remain open. "I…I don't know what to say. I'm overwhelmed…" she looked at Mr. DuPonte and the rest of the group. "And so happy and grateful to all of you." Tears openly fell down her cheeks.

Mr. DuPonte smiled, tears were in his eyes too. "You deserve it." He continued. "And as the owner of the Daily Gazette, it is my pleasure to present you with this check for $100,000!"

Mia's eyes widened. "I…I'm sorry. Did you say you're the

owner of the Gazette?" Mia asked him, her pulse racing.

Mr. DuPonte nodded. "That's right." He lifted the check and placed it in Mia's hands. It was heavier than expected and it almost slipped from her fingers. The camera crew had closed in, catching every moment.

"Do you know where Noah is?"

The surprise on Mr. DuPonte's face at Mia's question, was underscored by the bewilderment on the faces of everyone else from the Gazette who stood behind him. "Noah? I...he..." Mr. DuPonte checked his watch. "He should be at the airport by now."

Mia smiled warmly. "Thank you all! I'm so grateful for everything. But, I'm sorry. I can't do this right now. I have somewhere I need to be." She let the giant check slip from her hand, and turned on her heels. Seconds later she was in full-sprint back to Nadine's car.

CHAPTER 45

The airport app on Mia's phone told her they had just 15 minutes before the last plane to New York departed. Nadine zigzagged through traffic like Danica Patrick. If Mia hadn't been so consumed, she would have been terrified at all the near-misses from Nadine's driving. But Mia was focused – and she appreciated the speed. They careened through a traffic light at 20 above the speed limit. "I think that one was red," Nadine said.

"No, it was just yellow-adjacent."

"Yellow-adjacent, huh? That's a good spin. If I hadn't just been fired, I'd tell you to come work for me." Nadine joked, while swerving around a biker.

"You already tried that, remember? And this is where we ended up."

Nadine laughed. "Oh yeah."

Exactly seven minutes and six seconds later, Nadine skidded to a stop at the terminal drop-off. "Good luck!"

Mia hopped out of the car and ran inside. She had just over seven minutes left, according to her watch. No time to buy a ticket. She ran up to security and a friendly TSA agent smiled. "Boarding pass, please."

Mia smiled back. "I actually don't have a boarding pass." she said. "But I'm gonna buy one in a second. It's just…I have to stop the person I love from getting on a plane. Can you please let me through?"

The agent's eyebrows were arched all the way to the ceiling. After a long pause, he said, "Sorry, Ma'am. That's not how this works."

Mia was desperate. "Please. It's Christmas."

The agent's smile had evaporated. "Not for me. I'm Jewish, and I'm at work right now."

Mia looked at her watch again: four minutes left. "Well for Hanukkah then. Or for true love. Please"

The agent looked annoyed. "Ma'am, you're holding up the line, and to be honest, you're making me nervous. So, I'm going to ask you to leave one more time, or I'll be forced to involve security." He reached forward and grasped his walkie-talkie.

Mia took the hint and turned away. "Thanks."

Nadine's SUV slowed to a stop in front of Snow Valley Treasures. "Are you sure I can't take you all the way home?" she asked.

Mia smiled at her. "I'm good. I wanna check in here before heading back. But thank you again for everything you've done today."

As Mia climbed out of the car, the pair exchanged information and promised to remain in touch. Mia checked her phone as she walked toward the entrance: 27 missed calls; 104 unread texts; 7 voicemails. She scrolled through the missed calls first. Most were from Richard; several were from her friends; and a few were from unrecognized numbers. None were from Noah. Of the seven voicemails, Richard had left three, her friends, two, and two were from competing TV news stations wanting an interview. Mia made a mental note to call them back later. The texts didn't take very long to wade through. Most were "OMG"s and "I'm proud of you"s, followed by the "where are you??"s.

Mia tapped out a quick response to Richard – he'd been the

most insistent. "Hey! We did it! Yes, I'm still planning on Christmas Eve dinner. Edith can't make it anymore – she's eating with her daughter and granddaughter – but you won't get rid of me that easy. Just stopping at the store and I'll be there. I can't wait to see you!!"

Richard responded with a heart emoji and Christmas tree.

Snow Valley Treasures was locked up. All was dark inside except the winter wonderland window display shining in soft blue light. Mia unlocked the door and pushed inside. The place looked good, all things considered. Based on Richard's texts about how busy they'd been, she expected it to look like a WWI bunker. Mia walked around the room taking it all in. She looked at the shelves, and the toys; the various displays, and point of sale items. "You really don't know what you've got till it's gone," she thought. She was overwhelmed, exhausted, and felt torn in half – utter joy and intense loss; extreme relief and bitter pain. A wave of weariness hit her and she sat down on the carpet, leaned against a shelf, and shut her eyes. Her mind raced through the events of the last two weeks and everything that had brought her to that moment. Most of all she thought of Noah. Tears fell down her cheeks.

The jingle of the front door startled her. She opened her eyes and blinked as a figure approached. Mia's eyes were blurry, and she rubbed the tears away. The person was familiar. She shook off the daze. It was Noah.

"Looks like you forgot something," he said, holding up her giant check. "Should I put this in the register?"

Mia climbed to her feet. "Noah…I…how did you…they told me you moved to New York."

Noah laughed. "Who, my grandpa, the newspaper man? Didn't anyone ever tell you 'don't believe everything you read.'"

"I don't understand."

"I told my grandpa I was flying to New York – not moving there. I am gonna try to meet some agents and sell my manuscript."

"Oh." Mia chuckled at herself and felt a bit foolish for having rushed to the airport earlier. Mia's emotions welled inside her again. "Noah, I...I'm so happy you're here. There's so much I've wanted to say. I..."

"Wait," he interrupted. Noah set the check on the counter and moved toward her, smiling. From behind his back he pulled out a single white rose, identical to the one he'd plucked for her at the botanical garden. "Can you guess the name of this flower?"

Mia's laughed and wiped her cheeks. "It's a rose." she exclaimed and ran towards him. Mia wrapped her arms around him and drank in everything about him: his smell, his face, his laugh. She felt his strong arms reach around her and pull her close. It felt good to be in his embrace. "It's a rose," she said again.

Noah laughed. "That's correct. You solved the puzzle."

"What's my prize?"

They locked eyes, and stared at each other longingly. Noah closed his eyes and leaned toward her. She didn't wait. Mia leaned forward until she felt the warmth of his lips on hers. They kissed. It was a passionate, beautiful kiss and Mia never wanted the moment to end. When she finally opened her eyes, she noticed snow falling outside the window. Large beautiful flakes fell from the sky, each one unique as if they had been specially designed for this very moment. "It's snowing," she said. "I love snow at Christmas."

"I know." Noah said, with a smile. "I love it too."

She kissed him again.

EPILOGUE

Mia checked the flight number, then checked it again. 203 from La Guardia. She scanned the flight board. "It's on the ground," she said excitedly, and made her way to the security exit where she found a seat to wait. Travelers burdened by too many carry-on bags spilled out past her. After an eternity, Noah rounded the corner with a huge smile. He saw Mia and ran toward her. A dour TSA agent scowled at him. "No running," she barked. Noah smirked and slowed his pace to a speed walk. At last he passed through the gate and wrapped Mia in a warm embrace. He put both hands on her cheeks with his fingers behind her ears – she loved it when he did that – and pulled her in for a kiss. It was a kiss she'd been missing for the past week.

"How are you?" he asked. "And how is she?" Noah motioned with his head down to Mia's very cute, very pregnant belly.

Mia smiled. "She's kicking a lot. I think she's excited to hear her daddy."

Noah bent down and kissed Mia's belly.

She put his hand on the side of her stomach. "Feel." The baby kicked a few times and they giggled. They made their way to baggage claim and picked up Noah's suitcase. Then it was off to the parking garage. The Lemon Lime was a thing of the past. Mia pressed the unlock key on her keyfob and their shiny, black, SUV, just like Nadine's, beeped.

"I can drive," Noah offered.

"Honey, I'm pregnant, not in an iron lung."

Noah smiled. He loved his wife's sharp wit. "Better for me," he said as he climbed into the passenger seat and rested his feet on the dash.

Mia strapped in to the driver's seat and turned to Noah. "Quit holding out on me. What happened?"

His face contorted into a coy smile. "If I'm going to share that information, I'm gonna need another kiss. It's been a long flight after all."

Mia feigned frustration, even as she was laughing, and leaned over to kiss him. But instead of moving toward her lips, Noah leaned into Mia's ear and whispered. "They're publishing it."

Mia's mouth fell open. "What?" she yelled, right into his ear.

Noah laughed and cupped his ear. "Ouch." This time he shouted. "I said, they're publishing it!"

Mia let out a whoop and wrapped her arms around him. "I knew it! I'm so proud of you. A novelist. Just like your dad always knew you would be." Noah felt a twinge of sadness at the mention of his father, as his thoughts went to the typewriter. But it didn't matter. That had led him here and this was everything he ever wanted.

On the way home, Mia drove right past their house without even slowing. "Um, hon," Noah chuckled, "you just missed our house."

"Company Christmas party, remember?"

"Oh yeah!" But Noah was still confused when the car pulled to a stop in the Snow Valley Treasures parking lot. "I thought…"

"I just have to stop in for a sec, then we're outta here. I promise."

Noah pushed the door to SVT open and held it for his wife. The bells chimed and the people inside looked over. "Hi Harmony," Mia said joyfully.

"Hi, Mia," Harmony said, smiling. She was busy dusting a shelf, standing on a stepladder.

"Where's Nadine?"

"She's in back," Harmony said.

When she rounded the corner, Mia found Nadine buried in paperwork, a bit exasperated, as per usual. "Hi Mia, hi Noah," she said without looking up. "I'm going over these receipts for last month's expenses and one whole day is missing. I don't know where else to look."

Mia smiled knowingly to Noah, who grinned back. Nadine worked hard, sometimes a little too hard, and worked herself into a tizzy. "I'm sure it'll turn up. Have you talked to Richard?"

"Huh? No." she said. "He's been busy at our other location across town, all day. You think I should call him?"

"I will. You can kick your feet up a bit." Mia pulled out her phone and dialed a number.

"Snow Valley Treasures," came a voice from the other end.

"Hi Kate, is Richard there?"

"Oh, hi Mrs. Caffrey! Yeah, he's right here, hang on…"

Mia tried to respond, "You can call me…" but Kate had already put her on hold.

Richard answered. "Hello, Mrs. Caffrey," he said, teasingly.

Mia laughed. "Will you please remind Kate she can call me Mia?"

"Kate," Mia heard Richard say, "Mrs. Caffrey wants me to remind you that you can call Mrs. Caffrey, Mia."

Mia laughed again and rolled her eyes. "Listen, two things: first, Nadine is looking for the receipts for last month's expenses. Do you have any?"

Richard paused and Mia heard him rummaging through paperwork. "It looks like I have turned in everything. Wait. Except for the 8th. I have receipts for the 8th."

Mia looked at Nadine. "Is it the 8th that's missing?"

A look of relief washed over Nadine's face. "Yes! That's it."

"Good." Mia said into the phone. "Can you bring those with you tonight?"

"With me where?"

Mia mimed a dramatic face palm. "To the restaurant. Remember?"

"Ahhh. Yes. That. Ok, boss. Will do."

"See you in an hour. And make sure Kate comes too."

"You got it."

Mia disconnected the call and faced Nadine. "Feel better?"

"Much."

"You ready to go? Let's get outta here."

The three moved out of the back office and met Harmony upfront. She had changed out of her work apron and put on a pink Santa hat. The group laughed.

"If I was Santa," she said, "I'd wear this instead of red."

They all filed out the door and Mia was last to leave. She flipped out the lights and locked the back of the door handle. As she went to flip the "open" sign to "closed" she was struck by a thought. Only two years earlier on this exact date she and Richard had flipped the very same sign for what they thought was the last time. Mia smiled and turned the sign over, for what was definitely not the final time.

Dorothy met them at the restaurant, wearing her best floral print and pearls. She looked stunning. Edith, Renee and Harmony's daughter Tess, were also in attendance. After they were seated Mia looked out over her group of friends and smiled. These were the best people in the world, and she was proud to know them. She stood and clinked a glass with a fork to get their attention. After a few seconds, everyone looked over. "I'd like to propose a toast." Mia raised her glass of water as she spoke. The children, not wanting to miss out on the fun raised plastic cups filled with apple juice and chocolate milk, and everyone else held up flutes of champagne. Mia continued. "I'm overwhelmed by each of you and the impact you've all had on my life. I wouldn't be here without each of your love and support."

"Hear, hear!" Richard said, smiling.

"Tonight, I wanted to start this party off with a bit of good news: my husband, Noah, just found out from his agent his book is going to be published, with wide distribution!" A cheer went up from the group and everyone took turns congratulating him. He was embarrassed by the attention and shook his head at Mia, with a smile. "To Noah," Mia said and raised her glass. The group echoed and all took a drink. Mia stayed on her feet. "That's not all. There's another piece of good news. Richard and I found out from the bank we've been approved to open three new Snow Valley Treasures locations!" The group cheered and clapped. "So," Mia continued, "That means everyone here is getting a raise and a promotion." As soon as she'd said it, the table erupted in jubilation and pandemonium. Everyone hugged and chattered. Mia raised her glass. "Cheers and Merry Christmas!"

"Merry Christmas," the group shouted, almost in unison.

When things had died down a little and everyone was enjoying their meal, Mia leaned over and whispered in Noah's ear. "That's not the last surprise."

His eyes opened wide. "What else?"

"Follow me." Mia led him by the hand out of the restaurant to their car.

"Where are we going?" he queried. "We can't leave the party."

"We're not." Mia interlaced her fingers into Noah's and they walked around to the back of the car. She popped the backdoor open and revealed a blanket covering something. "Go ahead," she said. Noah looked at Mia with a glint of anticipation in his eyes. He slowly removed the blanket, and there, resting on the floorboard, was his dad's shiny, black, Excelsior typewriter.

Noah gasped. "I don't understand," he finally said, tears filling his eyes. "How did you…"

"I've been tracking it ever since you sold it. I knew it was at Kelly's Antiques so I just followed the chain of custody. I'm sorry it took so long. I didn't have the money to get it sooner."

Noah turned to Mia with tears of joy falling down his cheeks. "Thank you! I love you so much," he said. He wrapped her in his arms once again and, not for the last time, they kissed.

ABOUT THE AUTHOR

KB Badger lives with his wife and two kids in Metro Atlanta. In his spare time, he practices law. This is his first novel.

Made in the USA
Columbia, SC
17 November 2021